DICK CONTINO'S BLUES

James Ellroy was born in Los Angeles in 1948. His previous novels, *The Black Dahlia*, *The Big Nowhere*, *L. A. Confidential* and *White Jazz*, have won numerous awards and were international bestsellers. He lives with his wife in Connecticut.

DICK CONTINO'S BLUES
and Other Stories

James Ellroy

ARROW

First published 1994

1 3 5 7 9 10 8 6 4 2

James Ellroy's Introduction to *Dick Contino's Blues* first
appeared in the US edition of *GQ* magazine.

Dick Contino's Blues © James Ellroy 1993
High Dark Town © James Ellroy 1986
Dial Axminster 6–400 © James Ellroy 1987
Since I Don't Have You © James Ellroy 1988
Torch Number © James Ellroy 1990
Gravy Train © James Ellroy 1990

First published in the UK by Arrow in 1994
Random House, 20 Vauxhall Bridge Road, London
SW1V 2SA

Random House Australia (Pty) Limited
20 Alfred Street, Milsons Point, Sydney,
New South Wales, 2061, Australia

Random House New Zealand Limited
18 Poland Road, Glenfield
Auckland 10, New Zealand

Random House South Africa (Pty) Limited
PO Box 337, Bergvlei, South Africa

Random House UK Limited Reg No 954009

ISBN 0 09 941011 7

Photoset by Deltatype Ltd, Ellesmere Port, Cheshire
Printed and bound in Great Britain by
Cox & Wyman Ltd, Reading, Berks

To Alan Marks

Introduction

———

A man gyrating with an accordion – pumping his 'Stomach Steinway' for all its worth.

My father pointing to the TV. 'That guy's no good. He's a draft dodger.'

The accordion man in a grade Z movie: clinching with the blonde from the Mark C. Bloome tire ads.

Half-buried memories speak to me. Their origin remains fixed: L.A., my hometown, in the '50s. Most are just brief synaptic blips, soon mentally discarded. A few transmogrify into fiction: I sense their dramatic potential and exploit it in my novels, memory to moonshine in a hot second.

Memory: that place where personal recollections collide with history.

Memory: a symbiotic melding of THEN and NOW. For me, the spark point of harrowing curiosities.

The accordion man is named Dick Contino.

'Draft Dodger' is a bum rap – he served honorably during the Korean War.

The grade Z flick is *Daddy-O* – a music/hot-rod/romance stinkeroo.

Memory is contextual: the juxtaposition of large events and snappy minutiae.

In June of 1958 my mother was murdered. The killing went unsolved; I went to live with my father. I saw Dick Contino belt 'Bumble Boogie' on TV, noted my father's opinion of him and caught *Daddy-O* at the Admiral Theater a year or so later. Synapses snapped, crackled, popped: a memory was formed and placed in context. Its

1

historical perspective loomed dark: women were strangled and spent eternity unavenged.

I was ten and eleven years old then; literary instincts simmered inchoately in me. My curiosities centered on crime: I wanted to know the WHY? behind hellish events. As time passed, contemporaneous malfeasance left me bored – the sanguinary '60s and '70s passed in a blur. My imagination zoomed back to the decade preceding them, accompanied by a period soundtrack: golden oldies, Dick Contino slamming the accordion on the *Ed Sullivan Show*.

In 1965 I got kicked out of high school and joined the army. Everything about the army scared me shitless – I faked a nervous breakdown and glommed an unsuitability discharge.

In 1980 I wrote *Clandestine* – a thinly disguised, chronologically altered account of my mother's murder. The novel is set in 1951; the hero is a young cop – and draft dodger – who's life is derailed by the Red Scare.

In 1987 I wrote *The Big Nowhere*. Set in 1950, the book details an anti-Communist pogrom levelled at the entertainment biz.

In 1990 I wrote *White Jazz*. A major subplot features a grade Z movie being filmed in the same Griffith Park locales as *Daddy-O*.

Jung wrote: 'What is not brought to consciousness comes to us as fate.'

I should have seen Dick Contino coming a long time ago.

I didn't. Fate intervened, via photograph and video cassette.

A friend shot me the photo. Dig: it's me, age ten, on June 22, 1958. An L.A. *Times* photographer snapped the pic five minutes after a police detective told me that my mother had been murdered. I'm in minor-league shock: my eyes are wide, but my gaze is blank. My fly is at half-mast; my hands look shaky. The day was hot: the melting Brylcreem in my hair picks up flashbulb light.

The photo held me transfixed; its force transcended my many attempts to exploit my past for book sales. An underlying truth zapped me: my bereavement, even in that moment, was ambiguous. I'm already calculating potential advantages, regrouping as the officious men surrounding me defer to the perceived grief of a little boy.

I had the photograph framed, and spent a good deal of time staring at it. Spark point: late '50s memories reignited. I saw *Daddy-O* listed in a video catalog and ordered it. It arrived a week later; I popped it in the VCR.

Fuel-injected zoooom—

The story revolves around truck driver/drag racer/singer Phil 'Daddy-O' Sandifer's attempts to solve the murder of his best friend, while laboring under the weight of a suspended driver's license. Phil's pals 'Peg' and 'Duke' want to help, but they're ineffectual – addled by too many late nights at the Rainbow Gardens, a post-teenage doo-wop spot where Phil croons for gratis on request. No matter: Daddy-O meets slinky Jana Ryan, a rich girl with a valid driver's license and a '57 T-Bird ragtop. Mutual resentment segues into a sex vibe; Phil and Jana team up and infiltrate a nightclub owned by sinister fat man Sidney Chillis. Singer Daddy-O, cigarette girl Jana: a comely and unstoppable duo. They quickly surmise that Chillis is pushing Big 'H', entrap him and nail the ectomorph for the murder of Phil's best friend. A hot-rod finale; a burning question left unanswered: will Daddy-O's derring-do get him his driver's license back?

Who knows?

Who cares?

It took me three viewings to get the plot down anyway.

Because Dick Contino held me spellbound.

Because I knew – instinctively – that he held important answers.

Because I knew that he hovered elliptically in my 'L.A. Quartet' novels, a phantom waiting to speak.

Because I sensed that he could powerfully spritz narrative detail and fill up holes in my memory, bringing Los Angeles in the late '50s into some sort of hyperfocus.

Because I thought I detected a significant mingling of his circa '57 on-and-off-screen personas, a brew that thirty-odd intervening years would forcefully embellish.

Contino on-screen: a handsome Italian guy, late twenties, big biceps from weights or making love to his accordion. Dreamboat attributes: shiny teeth, dark curly hair, engaging smile. It's the '50s, so he's working at a sartorial deficit: pegger slacks hiked up to his pecs, horizontal-striped Ban-Lon shirts. He looks good and he can sing; he's straining on 'Rock Candy Baby' – the lyrics suck and you can tell this up-tempo rebop isn't his style – but he croons the wah-wah ballad 'Angel Act' achingly, full of baritone tremolos, quintessentially the pussy-whipped loser in lust with the 'noir' goddess who's out to trash his life.

And he can act: he's an obvious natural, at ease with the camera.

3

Dig: atrocious lines get upgraded to mediocre every time he opens his mouth.

And he's grateful to be top-lining *Daddy-O* – he doesn't condescend to the script, his fellow performers or lyrics like, 'Rock candy baby, that's what I call my chick. Rock candy baby, sweeter than a licorice stick!' – even though my threadbare knowledge of his life tells me that he's already been to much higher places.

I decided to find Dick Contino.

I prayed for him to be alive and well.

I located a half-dozen of his albums and listened to them, reveling in pure *Entertainment*.

'Live at the Fabulous Flamingo,' 'Squeeze Me,' 'Something for the Girls' – old standards arranged to spotlight accordion virtuosity. Main-theme bombardments; sentiment so pure and timeless that it could soundtrack every moment of transcendent schmaltz that Hollywood has ever produced. Dick Contino, show-stopper on wax: zapping two keyboards, improvising cadenzas, shaking thunderstorms from bellows compression. Going from whisper to sigh to roar and back again in the length of time it takes to think: tell me what this man's life means and how it connects to my life.

I called my researcher friend Alan Marks. He caught my pitch on the first bounce. 'The accordion guy? I think he used to play Vegas.'

'Find out everything you can about him. Find out if he's still alive, and if he is, locate him.'

'What's this about?'

'Narrative detail.'

I should have said *containable* narrative detail – because I wanted Dick Contino to be a pad-prowling/car-crashing/moon-howling/womanizing quasi-psychopath akin to the heroes of my books. I should have said, 'Bring me information that I can control and exploit.' I should have said, 'Bring me a life that can be compartmentalized into the pitch-dark vision of my first ten novels.'

'What is not brought to consciousness comes to us as fate.'

I should have seen the *real* Dick Contino coming.

Richard Joseph Contino was born in Fresno, California on January 17, 1930. His father was a Sicilian immigrant who owned a successful butcher shop; his mother was first-generation Italian-American. Dick had two younger brothers and a sister; a maternal uncle – Ralph

Giordano, aka Young Corbett – was briefly welterweight champion of the world.

The family was tight-knit, Catholic, only moderately tight-ass. Dick grey up shy, beset by fears of claustrophobic suffocation and separation from his loved ones. *Wicked bad fears*: the kind you recognize as irrational even as they rip you up.

Athletics and music allowed him to front a fearless persona. High-school fullback, five years of accordion study – good with the pigskin, superb with the squeezebox. Dick Contino, age seventeen, ready for a hot date with history: a strapping six-foot *gavonne* with his fears held in check by a smile.

Horace Heidt, late of Horace Heidt and his Musical Knights, was passing through Fresno looking for amateur talent. His *Door of Opportunity* radio program was about to debut – yet another studio audience/applause meter show – three contestants competing for weekly prize money and the chance to sing, play, dance or clown their way through to the grand finals, a five thou payoff and a dubious shot at fame. One of Heidt's flunkies heard about Dick and arranged an audition; Dick wowed him with a keyboard-zipping/bellows-shaking/mike-stand-bumping medley. The flunky told Horace Heidt: 'You've got to see this kid. I know the accordion's from squaresville, but you've got to *see* this kid.'

December 7, 1947: Horace Heidt slotted Dick Contino on his first radio contest. Dick played 'Lady of Spain' and 'Tico-Tico' and burned the house down. He won $250; horny bobbysoxers swarmed him backstage.

Horace Heidt hit first-strike pay dirt.

Dick Contino continued to win: week after week, traveling with the Heidt show, defeating singers, dancers, trombone players, comics and a blind vibraphonist. He won straight through to the grand finals in December '48; he became a national celebrity while still technically an amateur contestant. The Horace Heidt *Door of Opportunity* program soared on his coattails, zooming to #2 in the national radio ratings, sparking a 28 percent sales growth for their sponsor's product: Phillip Morris cigarettes.

The Fresno butcher's son now had four hundred fan clubs nationwide.

He averaged five thousand fan letters a week.

Teenage girls thronged his appearances, changing 'Dick-kie Cont-ino, we love you' to the tune of 'Lady of Spain'.

5

Horace Heidt was to say years later: 'You should have *seen* Dick play. If my show had been on television, Dick Contino would have been bigger than Elvis Presley.'

A Heidt tour followed the grand-finals victory. Other performers appeared with Contino – crypto-lounge acts backstopping the newly annointed 'Mr. Accordion'. Heidt had his cash cow yoked to a punk twenty-five-grand-a-year contract; Dick sued him and cut himself loose. Mr. Accordion flying high: record contracts, screen tests, top-liner status at the BIG ROOMS: Ciro's and the Mocambo in L.A.; the El Rancho Vegas; the Chez Paree in Chicago. Dick Contino, age nineteen, twenty, twenty-one: soaking up the spoils of momentum, making the squaresville accordion hip, unaware that public love is ephemeral. Too callow to know that idols who admit their fear will fall.

1951: the Korean War heating up. A vintage year for professional witch hunters, right-wing loonies and anti-Communist paranoics. Dick Contino goes from 'Valentino of the Accordion' to draft bait. A Selective Service notice arrives; he begs off his army induction, citing minor physical maladies. He's scared – but not of losing his BIG ROOM status, big paydays, and big poontang potential.

He's scared of all the baaaaad juju that could happen to you, might happen to you, *will* happen to you – shit like blindness, cancer, passing out on stage, your dog getting dognapped by vivisectionists, your mother getting raped, going punchy like your Uncle Ralph. The army looms – claustrophobia coming on like a steam-heated shroud. Fear – BIG-ROOM FEAR – crazy stuff so diffuse that you can't tell if it's outside you or inside you. Crazy stuff he might have outgrown if he hadn't been too busy on the Heartthrob Tour, jump-starting adolescent libidos.

Fear owned him now; it grew more vivid by the day. Dick went to the Mayo Clinic; three psychiatrists examined him and declared him psychologically unfit for army service. Dick's draft board wanted yet another opinion and shot him to their preferred headshrinker. The shrink conducted a cursory exam, contradicted the Mayo triumvarite and tagged Richard Contino 1-A.

Dick was inducted in April of 1951 and sent to Fort Ord, California. His fear became panic – he bolted the reception-station barracks and caught a bus to San Francisco. Now AWOL and a Federal fugitive, he trained down to his parents' new house outside L.A. He conferred with friends, a lawyer and a priest, got up some guts and turned himself in to the Feds.

6

The incident got front-page publicity. The papers played up a resentment number, harping on the BIG ROOM pay Dick Contino would be giving up if forced to serve as an army private. Dick's response: then take away my accordion for five years.

The Feds didn't buy it. Dick Contino went to trial for desertion; he fought his case with psychiatric testimony. Fear on trial, fear convicted – the U.S. Attorney liked Dick, considered him courageous and petitioned the judge to release him straight into the army. The judge refused – and hit Dick Contino with six months in the Federal joint at McNeil Island, Washington.

He did five months of the sentence, shaving four weeks off for good behavior. It could have been worse: he hauled pipes, did gardening work and put on a prisoners' Christmas show. Inside, the big fears seemed to subside: the business of day-to-day survival kiboshed that part of his imagination where terror flourished. Five months in, out, the ironic kicker: he got drafted and sent to Korea.

Where he served with distinction. Korea proved to be a mixed psychological bag: Dick's draft-trial notoriety won him friends, enemies and a shitload of invitations to play the accordion. Duty with a Seoul-attached outfit, back to the States early in '54. Richard Contino: honorably discharged as a staff sergeant; while overseas the recipient of an unsolicited presidential pardon signed by Harry S. Truman.

Dick Contino: back in the U.S.A.

Back to derailed career momentum, a long transit of day-to-day survival behind him.

The Big Room gigs were kaput. Momentum is at least 50 percent hype: it requires nurturing and frequent infusions of bullshit. Dick Contino couldn't play the game from McNeil Island and Korea. A bum publicity taint stuck to him: 'Coward' and 'Draft Dodger' throbbing in Red Scare neon.

He worked smaller rooms and dodged catcalls; he cut records and learned to sing as a hedge against dwindling interest in the accordion. A few journalists befriended him, but the basic show-biz take on Dick Contino was *this guy is poison*. Justifying yourself to the public gets old quick; 'Coward' may be the toughest American bullet to dodge. Liquor-store heisters/animal molesters/shyster lawyers – Americans prefer all of them to cowards.

Dick Contino learned to sing – Rock & Roll cut him off at the pass. He learned to act, top-lined a few 'B' films and faded in the wake of heartthrobs with un-derailed momentum. In 1956 he married actress Leigh Snowden, had three kids with her and settled down in Las Vegas – close to his hotel-lounge bread and butter. He continues to get small-room gigs and plays Italian fiestas in Chicago, Milwaukee, Philly and other paisano-packed venues.

Leigh Snowdon Contino died of cancer in 1982. The Contino kids would now be thirty-five, thirty-two and thirty.

My researcher's notes tapped out in '89. He said an obituary check turned up negative – he was certain that Dick Contino was still alive. A week later I got confirmation. 'I found him. He's still living in Las Vegas, and he says he'll talk to you.'

Before making contact, I charted the arc of two lives. A specific design was becoming clear – I wanted to write a novella featuring Dick Contino and the filming of *Daddy-O* – but a symbiotic pull was blunting my urge to get down to business, extract information and get out. I felt a recognition of my own fears binding me to this man: fear of failure, specific in nature and surmountable through hard work, and the very large fear that induces claustrophobic suffocation and causes golden young men to run from army barracks: the terror that anything might happen, could happen, *will* happen.

A merging in fear; a divergence in action.

I joined the army just as the Vietnam War started to percolate. My father was dying: I didn't want to stick around and watch. The army terrified me – I calculated plausible means of escape. James Ellroy, age seventeen, fledgling dramatist: pulling off a frantic stuttering act designed to spotlight his unsuitability for military service.

It was a bravura performance. It got me a quick discharge and a return trip to L.A. and my passions: booze, dope, reading crime novels and breaking into houses to sniff women's undergarments.

Nobody ever called me a coward or a draft dodger – the Vietnam War was reviled from close to the get-go, and extricating yourself from its clutches was held laudable.

I *calculated* my way out – and of course my fears remained unacknowledged. And I wasn't a golden young man sky-high on momentum and ripe for a public hanging.

I've led a colorful and media-exploitable life; my take on it has been picaresque – a stratagem that keeps my search for deeper meaning channeled solely into my books, which keeps my momentum building, which keeps my wolves of nothingness locked out of sight. Dick Contino didn't utilize my methods: he was a man of music, not of words, and he embraced his fears from the start. And he *continued*: the musicianship on his post-army-beef albums dwarfs the sides he cut pre-'51. He continued, and so far as I could tell, the only thing that diminished was his audience.

I called Contino and told him I wanted to write about him. We had an affable conversation; he said, 'Come to Vegas.'

Contino met me at the airport. He looked great: lean and fit at sixty-three. His *Daddy-O* grin remained intact; he confirmed that his *Daddy-O* biceps came from humping his accordion.

We went to a restaurant and shot the shit. Our conversation was full of jump cuts – Dick's recollections triggered frequent digressions and circuitous returns to his original anecdotal points. We discussed Las Vegas, the Mob, serving jail time, lounge acts, Howard Hughes, Korea, Vietnam, *Daddy-O*, L.A. in the '50s, fear and what you do when the audience dwindles.

I told him that the best novels were often not the best-selling novels; that complex styles and ambiguous stories perplexed many readers. I said that while my own books sold quite well, they were considered too dark, densely plotted and relentlessly violent to be chart toppers.

Dick asked me if I would change the type of book I write to achieve greater sales – I said, 'No.' He asked me if I'd change the type of book I write if I knew that I'd taken a given style or theme as far as it could go – I said, 'Yes.' He asked me if the real-life characters in my books ever surprise me – I said, 'No, because my relationship to them is exploitative.'

I asked him if he consciously changed musical directions after his career got diverted post-Korea. He said, yes and no – he kept trying to cash in on trends until he realized that at best he'd be performing music that he didn't love, and at worst he'd be playing to an audience he didn't respect.

I said, 'The work is the thing.' He said, yes, but you can't cop an attitude behind some self-limiting vision of your own integrity. You can't cut the audience out of its essential enjoyment – you have to give them some schmaltz to hold on to.

I asked Dick how he arrived at that. He said his old fears taught him to like people more. He said fear thrives on isolation, and when you cut

9

down the wall between you and the audience, your whole vision goes wide.

I checked in at my hotel and shadowboxed with the day's revelations. It felt like my world had tilted toward a new understanding of my past. I kept picturing myself in front of an expanding audience, armed with new literary ammunition: the knowledge that Dick Contino would be the hero of the sequel to the book I'm writing now.

Dick and I met for dinner the next night. It was my forty-fifth birthday; I felt like I was standing at the bedrock center of my life.

Dick played me a bebop 'Happy Birthday' on his accordion. The old chops were still there – he zipped on and off the main theme *rapidamente*.

We split for the restaurant. I asked Dick if he would consent to appear as the hero of my next novel.

He said yes, and asked what the book would be about. I said, 'Fear, courage and heavily compromised redemptions.'

He said, 'Good, I think I've been there.'

The night was cold; Las Vegas neon eclipsed every star overhead. The sky seemed to expand as I wondered what this time and place meant.

Dick Contino's Blues

I'm enjoying a half-assed renaissance these days.

Some dago fiesta gigs, some lounge work. A gooood spot on an AIDS telethon – my 'Lady of Spain' reprise goosed ten grand in contributions and got me a surreptitious blow job from a college girl working the phone lines. *Daddy-O* was released on video, and film critics hooked on '50s kitsch have been bugging me for interviews.

Their questions have my memory turning cartwheels. It's '58 again – I'm an accordionist/singer top-lining a 'B' flick for chump change. Did you write 'Rock Candy Baby' and 'Angel Act' yourself? Did you pour the pork to your costar, that blonde from the Mark C. Bloome tire ads? Who did your wardrobe, who did your stunts – how'd you get that '51 Ford airborne, the fuzz in hot pursuit – the footage looked real, but hastily spliced in.

I always try to answer truthfully.

I always write off the leaping car as movie magic.

In all candor, I made that supercharged/dual-quad/cheater-slicked motherfucker FLY. There's a story behind it – my loving farewell to L.A. back then.

1

I was bombing.

Atom-bombing: sweaty hands, shakes pending. My backup combo sounded off-sync – I knew it was *me*, jumping ahead of the beat. BIG-ROOM FEAR grabbed my nuts; headlines screamed:

CONTINO TANKS LACKLUSTER CROWD AT CRES-CENDO!

CONTINO LAYS PRE-EASTER EGG AT SUNSET STRIP OPENING!

'Bumble Boogie' to 'Ciribiribin' – a straight-for-the-jugular accordion segue. I put my whole body into a bellows shake; my brain misfired a message to my fingers. My fingers obeyed – I slammed out the 'Tico-Tico' finale. Contagious misfires: my combo came in with a bridge theme from 'Rhapsody in Blue'.

I just stood there.

House lights snapped on. I saw Leigh and Chrissy Staples, Nancy Ankrum, Kay Van Obst. My wife, my friends – plus a shitload of first-nighters oozing shock.

'Rhapsody in Blue' fizzled out behind me. BIG-ROOM FEAR clutched my balls and SQUEEZED.

I tried patter. 'Ladies and gentlemen, that was "Dissonance Jump", a new experimental twelve-tone piece.'

My friends yukked. A geek in the Legionnaire cunt cap yelled, 'Draft Dodger!'

Instant silence – big-room loud. I froze on Joe Patriot: booze-flushed, Legion cap, Legion armband. My justification riff stood ready: I went to Korea, got honorably discharged, got pardoned by Harry S. Truman.

No, try this: 'Fuck you. Fuck your mother. Fuck your dog.'

The Legionnaire froze. I froze. Leigh froze behind a smile that kissed off two grand a week, two weeks minimum.

The whole room froze.

Cocktail debris pelted me: olives, ice, whiskey-sour fruit. My accordion dripped maraschino cherries – I slid it off and set it down behind some footlights.

My brain misfired a message to my fists: kick Joe Patriot's ass.

I vaulted the stage and charged him. He tossed his drink in my face; pure grain spirits stung my eyes and blinded me. I blinked, sputtered, and swung haymakers. Three missed; one connected – the impact made me wah-wah quiver. My vision cleared – I thought I'd see Mr. America dripping teeth.

I was wrong.

Joe Legion – gone. In his place, cut cheekbone-deep by my rock-encrusted guinea wedding ring: Cisco Andrade, the world's #1 lightweight contender.

Sheriff's bulls swarmed in and fanned out. Backstopping them: Deputy Dot Rothstein, 200+ pounds of bull dyke with the hots for my friend Chris Staples.

Andrade said, 'You dumb son of a bitch.'

I just stood there.

My eyes dripped gin; my left hand throbbed. The Crescendo main room went phantasmagoric:

There's Leigh: juking the cops with 'Dick Contino, Red Scare Victim' rebop. There's the Legionnaire, glomming my sax man's autograph. Dot Rothstein's sniffing the air – my drummer just ducked backstage with a reefer. Chrissy's giving Big Dot a wide berth. They worked a lezbo entrapment gig once – Dot's had a torch sizzling ever since.

Shouts. Fingers pointed my way. Mickey Cohen with his bulldog Mickey Cohen, Jr. – snout deep in a bowl of cocktail nuts. Mickey, Sr., nightclub Jesus – slipping the boss deputy a cash wad.

Andrade squeezed my ratched-up hand – I popped tears. 'You play your accordion at my little boy's birthday party. He likes clowns, so you dress up like Chucko the Clown. You do that and we're even.'

I nodded. Andrade let my hand go and dabbed at his cut. Mickey Cohen cruised by and spieled payback. 'My niece is having a birthday party. You think you could play it? You think you could dress up like Davy Crockett with one of those coonskin caps?'

I nodded. The fuzz filed out – a deputy flipped me the bird and muttered, 'Draft Dodger.'

13

Mickey Cohen, Jr. sniffed my crotch. I tried to pet him – the cocksucker snapped at me.

Leigh and Chris met me at Googie's. Nancy Ankrum and Kay Van Obst joined us – we packed a big booth full.

Leigh pulled out her scratch pad. 'Steve Katz was furious. He made the bookkeeper prorate your pay down to one half of one show for one night.'

My hand throbbed – I grabbed the ice out of Chrissy's water glass. 'Fifty scoots?'

'Forty and change. They counted it down to the penny.'

Demons hovered: Leigh's obstetrician, the Yeakel Olds repo man. I said, 'They don't repossess babies.'

'No, but they do repossess three-month delinquent Starfire 88s. Dick, did you *have* to get the Continental Kit, "Kustom King" interior, and that hideous accordion hood ornament?'

Chrissy: 'It was an Italian rivalry thing. Buddy Greco's got a car like that, so Dick had to have one.'

Kay: 'My husband has an 88. He said the "Kustom King" interior is so soft that he almost fell asleep once on the San Bernardino Freeway.'

Nancy: 'Chester Boudreau, one of my *favorite* sex killers of all time, preferred Oldsmobiles. He said Oldsmobiles had a bulk that children found comforting, so it was easy to lure kids into them.'

Right on cue: my three-girl chorus. Chrissy sang with Buddy Greco and sold Dexedrine; Nancy played trombone in Spade Cooley's all-woman band and pen-palled with half the pervs in San Quentin. Kay: National President of the Dick Contino Fan Club. We go back to my army beef: Kay's husband Pete bossed the Fed team that popped me for desertion.

Our food arrived. Nancy talked up the 'West Hollywood Whipcord' – some fiend who'd strangled two lovebird duos parked off the Strip. Chris boohooed my Crescendo fracas and bemoaned the end of Buddy's Mocambo stand two weeks hence. Leigh let me read her eyes:

Your friends cosign your bullshit, but I won't.

Your display of manly pique cost us four grand.

You fight the COWARD taint with your fists, you just make it worse.

Radioactive eyes – I evaded them via small talk. 'Chrissy, did you catch Dot Rothstein checking you out?'

Chris choked down a hunk of Reuben sandwich. 'Yes, and it's been *five years* since the Barbara Graham gig.'

'Barbara Graham,' tweaked Nan the Ghoul. I elaborated:

'Chrissy was doing nine months in the Women's Jail downtown when Barbara Graham was there.'

Nancy, breathless: '*And?*'

'And she just happened to be in the cell next to hers.'

'*And?*'

Chris jumped in. 'Quit talking about me like I'm not here.'

Nancy: '*And?*'

'And I was doing nine months for passing forged Dilaudid prescriptions. Dot was the matron on my tier, and she was smitten by me, which I consider a testimonial to her good taste. Barbara Graham and those partners of hers, Santo and Perkins, had just been arrested for the Mabel Monohan killing. Barbara kept protesting that she was innocent, and the DA's Office was afraid that a jury might believe her. Dot heard a rumor that Barbara went lez whenever she did jail time, and she got this brainstorm to have me cozy up to Barbara in exchange for a sentence reduction. I agreed, but stipulated no Sapphic contact. The DA's Office cut a deal with me, but I couldn't get Barbara to admit anything vis-à-goddamn-vis the night of March 9, 1953. We exchanged mildly flirtatious napkin notes, which Dot sold to *Hush-Hush* Magazine, and they published with my name deleted. I got my sentence reduction and Barbara got the gas chamber, and Dot Rothstein's got herself convinced that I'm a lezzie. She still sends me Christmas cards. Have *you* ever gotten a lipstick-smeared Christmas card from a two-hundred-pound diesel dyke?'

The whole booth howled. Kay squealed with her mouth full – some club soda spritzed out and hit Leigh. A flashbulb popped – I spotted Danny Getchell and a *Hush-Hush* camera jockey.

Getchell spritzed headlines: ' "Accordion Ace Activates Lethal Left Hook at Crescendo Fistfest". "Draft Dodger Taunt Torches Torrid Temper Tantrum". "Quo Vadis, Dick Contino? Comeback Crumbles in Niteclub Crack-up".'

Nancy walked back to the pay phones. I said, 'Danny, this is publicity I don't need.'

'Dick, I disagree. Look at what that marijuana contretemps did for Bob Mitchum. I think this portrays you as a good-looking, hot-headed *gavonne* who's probably – excuse me, ladies – got a schvanze that's a yard long.'

15

I laughed. Danny said, 'If I'm lyin', I'm flyin'. Seriously, Dick, and again, excuse me, ladies, but this makes you look like you've got a yard of hard pipe and you're not afraid to show it.'

I laughed. Leigh sent up a silent prayer: save my husband from this scandal-rag provocateur.

Nancy shot me a whisper. 'I just talked to Ella Mae Cooley. Spade's been beating her up again . . . and . . . Dick . . . you're the only one who can calm him down.'

I drove out to Spade Cooley's ranch. Rain slashed my windshield; I tuned in Hunter Hancock's all-request show. The gang at Googie's got a call through: Dick Contino's 'Yours' hit the airwaves.

The rain got worse; the chrome accordion on my hood cut down visibility. I accelerated and synced bio-thoughts to music.

Late '47, Fresno: I glommed a spot on Horace Heidt's radio program. Amateur-night stuff – studio audience/applause meter – I figured I'd play 'Lady of Spain', lose to some local babe Heidt was banging and go on to college.

I won.

Bobbysoxers swarmed me backstage.

I turned eighteen the next month. I kept winning – every Sunday night – weeks running. I beat singers, comics, a Negro trombonist and a blind vibraphone virtuoso. I shook, twisted, stomped, gyrated, flailed, thrashed, genuflected, wiggled, strutted and banged my squeezebox like a dervish orbiting on Benzedrine, maryjane and glue. I pelvis-popped and pounded pianissimos; I cascaded cadenzas and humped harmonic hurricanes until the hogs hollered for Hell – straight through to Horace Heidt's grand finals. I became a national celebrity, toured the country as Heidt's headliner, and went solo BIG.

I played BIG ROOMS. I cut records. I broke hearts. Screen tests, fan clubs, magazine spreads. Critics marveled at how I hipsterized the accordion – I said all I did was make schmaltz look sexy. They said where'd you learn to *move* like that? I lied and said I didn't know.

The truth was:

I've always been afraid.

I've always conjured terror out of thin air.

Music and movement are incantations that help keep it formless.

1949, 1950 – flying high on fame and callow good fortune. Early '51: FORM arrives via draft notice.

16

FORM: day sweats, night sweats, suffocation fears. Fear of mutilation, blindness, cancer, vivisection by rival accordionists. 24-hour heebie-jeebies; nightclub audiences packing shrouds. Music inside my head: jackhammers, sirens, Mixmasters stripping gears.

I went to the Mayo Clinic; three headshrinkers stamped me unfit for army service. My draft board wanted a fourth opinion and sent me to their on-call shrink. He contradicted the Mayo guys – my 1-A classification stood firm.

I was drafted and sent to Fort Ord. FORM: the reception-station barracks compressed in on me. My heart raced and sent live-wire jolts down my arms. My feet went numb; my legs fluttered and dripped sweat. I bolted, and caught a bus to Frisco.

AWOL, Federal fugitive – my desertion made front-page news.

I trained down to L.A. and holed up at my parents' house. Reporters knocked – my dad sent them away. TV crews kept a vigil outside. I talked to a lawyer, worked up a load of show-biz panache and turned myself in.

My lawyer tried to cut a deal – the U.S. Attorney wasn't buying. I took a daily flailing from the Hearst rags: 'Accordion Prima Donna Suffers Stage Fright at Fort Ord Opening.' 'Coward', 'Traitor', 'Yellow Belly', 'Chicken-Hearted Heartthrob'. 'Coward', 'Coward', 'Coward'.

My BIG ROOM bookings were canceled.

I was bound over for trial in San Francisco.

Fear:

Bird chirps made me flinch. Rooms closed in coffin-tight the second I entered them.

I went to trial. My lawyer proffered Mayo depositions; I detailed my fear on the witness stand. The press kept resentment fires stoked: I had it all, but wouldn't serve my country. My response went ignored: so take away my fucking accordion.

The judge found me guilty and sentenced me: six months in the Federal pen at McNeil Island, Washington.

I did the time. I put on a sadistic face to deter butt-fuckers. Accordion slinging gave me big muscles – I hulked and popped my biceps. Mickey Cohen, in for income-tax evasion, befriended me. My daily routine: yard trusty work, squeezebox impromptus. Ingratiating showman/psycho con – a schizophrenic performance that got me through my sentence unmolested.

Released – January, '52. Slinking/creeping/crawling anxiety: *what happens next?*

Winter '52 – one big publicity watch. Big 'Contino Out of Jail' coverage – most of it portrayed me as a coward case-hardened by prison.

Residual fear: would I now be drafted?

Winter '52 – no gigs, BIG ROOM or otherwise. My draft notice arrived – this time I played the game.

Basic training, communications school, Korea. Fear back-burner-boogied; I served in a Seoul-based outfit and rose from private to staff sergeant. Acceptance/taunts/shoving matches. Resentment oozing off guys who envied what they thought I'd come home to.

I came home to tapped-out momentum and DRAFT DODGER in Red-bait neon. I received an unsolicited presidential pardon – my COWARD taint rendered it toilet paper. I became a vanishing act: BIG ROOM stints replaced by lounge gigs; national TV shots downgraded into local stuff. Fear and I played peekaboo – it always seemed to grab my balls and twist just when it felt like something inside me could banish all the bullshit forever.

I hit Victorville. L.A. radio had faded out – I'd been listening to shitkicker ditties. Apt: I pulled up to the Cooley ranch house soundtracked by Spade's own 'Shame, Shame on You'.

The porch reeked: marijuana and sourmash fumes. TV glow lit up windows blueish-gray.

The door stood ajar. I pressed the buzzer – hillbilly chimes went off. Dark inside – the TV screen made shadows bounce. George Putnam spritzed late local news: '... the fiend the Los Angeles County Sheriff's have dubbed the "West Hollywood Whipcord" claimed his third and fourth victims last night. The bodies of Thomas "Spike" Knode, thirty-nine, an out-of-work movie stuntman, and his fiancée Carol Matusow, nineteen, a stenographer, were discovered locked in the trunk of Knode's car, parked on Hilldale Drive a scant block north of the Sunset Strip. Both were strangled with a sash cord and bludgeoned postmortem with a bumper jack found in the backseat. The couple had just come from the Mocambo nightclub, where they had watched entertainer Buddy Greco perform. Authorities report that they have no clues as to the slayer's identity, and—'

18

A ratchet noise – metal on metal. That unmistakable drawl: 'From the size of your shadow, I'd say it's Dick Contino.'

'It's me.'

Ratch/ratch – trigger noise – Spade loved to get zorched and play with guns.

'I should tell Nancy 'bout that "Whipcord" sumbitch. She just might find herself a new pen pal.'

'She already knows about him.'

'Well . . . I'm not surprised. And this old dog, well . . . he knows how to put things together. My Ella Mae got a call from Nancy, and two hours later Mr. Accordion himself shows up. Heard you tanked at the Crescendo, boy. Ain't that always the way it is when proving yourself runs contrary to your own best interests?'

A lamp snapped on. Dig it: Spade Cooley in a cowboy hat and sequin-studded chaps – packing two holstered six-guns.

I said, 'Like you and Ella Mae. You beg her for details on her old shack jobs, then you beat her up when she plays along.'

Fluttering flags replaced George Putnam – KTTV signing off for the night. The National Anthem kicked in – I doused the volume. Spade slumped low in his chair and drew down on me. 'You mean I shouldn't have asked her if those John Ireland and Steve Cochran rumors were true?'

'You're dying to torture yourself, so tell me.'

Spade twirled his guns, popped the cylinders and spun them. Two revolvers, ten empty slots, one bullet per piece.

'So tell me, Spade.'

'The rumors were true, boy. Would I be sittin' here in this condition if those dudes were any less than double-digit bulls?'

I laughed.

I roared.

I howled.

Spade put both guns to his head and pulled the triggers.

Two loud clicks – empty chambers.

I stopped laughing.

Spade did it again.

Click/click – empty chambers.

I grabbed for the guns. Spade shot ME twice – empty chambers.

I backed into the TV. A leg brushed the volume dial – the Star-Spangled Banner went very loud, then very soft.

Spade said, 'You could have died hearing your country's theme song, which might have gotten you the posthumous approval of all them patriotic groups that don't like you so much. And you also could have died not knowing that John Ireland had to tape that beast of his to his leg when he wore swimming trunks.'

A toilet flushed upstairs. Ella Mae yelled, 'Donnell Clyde Cooley, quit talking to yourself or God knows who, and come to bed!'

Spade aimed both guns at her voice and pulled the triggers.

Two empty chambers.

Four down per piece, two to go – fifty-fifty odds next time. Spade said, 'Dick, let's get blotto. Get me a fresh bottle from the kitchen.'

I walked to the bathroom and checked the medicine cabinet. Yellow jackets on a shelf – I emptied two into a glass and flushed the rest.

Kitchen recon – a Wild Turkey quart atop the icebox.

I dumped it down the sink – all but three fingers' worth.

Loose .38 shells on a shelf – I tossed them out the window.

Spade's maryjane stash – right where it always was in the sugar bowl.

I poured it down the sink and chased it with Drano.

Spade yelled, 'I am determined to shoot somebody or something tonight!'

I swirled up a cocktail: bourbon, Nembutal, buttermilk to kill the barbiturate taste. Spade yelled, 'Go out to your car and get your accordion, and I'll put it out of its misery!'

On the breakfast table: a TV remote-control gizmo.

I grabbed it.

Back to Spade. On cue: he put down one gun and grabbed his drink. One six-shooter on the floor – I toed it under his chair.

Spade twirled gun #2.

I stood *behind* the chair. Spade said, 'I wonder if John used masking tape or friction tape.'

Blip, blip – I pushed remote-control buttons. Test pattern, test pattern, Rock Hudson and Jane Wyman in some hankie epic.

I nudged Spade. 'I heard Rock Hudson's hung like a horse. I heard he put the make on Ella Mae back when she played clarinet on your old Hoffman Hayride Show.'

Spade said, 'Ixnay – Rock's a fruit. I heard he plays skin flute with some quiff on the Lawrence Welk program.'

Shit – no bite. Blip, blip, Caryl Chessman fomenting from his death-row cell. 'Now there's your double-digit dude, Spade. That cat is legendary in criminal annals – Nancy Ankrum told me so herself.'

'Nix. Shitbird criminals like that are always underhung. I read it in *Argosy* Magazine.'

Blip, blip, blip – *beaucoup* test patterns. Blip, blip, blip – test-drive the new '58 Chevy, Ford, Rambler, et fucking al. Blip – Senator John F. Kennedy talking to reporters.

Spade pre-empted me. 'Hung like a cashew. Gene Tierney told me he screws from hunger. Hung like a cricket, and he expects a standing ovation for a two-minute throw.'

Shit – running out of channels. Blip – an American Legion chaplain with 2:00 A.M. prayers.

'. . . and as always, we ask for the strength to oppose our Communist adversary at here and abroad. We ask—'

Spade said, 'This is for Dick Contino,' raised his gun and fired. The TV screen imploded – wood splintered, tubes popped, glass shattered.

Spade passed out on the floor rag-doll limp.

TV dust formed a little mushroom cloud.

I carried Spade upstairs and laid him down in bed next to Ella Mae. Cozy: inside seconds they were snoring in unison. I remembered Fresno, Christmas '47 – I was young, she was lonely, Spade was in Texas.

Keep it hush-hush, dear heart – for both our sakes.

I walked out to my car. February 12, 1958 – what an all-time fucker of a night.

2

Bad sleep left me fried – hung over from my rescue run.

The baby woke me up. I'd been dreaming: I was on trial for Crimes Against Music. The judge said the accordion was obsolete; a studio audience applauded. Dig my jury: Mickey Cohen's dog, Jesus Christ, Cisco Andrade.

Leigh had coffee and aspirin ready. Ditto the A.M. *Mirror*, folded to the entertainment page.

'Brawl Deep-Sixes Contino Opening. Nightclub Boss Calls Accordion King "Damaged Goods".'

The phone rang – I grabbed it. 'Who's this?'

'Howard Wormser, your agent, who just lost 10 percent of your Crescendo money *and* 10 percent of your sixty-day-stand at the Flamingo Lounge. Vegas called early, Dick. They get the L.A. papers early, and they don't like to sit on bad news.'

A *Mirror* subhead: 'Draft Dodger Catcalls Plague Fading Star.'

'I was busy last night, or I would have seen this coming.'

'Seeing things coming is not your strong suit. You *should* have accepted Sam Giancana's invitation to be on call for Chicago Mob gigs, and if you did you'd be playing big rooms today. You *should* have testified before that grand jury and named some Commies. You *should*—'

'I don't know any Commies.'

'No, but you *could* have gotten a few names from the phone book to make yourself look good.'

'Get me some movie work, Howard. Get me a gig where I can sing a few songs and get the girl.'

Howard sighed. 'There is a certain wisdom to that, since young snatch *is* your strong suit. I'll look into it. In the meantime, play a few bar mitzvahs or something and stay out of trouble.'

'Can you get me a few bar mitzvahs?'

22

'That was just a figure of speech. Dick, be calm. I'll call when I've got you 90 percent of something.'

Click – one abrupt hang-up faded into noise outside – brake squeals, gear crunch. I checked the window – fuck – a tow truck had my car bumper-locked.

I ran out. A man in a Teamster T-shirt held his hands up. 'Mr. Contino, this wasn't my idea. I'm just a poor out-of-work union man with a family. Bob Yeakel said to tell you enough is enough, he read the papers this morning and saw the writing on the wall.'

The bumper winch ratched my trunk open. Record albums flew out – I grabbed an *Accordion in Paris*.

'What's your name?'

'Uh . . . Bud Brown.'

I pulled the pen off his clipboard and scrawled on the album cover. 'To Bud Brown, out-of-work union man, from Dick Contino, out-of-work entertainer. Dear Bud, why are you fucking with my beautiful Starfire 88, when I'm just a working stiff like you? I know that the evil McClellan Committee is harassing your heroic leader Jimmy Hoffa, in much the same way I was harassed during the Korean War, and thus you and I share a bond that you are trespassing on in your current scab status. Please do not fuck with my beautiful Starfire 88 – I need it to look for work.'

The tow-truck driver applauded. Bud Brown fisheyed me – my McClellan shtick hit him weird.

'Mr. Contino, like I said, I'm sorry.'

I pointed to the albums.

'I'll donate those to your Teamster local. I'll autograph them. You can sell them yourself and keep the money. All I'm asking is that you let me drive this car out of here and hide it somewhere.'

Raps on the kitchen window – Leigh holding baby Merri up. Brown said, 'Mr. Contino, that's fighting dirty.'

Worth the fight: my baby-blue/whitewall-tired/foxtail-antennaed sweetie. Sunlight on the accordion hood hanger – I almost swooned.

'Have you guys got kids with birthdays coming up? I'll perform for free, I'll dress up like a—'

The tow-truck radio crackled; the driver listened and rogered the call. 'That was Mr. Yeakel. He says Mr. Contino should meet him at the showroom pronto, that maybe they can work out a deal on his delinquent.'

'. . . and you know I've got my own TV show, *Rocket to Stardom*. My brothers and I do our own commercials and give amateur Angeleno talent a chance to reach for the moon and haul down a few stars. We put on a show here at the lot every Sunday, and KCOP broadcasts it. We dish out free hot dogs and soda pop, sell some cars and let the talent perform. We usually get a bunch of hot-dog scroungers hanging around – I call them the "Yeakel Yokels". They applaud for the acts, and whoever gets the most applause wins. I've got a meter rigged up – sort of like that thingamajig you had on the Heidt show.'

Bob Yeakel: tall, blond, pitchman shrill. His desk: covered with memo slips held down by chrome hubcaps.

'Let me guess. You want me to celebrity MC one of your shows, in exchange for which I get to keep my car free and clear.'

Yeakel yuk-yuk-yukked. 'No, Dick, more along the lines of you produce *and* celebrity MC at least *two* shows, *and* perform at the Oldsmobile Dealers of America Convention, *and* spend some afternoons here at the lot auditioning acts and bullshitting with the customers. In the meantime, you get to keep your car, and we stop the clock on your delinquent interest payments, but not on the base sum itself. Then, if *Rocket to Stardom*'s ratings zoom, I might just let you have that car free and clear.'

'Is that *all* I have to do?'

Yuk-yuk-yuk. 'No. You also have to pitch all your potential contestants on the '58 Oldsmobile line. And no jigaboos or beatniks, Dick. I run a clean family show.'

'I'll do it if you throw in two hundred a week.'

'A hundred and fifty, but off-the-books with no withholding.'

I stuck my hand out.

Work:

The Oldsmobile Dealers Convention at the downtown Statler. Dig it: five hundred car hucksters and a busload of hookers chaperoned by a VD doctor. Bob Yeakel opened for me – shtick featuring 'Peaches, the Drag Queen with an Overbite.' Chris Staples sang, 'You Belong to Me', and 'Baby, Baby, All the Time' – Yeakel ogled her and cracked jokes about her 'Tail Fins'. I killed the booze-fried crowd with a forty-minute set and closed with the *Rocket to Stardom* theme song.

Work:

Birthday parties – Cisco Andrade's son, Mickey Cohen's niece. The Cisco gig was East L.A. SRO – Mex fighters and their families wowed by Dick Contino as 'Chucko the Birthday Clown'. Degrading? Yeah – but the guests shot me close to a C-note in tips. The Cohen job was more swank: a catered affair at Mickey's pad. Check the guest list: Lana Turner and Johnny Stompanato, Mike Romanoff, Moe Dalitz, Meyer Lansky, Julius La Rosa, and the Reverend Wesley Swift – who explained that Jesus Christ was an Aryan, not a Jew, and that *Mein Kampf* was the lost book of the Bible. No gratuities, but Johnny Stomp kicked loose two dozen cases of Gerber's Baby Food – he bankrolled a fur-van hijack, and his guys hit the wrong truck.

Work – long days at the Yeakel Olds lot.

I called the girls in to help me: Leigh, Chrissy, Nancy Ankrum, Kay Van Obst. Word spread quick: Mr. Accordion and female coterie LIVE at Oldsmobile showroom!

We bullshitted with browsers and referred hard prospects to salesmen; we spritzed the '58 Olds lineup nonstop. We grilled burgers on a hibachi and fed the mechanics and Bud Brown and his repo crew.

Nancy, Kay and Leigh screened *Rocket to Stardom* applicants – I wanted to weed out the more egregious geeks before I began formal auditions. Bob Yeakel drooled whenever Chris Staples slinked by – I convinced him to put her on the payroll as my assistant. Grateful Chrissy gave Bob a thank-you gift: her *Nugget* Magazine foldout preserved via laminated wall plaque.

My Yeakel run nine days in: a righteous fucking blast.

Nine days sans 'Draft Dodger' jive – some kind of Contino world record.

We held auditions in a tent behind the lube rack; Bud Brown stood watchdog to keep obvious lunatics out. The girls had compiled a list: forty-odd individuals and acts to be winnowed down to six spots per show.

Our first finalist: an old geezer who sang grand opera. I asked him to belt a few bars of *Pagliacci*; he said that he possessed the world's largest penis. He whipped it out before I could comment – it was of average length and girth. Chrissy applauded anyway – she said it reminded her of her ex-husband's.

Bud hustled the old guy out. Pops was gone – but he'd set a certain tone.

Check this sampling:

Two roller-skating bull terriers – sharklike dogs with plastic fins attached to their backs. Their master was a Lloyd Bridges look-alike – the whole thing was a goof on the TV show *Sea Hunt*.

Nix.

An off-key woman accordionist who tried to slip me her phone number with Leigh right there.

Nix.

A comic with patter on Ike's golf game – epic snoresville.

Nix.

A guy who performed silk-scarf tricks. Deft and boring: he cinched sashes into hangman's knots.

Nix.

Over two dozen male and female vocalists: flat, screechy, shrill, hoarse – dud Presley and Patti Page would-bes.

A junkie tenor sax, who nodded out halfway through a flubbed-note 'Body and Soul.' Bud Brown dumped him in a demo car; the fucker woke up convulsing and kicked the windshield out. Chrissy summoned an ambulance; the medics hustled the hophead off.

I confronted Nancy. She said, 'You should have seen the ones that *didn't* make the cut. I wish the "West Hollywood Whipcord" had a viable talent – it would be fun to put him on the show.'

I braced Bud Brown. 'Bud, the show's forty-eight hours off, and we've got nobody.'

'This happens sometimes. When it does, Bob calls Pizza De-Luxe.'

'What—'

'Ask Bob.'

I walked into Yeakel's office. Bob was eyeballing his wall plaque: Miss Nugget, June '54.

'What's Pizza De-Luxe?'

'Are your auditions going *that* bad?'

'I'm thinking of calling those roller-skating dogs back. Bob, what's—'

'Pizza De-Luxe is a prostitution racket. An ex-Jack Dragna goon who owns a greasy spoon called the Pizza Pad runs it. He delivers pizza twenty-four hours a day legit, and if you want a girl or a dicey boy on the side, a female or male prostitute will make the delivery. All of the hookers are singers or dancers or Hollywood riffraff like that, you know, selling some skin to make ends meet until they get their so-called "big break". So . . . if I get strapped for decent contestants I call

26

Pizza De-Luxe. I get some good pizza, some good "amateur" talent, and my top-selling salesman of the month gets laid.'

I checked the window. A transvestite dance team practiced steps by the grease rack – Bud Brown and a cop type shooed them off. I said, 'Bob, call Pizza De-Luxe.'

Yeakel blew his wall plaque kisses. 'I think Chrissy should win this next show.'

'Chrissy's a professional. She's singing backup for Buddy Greco at the Mocambo right now.'

'I know that, but I want to do her a solid. And I'll let you in on a secret: my applause meter's rigged.'

'Yeah?'

'Yeah. It's a car battery hooked up to an oscilloscope screen. I've got a foot pedal I tap to goose the needle. I'm sure Chris would like to win – it's a C-note and a free down payment on a snappy new Oldsmobile.'

I laughed. 'With debilitating *monthly* payments?'

'Normally, yes. But with Chrissy I'm sure we could work something else out.'

'I'll tell her. I'm sure she'll play along, at least as far as the "free" down payment.'

Bob's phone rang – he picked up, listened, hung up. I scoped the window – Bud Brown and the fuzz type saw me and turned away, nervous.

Bob said, 'I might have a way for you to buy out of your second *Rocket to Stardom* commitment.'

'I'm listening.'

'I've got to think it over first. Dick, I'm going to call Pizza De-Luxe right now. Will you . . .'

'Talk to Chrissy and tell her she just won an amateur talent contest rigged by this car kingpin who wants to stroke her "Tail Fins"?'

'Right. And ask for what she wants on her pizza.'

Chris was outside the sales shack, smoking.

I spilled quick. 'Bob's bringing in some quasi-pro talent for Sunday's show. He wants you to sing a couple of songs. You're guaranteed to win, and he's got mild expectations.'

'If he keeps them mild, he won't be disappointed.'

Smoke rings drifted up – a sure sign that Chrissy was distracted.

'Something on your mind?'

27

'No, just my standard boogeyman.'

'I know what you mean, but if you tell me, you'll probably feel better.'

Chris flicked her cigarette at a Cutlass demo. 'I'm thirty-two, and I'll always earn a living as an entertainer, but I'll never have a hit record. I like men too much to settle down and have a family, and I like myself too much to sell my tush to clowns like Bob Yeakel.'

'And?'

'And nothing. Except that a car followed me after my Mocambo gig last night. I think it's Dot Rothstein. I think she got rehipped on me after she saw me at your show at the Crescendo.'

'Was she at the Mocambo last night?'

'Yes. And it's in L.A. *County* jurisdiction, and she's an L.A. County Deputy Sheriff, which means . . . shit, I don't know. Dick, will you and Leigh come to Buddy's show tonight? Dot knows you're friends with Mickey Cohen, and it might discourage her from making any moves.'

'We'll be there.'

Chris hugged me. 'You know what I envy about your career?'

'What?'

'That at least you're *notorious*. At least that draft dodger thing gives you something to . . . I don't know, at least *overcome*.'

A lightbulb went POP! – but I didn't know what it meant.

3

The Mocambo JUMPED.

Buddy Greco was belting 'Around the World' – working it scat-man style. Buddy not only sells you the song – he drives it to your house and installs it. Chrissy and another girl sang counterpoint – nightclub eyeball magnets.

Leigh and I perched at the bar. She was pissed: I'd told her Bob Yeakel gave me an out on *Rocket to Stardom* # 2 – work repo backup for Bud Brown and another finance clown named Sid Elwell. Bob had a shitload of Darktown delinquents – I was to divert the owners while Bud and Sid grabbed their sleds.

I accepted Bob's offer – the repo runs were scheduled for tomorrow. Leigh's response: it's another courage test. You don't know how to pass on things like that.

She was right. Chrissy's lightbulb POP! flickered: 'At least the draft dodger thing gives you something to *overcome*.'

Buddy snapped lyrics – 'I traveled on when love was gone, to keep a big fat swingin' rendezvous' – the crowd snapped fingers along with him. Danny Getchell hopped ringside tables – snouting for *Hush-Hush* 'Sinuendo'. Check Dot Rothstein by the stage: measuring Chrissy for a bunk at the Dyke Island Motel.

Leigh nudged me. 'I'm hungry.'

I leaned close. 'We'll go to Dino's Lodge. It won't be long – Buddy usually closes with this number.'

'No more will I go all around the world, 'cause I have found my world in you – ooblay-oooh-oooh-baa-baa-doww!'

Big-time applause – jealousy ditzed me. Dot sidled up to the bar and dug through her purse. Check it out: KY Jelly, .38 snubnose.

She threw me a sneer. Check her outfit: Lockheed jumpsuit, tire-tread sandals. Chrissy signalled from the stage door – the parking lot, five minutes.

Dot chug-a-lugged a Scotch; the bartender refused payment. I stood up and stretched – Dot bumped me passing by. 'Your wife's cute, Dick. Take good care of her or someone else will.'

Leigh stuck a leg out to trip her; Dot sidestepped and flipped me the finger. The barman said, 'She's supposed to be here on a stakeout for the West Hollywood Whipcord, but all she does is drool for the chorus girls.'

'Beautiful women can get away with anything.'

The barman roared. I doubled his tip and followed Leigh out to the parking lot.

Chrissy was waiting by the car. Dot Rothstein stood close by – bugging loiterers for IDs. She kept one eyeball on Chris: strictly X-ray, strictly a scorcher.

I unlocked the sled and piled the girls in. Ignition, gas, zoom – Dot's farewell kiss fogged my back windshield.

Heavy traffic on the Strip – we slowed to a crawl. Chris said, 'I'm hungry.'

I said, 'We'll hit Dino's Lodge.'

'Not there, *please.*'

'Why?'

'Because Buddy's taking a group from the club there, and I'm betting Dot will crash the party. Really, Dick, anyplace but Dino's.'

Leigh said, 'Canter's is open late.'

I hung a sharp right. Headlights swept my Kustom King interior – the car behind us swung right abruptly.

South on Sweetzer, east on Fountain. Dildo Dot had me running edgy – I checked my back mirror.

That car was still behind us.

South on Fairfax, east on Willoughby – that car stuck close. A sports job – white or light gray – I couldn't make out the driver.

Odds on: Deputy Dot Rothstein.

South on Gardner, east on Melrose – those headlights goose goose goosed us. Leigh said, 'Dick, what are you doing?'

'We're being followed.'

'What? Who? What are you—'

I swung into a driveway sans signal; my tired plowed some poor fucker's lawn. The sports car kept going; I backed out and chased it.

It zooooomed ahead; I flicked on my brights and blipped its tail. No fixed license plate – just a temp sticker stuck to the trunk. Close, closer – a glimpse of the last four digits: 1116.

The car ran a red on 3rd Street. Horns squealed; oncoming traffic held me back. Taillights flickered eastbound: going, going, gone.

Leigh said, 'I've got no more appetite.'

Chris said, 'Can I sleep at your place tonight?'

4

Repo adventures.

Cleotis De Armand ran a crap game behind Swanky Frank's liquor store on 89th and Central, flaunting his delinquent 98 right there on the sidewalk. Bud Brown and Sid Elwell came in cereal-box badges and shook him down while I fed Seconal-laced T-Bird to the winos guarding the car. BIG fear: this was combustible L.A. Darktown, cop-impersonation beefs probable if the ubiquitous LAPD swooped by. They didn't – and *I* was the one who drove the sapphire-blue jig rig to safety while the guard contingent snored. Beginner's luck: I found a bag of maryjane in the glove compartment. We toked a few reefers en route to our next job: boost a '57 Starfire off Big Dog Lipscomb, the Southside's #1 streetcorner pimp.

The vehicle: parked by a shoeshine stand at 103 and Avalon. Customized: candy-apple-red paint, mink interior, rhinestone–studded mud flaps, radio aerials topped with plastic streamers. Bud said, 'Let's strip the upholstery and make our wives fur stoles' – Sid and I were thinking the same thing.

The team deployed.

I unpacked my accordion and slammed 'Lady of Spain' right there. Sid and Bud walked point on Big Dog Lipscomb: across the street browbeating whores. Someone yelled, 'Hey, that's Dick Contino' – Watts riffraff engulfed me.

I was pushed off the sidewalk – straight into Big Dog's coon coach. An aerial snapped; my back hit the hood; I played prostrate and didn't miss a note.

Look, Mom: no fear.

Foot scrapes, yells – dim intrusions on my reefer reverie. Hands yanked me off the hood – I went eyeball to eyeball with Big Dog Lipscomb.

He swung on me – I blocked the shot with my accordion. Contact:

his fist, my keyboard. Sickening cracks: his bones, my bread-and-butter baby.

Big Dog yelped and clutched his hand; some punk kicked him in the balls and picked his pocket. Car keys in the gutter – Bud Brown right there. Flipped, tossed, sprawled – in fur and chauffeur-driven: Sid with white knuckles on a mink steering wheel.

Look, Mom: no fear.

We rendezvoused at Teamster local 1819 – Bud brought the backup sled. My accordion needed a face-lift – I was too weed-wafted to sweat it.

Sid borrowed tools and stripped the mink upholstery; I signed autographs for goldbricking Teamsters. That lightbulb POP! flickered anew: 'Draft dodger thing . . . gives you something to overcome.' That car chase crowded my brain: temp license 1116; Dot Rothstein after Chrissy or something else?

Bud shmoozed up the Local prez – more information pump than friendly talk. A teamster begged me to play 'Bumble Boogie' – I told him my accordion died. I posed for pix instead – the prez slipped me a local 'Friendship Card'.

'You never can tell, Dick. You might need a real job someday.'

Too true – a wet towel on my hot fearless day.

Noon – I took Sid and Bud to the Pacific Dining Car. We settled in behind T-bones and hash browns – small talk came easy for a while.

Sid put the skids to it. 'Dick . . . ask you something?'

'Sure.'

'You know . . . your army rap?'

'What about it?'

'You know . . . you don't impress me as a frightened type of guy.'

Bud piped in: 'As Big Dog Lipscomb will attest to. It's just that . . . you know.'

I said, 'Say it. It feels like I'm close to something.'

Sid said it. 'You know, it's like this. Someone says "Dick Contino", and the first thing you think of is "coward" or maybe "draft dodger". It's like a reflex, when you should be thinking "accordion player" or "singer" or "good repo backup".'

I said, 'Finish the thought.'

Bud: 'What Sid's saying is how do you get around that? Bob Yeakel says it's a life sentence, but isn't there something you can *do*?'

Closer now – lightbulb hot – so HOT I pushed it away. 'I don't know.'

Sid said, 'You can always do something, if you've got nothing to lose.'

I changed the subject. 'A car was tailing me last night. I think it might be this lezbo cop who's hipped on Chrissy.'

Bud whooped. 'Put her on *Rocket to Stardom*. Let her sing "Once I Had a Secret Love".'

'I'm not 100 percent sure it's her, but I got the last four digits of the license plate.'

'So it was just a temporary sticker? Permanent plates only have three letters and three digits.'

'Right, 1116. I thought Bob could call the DMV and get a make for me.'

Bud checked his watch, antsy. 'Not without all nine digits. But ask Bob anyway, *after* the show tomorrow. It's a Pizza De-Luxe gig, and he always bangs his favorite "contestant" *after* the show. Mention it to him then, and maybe he'll call some clerk he knows and tell him to look up all the 1116s.'

A waitress crowded up, menu first. 'Are you Dick Contino? My daddy doesn't like you 'cause he's a veteran, but my mom thinks you're *real* cute. Could I have your autograph?'

'Ladies and Gentlemen, this is Dick Contino, welcoming you to *Rocket to Stardom* – where tomorrow's stellar performers reach for the moon and haul down a few stars! Where all of you in our television audience and here at Yeakel Oldsmobile can seal your fate in a Rocket 88!'

Canned applause/hoots/yells/whistles – a rocket launch straight for the toilet.

Somebody spiked the punch – our live audience got bombed pre-showtime.

Sid Elwell ID's the crowd: mostly juiceheads AWOL from the county dry-out farm.

Act #1 – a Pizza De-Luxe male hooker. Topical patter deluxe: Eisenhower meets Sinatra at the 'Rat Pack Summit'. Ring-a-fucking-ding: Ike, Frank and Dino swap stale one-liners. The crowd booed; the applause meter went on the fritz and leaked steam.

Act #2 – a Pizza De-Luxe prostie/songbird. Tight Capris, tight sweater – mauling 'Blue Moon' made her bounce in two directions. A pachuco by the stage kept a refrain up: 'Baby, are they real?' Bud

34

Brown sucker-punched him silent off-camera; the sound man said his musings came through unsquelched.

Act #3 – 'Ramon and Johnny' – two muscle queen acrobats. Dips, flips, cupped-hand tosses – nice, if you dig shit like that.

Whistles, applause. Bob Yeakel said the guys worked shakedowns: extorting married fags with sodomy pix.

Some spurned lover out of nowhere yelled, 'Ramon, you bitch!'

Ramon blew the audience a pouty kiss.

Johnny spun in mid-toss; Ramon neglected to catch him. Johnny hit the stage flat on his back.

The crowd went nuts; the applause meter belched smoke. Kay Van Obst drove Johnny to Central Receiving.

#4, #5 – Pizza De-Luxe torch singers. Slit-legged gowns, cleavage, goosebumps – both sang Bob Yeakel-lyricked ditties set to hit records. 'The Man I Love' became 'The Car I Love'; 'Fly Me to the Moon' got raped thusly: 'Fly me to the stars, in my souped-up 88; it's got that V-8 power now, and its traction holds straight! In other words, OLDS IS KING!!!'

Cleavage out-tractioned lyrics – the drunks cheered. Sid Elwell hustled a new car battery/applause meter on stage for Chris Staples' bit and final bows.

Chrissy:

Running on fear – that car chase spooked her. I told her I'd have Bob Yeakel tap some DMV slave to trace the license – my backstage pitch shot her some last-minute poise.

Chrissy:

Scorching 'Someone to Watch Over Me' like the Gershwins ALMOST wrote it for her – going hushed so her voice wouldn't crack – the secret of mediocre songsters worldwide.

Chrissy:

Shaking it to 'You Make Me Feel So Young'; putting the make out implicit: *she'd* call *you* at 3:00 in the morning.

Chrissy:

Wolf whistles and scattered claps first time out. Better luck at final bow time: Bob Yeakel hooked the applause rig up to an amplifier.

Chrissy won.

The crowd was too drunk to know they got bamboozled.

Bob congratulated Chris and stroked her tail fins on-camera – Chris swatted his hand.

Ramon moaned for Johnny.

The sales crew snarfed Pizza De-Luxe pizza.

Leigh called to say she'd caught the show on TV. 'Dick, you were better off as Chucko the Clown.'

I grabbed Chrissy. 'Tell Bud and Sid to meet us at Mike Lyman's. You gave me an idea the other day.'

Bud and Sid made Lyman's first. I slipped the headwaiter a five-spot; he slipped us a secluded back booth.

We huddled in, ordered drinks and shot the shit. Topics covered: *Rocket to Stardom* as epic goof; would my repo work spring me from my second producing gig? Bud said he spieled the car chase to Bob Yeakel; Bob said he'd try to DMV-trace the temp license. Sid reprised the Big Dog repo – I used it to steer talk down to biz.

'I've been stuck with this "Coward" tag for years, and I'm tired of it. My career's going nowhere, but at least I've got a name, and Chrissy doesn't even have that. I've got an idea for a publicity stunt. It would probably take at least two extra men to pull off, but I think we could do it.'

Bud said, 'Do *what*?'

Chris said, 'I've got a hunch I know where this is going.'

I whispered. 'Two hoods kidnap Chrissy and me at gunpoint. The hoods are psycho types who've got this crazy notion that we're big stars who can bring in ransom money. They contact Howard Wormser – he's the agent who gets both of us work – and demand some large amount. Howard doesn't know the gig's a phony, and either calls the fuzz or doesn't call the fuzz. In either case, Chrissy and I heroically escape. We can't identify the kidnappers, because they wore masks. We fake evidence at the place where we were held hostage and tough it out when the cops question us. We're bruised-up and fucked-up from the ordeal. The kidnappers, of course, remain at large. Chrissy and I get a boatload of publicity and goose our careers. We pay off the fake kidnappers with a percentage of the good money we're now making.'

Three deadpans.

Three-way silence – I clocked it at one minute.

Sid coughed. 'This is certifiably nuts.'

Chris coughed and lit a cigarette. 'I like it. If it works, it works. If it doesn't, Dick and I go to jail. We've both been to jail, so we know we can survive. I say maybe this is the real *Rocket to Stardom*, and if it isn't, *c'est la* goddamn *guerre.* I say better to try it than not to. I say the entertainment business thrives on bullshit, so why not try to shovel some of our own?'

Bud strafed me: wary eyes, working on sad. 'It's dangerous. It's illegal, probably to the tune of a couple of years in jail. And you're what the cops would call a "known associate" of me and Sid. I could probably set you up with some guys more removed, so the cops couldn't link you to them. See, Dick, what I'm thinking is: if you're *determined* to do it, then maybe we could make some money by cutting down the chance you'll get caught. *If you're determined to do it, hell or high water.*'

Those eyes — why so *sad?*

'I'm determined.'

Bud pushed his drink aside. 'Then it has to look real. Let's go, there's a place you should see.'

We convoyed up to Griffith Park and went hiking. There it was: a shack tucked into a box canyon a mile north of the Observatory.

Hard to spot: scrub bushes blocked the canyon entrance off.

Tumbleweeds covered the roof — the shack couldn't be seen from the air.

The door was open. Stink wafted out: dead animals, dead something. Dig the interior: a mattress on the floor, blood-encrusted pelts stacked on a table.

Chris said, 'Scalps,' and covered her nose.

I looked closer — yeah — SCALPS.

Sid crossed himself. Bud said, 'I found this place a few years ago. I was on a hiking jaunt with a buddy and stumbled onto it. Those scalps spooked the living bejesus out of me, and I checked with this cop pal of mine. He said back in '46 some crazy Indian escaped from Atascadero, killed six people and scalped them. The Indian was never captured, and if you look close, you'll see six scalps there.'

I looked close. Six scalps, all right — one replete with braids and a plastic barrette.

Chris and Sid lit cigarettes — the stink diminuendoed. I said, 'Bud, what are you saying?'

'That at least one of your kidnappers should be made up to look like an Indian. That this dump as the kidnappers' stash place would gain you some points for realism. That a psycho Indian who might be long dead makes a good fall guy.'

37

Chris said, 'If this works and my career takes off, I'll give you each 10 percent of my gross earnings for the next ten years. If it doesn't work, I'll cash in some stocks my dad left me and split the money between you, and I'll sleep with both of you at least once.'

Sid howled. Chris poked a scalp and said, 'Ick. Icky lizard.'

I said, 'Count me in, minus the bed stuff. If the gig doesn't fly or get results, I'll fork over the pink slip on my 88.'

Four-way handshakes. A bird squawked outside – I flinched wicked bad.

5

Scalps.

Indian fall guys.

Teamster goons.

Encore: Dick Contino, truculent guinea hood.

Who *didn't* tell his wife: I'm knee-deep in a hot kidnap caper.

Monday morning twinkled new-beginning-bright. I walked out for the paper – a fuzz type was lounging on my car. I'd seen him before: hobnobbing with Bud Brown at Yeakel Olds.

I eeeased over guinea-hood coool. Fear: my legs evaporated.

He held up a badge. 'My name's DePugh. I'm an investigator for the McClellan Senate Rackets Committee. Bud Brown snitched you for Conspiracy to Kidnap, Conspiracy to Defraud and Conspiracy to Perpetrate a Public Hoax, and believe me, he did you a big favor. Hand me the contents of your outside jacket pockets.'

I complied. Felony bingo: repo-run reefers. Bud Brown: lying rat motherfucker.

DePugh said, 'Add Possession of Marijuana to those charges, and put that shit back in your pockets before your neighbors see it.'

I complied. DePugh whipped out a sheet of paper.

Dear Dick:

I couldn't let you and Chrissy go through with it. You would have gotten caught in your lies and everybody would have gotten hurt, me and Sid included. I told Mr. DePugh, who is a nice guy, so that he would stop you but not get you in trouble. Mr. DePugh said there is a favor you could do for him, so my advice is to do it. I'm sorry I finked you off, but I did it for your own good.

Your pal, Bud Brown.

My legs returned – this wasn't a jail bounce. Shit clicked in late: Bud pressing the Teamster prez for info: Bud hinky on the kidnap plan from jump street. 'Brown's an informant for the McClellan Committee.'

'That's correct. And I am a nice guy with a beautiful and impetuous nineteen-year-old daughter who may be heading for a fall that you can help avert.'

'*What?*'

DePugh smiled and clicked into focus: a cop from Moosefart, Minnesota, with a night-school law degree. 'Dick, you are one good-looking side of beef. My daughter Jane, God bless her, goes for guys like you – although I'm pretty sure she's still a virgin, and I want to keep her that way until she finds herself some nice pussy-whipped clown that I can control and marries him.'

'*What?*'

'Dick, you keep asking me that, so I will now tell you that one hand washes the other, a stitch in time saves nine, and if you scratch my back I'll scratch yours: i.e., I'll let your fake kidnapping happen, and I'll even supply you with some muscle far superior to Bud and Sid – if you do me a favor.'

I checked the kitchen window – no Leigh – good. 'Tell me about it.'

DePugh tossed an arm around me. 'Jane's an undergrad at UCLA. She's flirting with pinko politics and attending some sort of quasi-Commie coffee klatch every Monday night. The klatch is an open thing, so anybody can show up, and with that bum Korean War deal of yours, you'd be a natural. See, Dick, I'm afraid the Feds have infiltrated the group. I'm afraid Janie's going to get her name on all kinds of lists and fuck her life up. I want you to infiltrate the group, woo Janie, but don't sleep with her, and make it look like she just joined the group to chase men, which Janie implied to her mother is true. You join the "Westwood People's Study Collective", put some moves on Jane DePugh and pull her out before she gets hurt. Got it?'

Holy Jesus Christ.

'And no reprisals against Bud and Sid. Really, Dick, Bud did you an all-time solid by bringing me into this scheme of yours. You'll see, I'll find you some good boys.'

I said, 'I like the scalp angle. I want to keep it.'

DePugh pulled out photos. The top one: a dead Indian on a morgue slab. Three bullet holes in his face; 'Sioux City, S.D. Coroner's Office 9/18/51' stamped on back.

'Bud Brown and I are old pals from Sioux City. When I was on the Sheriff's there, Chief Joe Running Car here got drunk and scalped his wife. I picked him up, and he copped to those Griffith Park snuffs.

40

Chief tried to escape, and I killed him. Bud and I are the only ones who know that he confessed to the L.A. killings, and the only ones who've got the shack pegged. Chief Joe here – he's your fall guy.'

Three bullet holes/one tight circle – DePugh took on a new panache. 'Show me the other picture.'

He held it up. 'Aah, my Janie.'

Nice: a redhead hot for some mischief. Sleek – Julie London minus 10,000 miles.

Leigh banged on the window and drew a question mark.

DePugh caught it. 'You'll think of something. Just don't fuck my daughter, or I'll kill you.'

6

Green eyes scorched me – I shaved a few miles off Jane DePugh's odometer.

In session: the Westwood People's Study Collective.

The boss pinko droned on: the labor strike aesthetic, blah, blah. Some collective: me, a few beatniks, a Hollywood 'producer' named Sol Slotnick – a wolf with fangs for sweet Janie.

My mind wandered. Sol and Jane made me walking in – Jane's horns grew right on cue. Now it was Commie biz as usual.

Blah, blah – the LAPD as management enforcers. A cheap one-room pad; shit-strewn cat boxes placed strategically. Bum furniture – my chair gouged my ass.

'It is well known that Chief William H. Parker has formed anti-labor goon squads at the request of wealthy contributors to LAPD fund drives.'

I called Chrissy and spilled on Dave DePugh's shakedown – she agreed not to tell Leigh about it. I told her the kidnap scheme was still on – with DePugh supplying some pro muscle. Scared Chris: a light-colored sports car tailed her briefly last night. I mentioned Yeakel's DMV contacts – a temp license trace might be possible.

'. . . it is thus not untoward to state that police violence is violence aimed at subjugating the lower stratas of society.'

I flicked a cat turd off my chair. Jane crossed her legs my way – ooooooh, daddy!

A man walked in and sat down. Thirty-fiveish, hipster garb: sandals, Beethoven sweatshirt. *I* made *him*: an FBI face in the crowd at my desertion trial.

He made *me*: a half-second quizzical look.

He didn't make *me* make *him* – I glued on a deadpan quicksville.

Fed sharks circling – Janie, watch your mouth.

The Head Red called for questions. Jane said, 'My dad's an

42

investigator with the McClellan Committee. They're investigating corrupt labor unions, so I hope you're not going to tell us that all unions are squeaky-clean.'

Sol Slotnick raised a hand. 'I ditto that sentiment. I made a picture once called *Picket Line!* I had some connections in the garment rack – I mean trade, and I had a kickback – I mean a reciprocal agreement going with the owner of a sweat sh– I mean factory, who let me film his peons – I mean workers, at work. Uh . . . uh . . . uh, I saw good on both sides of the picket line, which . . . uh . . . is why *Picket Line!* was the title of the movie.'

Sol looked at Jane. Jane looked at me. The Fed inched his chair away from a cat box.

The beatniks walked out, oozing boredom. The Commie commissar harrumphed.

Sol, eyes on Jane: 'I'm, uh, thinking of making a picture about that killer that's strangling those kids up on the Strip. You know, the West Hollywood Whipcord. I want to show him as a . . . uh . . . out-of-work union guy who got fucked – I mean loused up by corrupt management practices. And . . . uh . . . when the cops shoot him, he's gonna decry the corruption of the system while he spits blood and repents. It's gonna be like *Picket Line!* I'm gonna show good and bad on both sides of the fence. I might even go the whole hog and have a Negro cop! See, this shvartze gas-station attendant I know has taken some acting classes. I think I could do good business with this picture and do some social good to boot. I think I'll call it *Sunset Strip Strangler!*'

Sol looked at Jane.

Jane looked at me.

The Fed looked at Sol.

The boss pinko said, 'Mr. Contino, you're acquainted with the dark side of the police experience. Would you care to offer comments?'

'Yeah. I agree with everything Jane said.'

Jane threw me a swoon. Sol muttered, 'Goyishe prick' – I barely caught it. Mr. Commissar sighed. 'Sometimes I think I'm running a lonely-hearts club. And on that note, let's call it a night. We'll have coffee at the usual place, and I'll do my best to upgrade the conversation.'

We hit Truman's Drive-In and comandeered a booth. Sol slid in next to Jane; I sandwiched her from the flip side.

The Fed and the Red sat buddy-buddy close. Jane pressed into me – her nylons went scree-scree.

I signaled a waitress – coffee all round.

The Fed said, 'My name's Mitch Rachlis.'

Introductions flew quick – the Commie tagged himself Mort Jastrow. I ditzed Rachlis: 'You look familiar, Mitch.'

Smart fucker: 'My wife's a fan of yours. We caught you at the El Rancho Vegas way back when, and a couple of times at the Flamingo Lounge. We always sit up close, so maybe that's why I look familiar.'

Smark fucker/good improvisor.

Sol moved on Jane. 'Have you ever considered a career in motion pictures?'

Jane scrunched my way. 'I'm keeping that option open. In fact, right now I've narrowed my career choices down to doctor, lawyer or movie star.'

'I could help you. If *Sunset Strip Strangler!* floats, you could play one of the victims. Can you sing?'

'I certainly can. In fact, that's my fourth career option: recording star.'

'Sweetie, that's wonderful. See, I could cast you as a nightclub songstress that attracts men like flies on sh– I mean like moths to the flame. The West Hollywood Whipcord gets a big boner – I mean a big thing going for you, and you get to perform a few numbers to showcase your singing skills.'

Mitch Rachlis butted in. 'What are you working on now, Mr. Slotnick?'

'A picture called *Wetback!* It blows the lid off the treatment of migrant fruit pickers. It's gonna stir up a load of shit – I mean controversy, and establish me as a producer of socially conscious pictures that deliver a message but don't fuck with – I mean sacrifice a good story in the process. Sweetie, write your number down for me. I might need to call you soon for an audition.'

Jane complied – twice. One napkin slip went to Sol; one snaked into my pants pocket. Jane's hand/my thigh – oooh, daddy!

Mitch the Fed looked at Sol – stone puzzled. Mort the Red scoped the whole group – stone disgusted.

Janie pressed up to me. 'We should get together. I'd love to hear about your political struggle and what it's like to play the accordion.'

'Sure, I'd like that,' came out hoarse – our leg-to-leg action crossed the line.

The Fed said, 'See you all next week,' and hotfooted it. Jane lit a cigarette – Miss Teen Sophisticate, 1958. I checked the window – and spotted Rachlis outside by the pay phones.

Janie smiled – teen steam wilted my pompadour. I put a dollar on the table, mumbled good nights and split.

The parking lot spread out behind the phone bank. Rachlis stood in an open booth, his back to me. I eased by just inside earshot.

'. . . and of all people, Dick Contino was at the meeting.'

'. . . The whole thing wasn't exactly what you'd call subversive.'

'. . . No, I don't think Contino made me . . . Yeah, right, I was there at his trial.'

'. . . Yes, sir . . . Yes, sir . . . Slotnick *is* the one we're interested in. Yes, that wetback movie does sound pro-Communist . . . Yes, sir, I'll . . .'

I walked down Wilshire, relieved: Joe Fed wasn't after Jane – or me. Then guilt goosed me: this extortion gig felt like a blight on my marriage. Another phone bank by the bus stop – I called Chrissy.

Her service answered: 'Miss Staples will be spending the night at OL-24364.'

My number. Chris probably called Leigh and asked to sleep over – that car probably tailed her again.

Shit – no kidnap scheme/extortion scheme confidante.

A directory by the phone. I looked up Truman's, dialed the number and paged trouble.

Jane came on. 'Hello?'

'This is Dick. Would you like to have dinner tomorrow night?'

'Oh, yes! Yes, I would!'

Please God: get me out of this morass intact and protect me from myself and this Teen Temptress—

7

The mail arrived early. I went through it on the sly – half expecting notes from the dangerous DePughs. Irrational: I only met them yesterday.

Leigh was still asleep; Chrissy sawed wood on the couch. She confirmed it last night: the light-colored sports car tailed her again. I insisted: you're our guest until this bullshit resolves. Her DePugh Dilemma advice: warn Sol Slotnick on the Feds and let Jane down easy. Buy her dinner, be her pal – but no wanka-wanka. PROTECT OUR RELATIONSHIP WITH DAD AND OUR BOSS KIDNAP CAPER.

Bills, *Accordion Quarterly* magazine. A letter to Miss Christine Staples, no return address on the envelope.

Waa! Waa! – baby Merri back in her bedroom.

Chrissy stirred and yawned. I said, 'There's a letter here for you.'

'That's odd, because nobody knows I've been staying here on and off.'

I tossed the envelope over; Chris opened it and pulled a sheet of paper out. Instant heebie-jeebies – she trembled like Jell-O with the DT's.

I grabbed it – one yellow legal-pad page.

Swastika decals circling the borders – model-airplane stuff. Glued-on newspaper letters: *I WANT TO FUCK YOU TO DEATH.*

My brain zipped:

Dot Rothstein? The tail car, temp license 1116 – who? The tail-car geek might have followed Chris here and glommed the address – but why send a letter here? The fiend might have seen Chris and me on *Rocket to Stardom*; he could have bagged my address from the phone book. Long shot: he could have resumed his tail after *I* chased *him* that first night Chrissy slept here.

Chris reached for her cigarettes; a half-dozen match swipes got one lit. I said, 'I'll take this to the cops. We'll get you some proper protection.'

'No! We can't! It'll screw the kidnap thing up if we've got cops nosing around!'

'Sssh. Don't wake Leigh up. And don't mention the kidnap gig when she might hear you.'

Chris spoke sotto voce. 'Talk to Bob Yeakel about checking with his DMV people on the license again. Maybe we can get a name that way, and turn it over to Dave DePugh. Then maybe he can lean on the guy to make him stop. I don't think this is Dot Rothstein, because I don't think she could squeeze into a sports car.'

'I'll talk to Bob. And you're right, this isn't Dot's style.'

Chris stubbed her cigarette out. Shaky hands – the ashtray jittered and spilled butts. 'And ask Bob to give us some time off. Remember, he said he'd cut you loose on your second show if you helped out with those repossessions.'

I nodded. Leigh walked in cinching her robe; Chris held her mash note up show-and-tell style. My stoic wife: 'Dick, go to your father's house and get his shotguns. I'll call Nancy and Kay and have them bring some ordnance over.'

My dad kicked loose two twelve-gauge pumps. I called Bob Yeakel and batted 500: yes, Chris and I could have a few more days off; no, his DMV contact was out of town – there was no way he could initiate a license check. I buzzed Dave DePugh's office to pitch a kidnap skull session – the fucker was 'out in the field'.

The White Pages listed Sol Slotnick Productions: 7481 Santa Monica Boulevard. I drove out to West Hollywood and found it: a warehouse down the block from Barney's Beanery.

I shoved the door open; industrial smells wafted up. Sweatshop City: rows of garment racks, sewing machines and pressers. Signs in Spanish posted, easy to translate: 'Faster Work Means More Money'; 'Mr. Sol Is Your Friend'.

I yelled – nobody answered.

Cramped – I scissor-walked to the back. Three Border Patrol cars stood on blocks; a nightclub set stood on a platform: bar, tables, dance floor.

Homey: sleeping bag, portable TV. Foodstuffs on the bar: crackers, Cheez Whiz, canned soup.

47

'Yeah, yeah, I live here. And now that you have witnessed this ignominy, state your business.'

Sol Slotnick, popping through bead curtains in a bathrobe.

'I also swiped this robe from the Fountainbleu Hotel in Miami Beach. Contino, what is this? First you steal Jane DePugh's heart, and now you come to torment me?'

Why mince words?

'I'm happily married, and I've got no interest in Jane. I was sent in to pull her out of that Commie group before she hurts herself. You should get out, too. There's an FBI plant in the group, and he's interested in *you*. The local FBI's got some bee in its bonnet that *Wetback!* is pro-Red.'

Sol grabbed a bar stool and steadied himself. Rainbow time: he went pale, then flushed bright red. Lunch time: he wolfed a stack of saltines and Cheez Whiz.

His color stabilized. A belch, a smile – this clown digested grief fast. 'I'll survive. I'll shift gears like when I lost my backing for *Tank Squadron!* and doctored the script into *Picket Line!* Besides, I just joined that *fakoktah* group to chase trim. I saw Jane on the street up by UCLA and followed her to my first meeting. You know, I think I want to marry her as well as drill her. I'm forty-nine years old, and I've had three attacks, but I think a young cooze like that could add another twenty years to my lifespan. I think this is one Jew she could seriously re-*JEW*vinate. I could make her a star, then trade her in for some younger poon before she starts cheating on me with handsome young greaseballs like you. Contino, tell me, do you think she'd consent to a nude screen test?'

The spritz had me reeling. Sol built a cracker/Cheez Whiz skyscraper and snarfed it. Fish-belly white to red and back again – the spritz hit overdrive. 'You know, I'd love to use *you* in a movie – you and Janie, what a pair of filmic lovebirds you could be. Most of your publicity has been poison, but it's not like you're Fatty Arbuckle, banging starlets with Coke bottles. Dick, a wholesome young slice of low-fat cheese like Jane DePugh could ream me, steam me, dry-clean me and get me off this B-movie treadmill to Nowheresville that has had me exploiting aggrieved shvartzes and taco benders to glom the cash to make these lox epics that have given me three heart attacks and a spastic colon. 'Dick, I own this factory. I hired illegal aliens to sew

48

cut-rate garments until the INS nailed me for harboring wetbacks, because I let them sleep here on the premises in exchange for a scant one-half of their pay deducted from their checks. The INS nailed me and fined me and shipped most of my slaves – I mean workers – back to Mexico, so I glommed some Border Patrol cars for bupkis at a police auction and decided to make *Wetback!* to atone for my exploitation sins and defer the cost of my fine. Now the Feds want to crucify me for my egalitarian tendencies, so I won't be able to shoot *Wetback!* I've got these Mex prelim boxers lined up to play illegals, but they're *really* illegals, so if I shoot the movie, the INS will round them up and put them on the night bus to Tijuana. Dick, all I want to do is make serious movies that explore social issues and turn a profit, and slip to schnitzel to Jane DePugh. Dick, I am at a loss for words. What do *you* recommend?'

My head whizzed. I ate a cracker to normalize my blood sugar. Sol Slotnick stared at me.

I said, 'I've got a date with Jane tonight, and I'll put in a good word for you. And I know an FBI man pretty well. I'll tell him that you're not making *Wetback!*, and ask him to pass the word along.'

'*You're* friends with one of J. Edgar Hoover's minions?'

'Yeah, Special Agent Pete Van Obst. His wife's the President of my National Fan Club.'

'What's the current membership? We might make a picture together, and statistics like that impress financial bankers.'

'The current membership is sixty-something.'

'So you add a few zeros and hope they don't check. Dick, be a gentleman with Jane tonight. Tell her I think she has movie-star potential. Tell her you've heard rumors that I'm hung like Roy Rogers' horse Trigger.'

Dismissal time – Sol looked exhausted. I grabbed a few crackers for the road.

Kay Van Obst brought three .45 autos – FBI issue, 'borrowed' from husband Pete. Nancy Ankrum brought a sawed-off loaded with rat-poison-dipped buckshot – Caryl Chessman told her where to find one. Add my dad's twelve-gauge pumps and call the pad 'Fort Contino' – L.A.'s cut-rate Alamo.

Ammo boxes on the coffee table.

Front-and back-window eyeball surveillance – four women in rotating shifts.

Four women packing kitchen knives in plastic scabbards – Kay hit a toy store on her way over.

Time to kill before my 'date' – I took a snooze.

Ink-smeared dreams:

COWARD REDEEMED; KIDNAPPERS STILL AT LARGE!

CONTINO FOILS FIENDS; SAVES BACKUP SINGER FROM TORTURE AND RAPE!

L.A. FUZZ NIX PUBLICITY STUNT SPECULATION: 'THIS CAPER WAS REAL!'

Chris held down by salivating psychopaths.

Cops swarming the kidnap shack.

Chief William H. Parker holding up scalps.

CONTINO KIDNAP PLOT REVEALS BIZARRE LINKS TO UNSOLVED MURDERS!!!

REDSKIN RESERVATIONS RAIDED IN SEARCH FOR KIDNAPPERS!!!

APACHE CHIEF SAYS, 'HEAP BAD BUSINESS! ME SEND UP SMOKE SIGNALS TO TRAP SCALP KILLER!'

Chris woke me up. 'You should get ready. I told Leigh you were jamming with some studio guys, so take your accordion.'

A last headline flickered out:

CONTINO CONQUEST CONTINUES! KIDNAP TOPS LINDBERGH SNATCH IN POPULAR POLL!

'I'm sure you must think that I'm just a naive young thing. You must think that any girl who hasn't narrowed her career choices down any better than doctor, lawyer, movie star or recording star must be rather silly.'

Jane picked the restaurant: a dago joint off Sunset and Normandie. The Hi-Hat Motel stood catty-corner – 'Vacancy' in throbbing neon made me sweat.

I drank wine. Jane drank ginger ale under protest – feeding minors liquor was a contributing beef.

'I don't think you're silly. When I was nineteen I was a recording star, but I just fell into it. You should finish college and let things happen to you for a while.'

'You sound like my Dad. Only he doesn't push the "let things happen" part, because he knows that I have the same appetites my Mom had when I was her age. I look like my Mom, I act like my Mom

50

and I talk like my Mom. Only my Mom married this rookie cop from Sioux Falls, South Dakota, who got her pregnant when she was eighteen, and I'm too smart for that.'

Scorch/scorch/twinkle – green eyes offset by Chianti-bottle candlelight. 'Sol Slotnick might fit that "let things happen to you" bill. He likes you, and he's a legit movie producer who could get you work.'

Jane futzed with her bread plate. 'He's a lech and a fatty-patty. He followed me to my first collective meeting, so he's one step up from a wienie-wagger. My Dad used to drive me around when he was a detective in Sioux Falls. He wanted to show me what I had to look forward to as far as men were concerned. He showed me all the pimps and panty-sniffers and winos and wienie-waggers and rag-sniffers and gigolos that he dealt with, and believe me, Sol Slotnick fits right in. Besides, he has small hands, and my Mom told me what *that* means.'

I sipped dago red. Jane said, 'You have *big* hands.'

'Vacancy' throbbed.

Questions throbbed: who's gonna know? Who's gonna care? Who's gonna tell?

Easy – you/you/you – straight across.

'Jane, Sol's the kind of guy that makes dreams come true.'

'Sol Slotnick is a long-distance wrong number. My Mom reads *Variety*, and she said *Picket Line!* was one of the big low-grossing losers of 1951. Sol Slotnick, ick.'

I dipped some bread in my wineglass and bit off a crust. Jane said, 'You're both earthy and sensitive. You're politically aware, but not didactic. You've been wronged by society, but you're not a martyr. My Mom said that men with ambiguous qualities like that make the best lovers, because they keep you guessing, and that postpones the inevitable letdown of sex getting stale.'

'Your dad must be quite a guy.'

Jane giggled. 'You mean my Dad's brother Phil. I figured that out because Uncle Phil used to come around a lot when my dad was out of town on extradition assignments, and I got sent to the movies all the time. *And,* I used to sneak peeks at my Mom's diaphragm, which sure was out of its case a lot when Uncle Phil was around. And you know what? Uncle Phil's hands were *much* bigger than my Dad's.'

I checked out my own mitts. Big – accordion practice gave them their girth.

51

A waiter hovered – I signaled him away. Jane laced fingers with me. 'Did you ask me out just to shill for Sol Slotnick?'

'Did you join the Westwood People's Collective just to chase men?'

'Not fair. You answer first.'

I pulled my hands free. 'I was bored and shopping around for kicks, so I went to the meeting. You looked like kicks, but I've decided not to cheat on my wife.'

Hot potato – Jane winced. 'Okay, so I joined the group for the same reason. And you can tell Sol Slotnick that I won't sleep with him until the twelfth of never, but I will audition and strip down to a bikini if you'll chaperone me.'

'I'll tell him, and I'll chaperone you. And I'll warn you now: you should quit going to those meetings, or your name will end up on some goddamn blacklist that could break your heart.'

Jane smiled. My heart swelled – just a little.

'There's a meeting tomorrow night that I *have* to go to, because Mort's going to discuss FBI malfeasance, and I want to get some lines to tease my Dad with. Besides, that man with the Beethoven sweatshirt looks cute.'

'He's an FBI agent taking names.'

'Well, then at least my Dad will approve of him. My Dad's *so* right-wing. He thinks that slavery should be reinstated and that streets should be privately owned, so the owners can charge protective tariffs. My Mom's a liberal, because she had a Brazilian lover once. He had really big hands, but he tried to pimp her out to cover some track bets he made, and my Mom said "No, sir," and called a cop.'

'What did the cop do?'

'The cop was my Dad. He got her pregnant.'

I called for the check. 'Come on, I'll drive you home.'

Jane snuggled close in the car. Channel No 5 tickled my nose – I cracked the window for relief. The McGuire Sisters on the radio – I let 'Sincerely' wash over me like Jane and I were for real.

It started drizzling. I hit the wipers and adjusted the rearview – a car was glued to my back bumper.

Spooky.

I punched the gas; the car behind us accelerated.

Jane slid off my shoulder and into my lap.

I hung a sharp left, sharp right, sharp left – that car bird-dogged collision-close.

Jane burrowed into my lap.

I felt myself responding.

Left turn, right turn – the steering wheel brushed Jane's hair. Hands on my zipper – something told me to hit the brakes.

BAM! Two-car bumper-locked pileup – in the middle of a pissant L.A. side street.

I quit responding. Jane said, 'Shit, I think I chipped a tooth.'

I got out. French-kissing: my Continental Kit and a '56 De Soto grille.

??? – no white sports job – ???

I ran back.

The De Soto driver got out, weak-kneed. Streetlamp glow lit him up good: Danny Getchell, *Hush-Hush* Magazine.

'Dick, don't hit me, I've got pictures!'

I charged him. A flashbulb popped and blinded me – Getchell bought some seconds.

'The waiter at the restaurant recognized you and called me!'

My sight came back blurry – I charged and sideswiped a tree.

'Dick, I've got pix of you and the redhead holding hands!'

Flashbulb pop – I picked myself up seeing stars.

'I've got a shot of you and the twist walking by the Hi-Hat Motel!'

I charged the voice – 'Dick, you can buy out with money or trade out with a story! Don't you know some queers you can rat?'

I tripped on a hubcap and went sprawling. Jane yelled, 'My dad's a policeman *and* a lawyer, you extortionist cocksucker!'

Flashbulb pop-pop-pop – my whole world went bright white.

'Dick, your zipper's down!'

I flailed on my knees and glimpsed trouser legs. Those legs went spastic – I caught a blurred shot of Jane shoving Getchell.

Gray flannel up close – I grabbed and yanked. Getchell hit the pavement; Jane smashed his camera on the curb.

'I dropped the film off, you dumb guinea shitbird!'

My hands/his neck – made for each other. *My* voice, surreal to *my* own ears: 'If you tell Leigh, I'll kill you. I've got no money, and the only story I've got is too good for you.'

Choking out raspy: 'You bluff. I call.'

I tightened my grip. Choking out bone-dry: 'You bluff. I call.'

Door slams, background voices. Jane said, 'Dick, there's witnesses. My Dad says eyewitnesses get killers the death penalty.'

Getchell, bedrock bone-dry: 'You bluff. I call.'

I let go. Getchell hunkered up and ass-scooted away. I pulled him back by the hair and whispered, 'I'm working out a fake kidnap thing with some pros. I won't give you the exclusive, but I'll give you first crack at my own account.'

Getchell choked out, 'Deal.'

Jane helped me up. Miss Teen Temptress was snaggle-toothed now.

8

Fort Contino, cabin-fevered up.

Leigh and Chris practiced knife throws: the 'I WANT TO FUCK YOU TO
DEATH' note corkboard-mounted served as a target. Nancy Ankrum
kept her snout stuck in the *Herald*: the West Hollywood Whipcord hit
again. Kay Van Obst on maintenance duty: oiling pistols and shotguns.

The girls had spent the night – 'Barracks Contino'. Bob Yeakel sent
a food supply over: a half-dozen Pizza De-Luxe pizzas. A note
accompanied them: *Chrissy Dear, be of strong heart. My pal at the DMV
goes back to work in a week, and I'll have him start checking temporary
licenses then. Dinner soon? Romanoff's or Perino's?*

Leigh kept me under fisheye surveillance: I came home last night
with ripped pants and a mangled car. My excuse: some punks tried to
hijack my accordion. Leigh was skeptical. I kept smelling Jane's
shampoo – maybe Alberto VO5, maybe Breck.

I got Kay alone. 'Can you call Pete and deliver sort of a cryptic
message? I'll explain later.'

'Well . . . sure.'

'Tell him to talk to the agent assigned to the Westwood People's
Study Collective. Tell him to tell the agent that I know for a fact that
Sol Slotnick is not going to shoot the movie *Wetback!* Tell Pete that
Slotnick is *not a Red*, he's just a movie clown trying to make money and
get laid.'

Kay got it straight and grabbed the hall phone; I covered her so
Leigh wouldn't hear. Whispers, whispers – a nudge in my back.

'Pete said he'll pass it along, and he said that you've got a certain
credibility. He said that if the agent isn't at the meeting tonight, you'll
know he bought your story.'

Good – some intrigue resolving my way. The doorbell rang – Nancy
checked the peephole and opened up smiling.

Pizza De-Luxe with three piping-hot pies. Sizzling cheese and anchovies – unmistakable. Ramon of 'Ramon and Johnny' trilled, 'Buon appetite!'

I got lost: lunch by myself, a cruise to the beach, dinner solo. I stewed, I fretted – shakedown Danny Getchell, my ratched-up car. Dave DePugh and Janie, Sol Slotnick, the kidnap – some four-or-five-or-six-horse parlay buzz-bombed my brain. Wires crossed, sputtered and finally made contact – I drove straight to the Westwood Collective and parked with an eye on the door.

7:58 – Sol Slotnick walked in.

8:01 to 8:06 – assorted beatniks walked in.

8:09 – Jane DePugh walked in.

8:09 to 9:02 – no Fed man in sight – Pete Van Obst probably put the fix in.

9:04 – I stationed myself by that door.

Jane and Sol walked out first; I gathered them up in one big embrace. 'Not *Wetback!*, *Border Patrol!* You've got the cars, and you can hire some non-illegals to play illegals! The movie stars Janie and me, and we can start working on the script tonight! Sol, I pulled the Feds off your ass, so now we can work this deal free and clear!'

Jane said, 'I'll call my Dad and tell him I'll be home late.'

Sol said, '*Border Patrol!* . . . Riiiiiiight . . .'

I zoomed by Googie's and copped some bennies off Gene the Queen, this transvestite that deals shit from the men's room. Va va voom! I chased a handful with coffee and hit Sol's warehouse hummingbird buzzed.

Sol and Jane filled their fuel tanks: Maxwell House, double ×Benzedrine. Pencils, notebooks, the *Wetback!* script to work from, go—

We changed heroic fruit picker Pedro to Big Pete – a Border Patrolman/accordionist hot to foil a Communist band exporting wetbacks to a secret slave-labor camp in the Hollywood Hills. Big Pete is in love with torch singer Maggie Martell, formerly leftist earth mother Maria Martinez. Maggie is being pursued by evil scientist Dr. Bob Khruschev, who's brainwashing the wetbacks and implanting slogan devices inside their heads. Big Pete/Maggie/Khruschev – a hot love triangle!!! Big Pete serenades illegals from the back of a truck; his accordion lures them into surrender and deportation! Khruschev sends his sloganeering robots into the bracero community, where they spout Commie rebop and corrupt a youth group that Big Pete has been indoctrinating into Americanism. The robots and corrupted youths advance on a Border Patrol station; Big Pete makes an impassioned anti-Red speech that instantly uncorrupts the young pachucos and inspires them to attack their corruptors. The robots are demolished; Dr. Bob Khruschev makes a last-ditch effort to corrupt Maggie with a pinko love potion that makes all Commies and fellow-travelers irresistible! Maggie unknowingly drinks the evil brew and puts the make on a roomful of visiting Soviet spies! Big Pete arrives on the scene, lures the spies outside with accordion music and guns them down! The movie ends with a citizenship swear-in: all the wetbacks that fought the Reds are issued green cards!

We finished the script at 6:00 A.M. – Benzedrine-blasted, exultant. Jane called her dad to say she was a movie star – Sol just offered her five hundred scoots to play Maggie Martell.

I wondered how 'Dad' would react.

Jane cupped a whisper. 'Dick, Dad wants to talk to you.'

I grabbed an extension; Jane hung up. DePugh came on the line. 'I approve, Contino. But I want this Slotnick clown to up the payoff to *six* hundred. Plus: no gratuitous cleavage during her nightclub scenes. Plus: no heavy make-out scenes with you. Plus: I say we tie the kidnapping in to the movie. I say we do it just as the movie starts shooting. I've got some Teamster guys to play the kidnappers, and I think you should audition them. Dick, this caper is tied to Janie's career now, so I want to do this right. We want a realistic abduction backed by eyewitness testimony. We want—'

Rabid-dog stage daddy – whoa!

'We want—'

I said, 'Dave, I'll call you,' and hung up. Sol was taking his benny-jacked pulse – at 209 when I walked over.

'Can you stand some more excitement?'

'Just barely. The way Jane rewrote that love scene is gonna get us Auschwitz'd by the Legion of Decency.'

I whispered. 'I'm getting kidnapped right before we start shooting. It's a put-up job with some pro muscle working back-up.'

Sol whispered. 'I like it, and you can count on me to keep mum. What about Jane as your co-victim? Add cheesecake to beefcake for a *real* publicity platter.'

57

'That spot's already filled.'

'Shit. Why are we whispering?'

'Because amphetamines induce paranoia.'

The warehouse door slid open; two pachucos struck lounging poses. Slit-bottom khakis, Sir Guy shirts – bantamweight punks on the stroll.

'Hey, Mr. Sol. You got *trabajo*?'

'When we get our movie work? Hey, Mr. Sol, what you got for us?'

Sol flipped. 'I'm doing a new picture! No *trabajo*! No work! Get your green cards and you can play robots in *Border Patrol!* Amscray! Get out of here, I'm having a heart attack!'

The punks split with middle-finger farewells; Sol broke out the saltines, took his pulse and noshed simultaneously. My fair co-star: dozing in a Border Patrol car.

I walked outside for some air. *Herald*s in a curbside newsrack – 'New Whipcord Slayings!' on page one. Photos of the dead couple – the woman looked oddly like Chris Staples.

My benny jag was wearing down – I stifled a yawn. A carload of pachucos cruised by; one *vato* eyeballed me mean. I walked back to give the script a last look.

Sol had a saltine Dagwood going: peanut butter, lox spread, sardines. Jane was scoping her chipped tooth in a compact. I said, 'Get your dad to set you up with a good dentist.'

'No. I've decided it will be my trademark. Dick, we were so close when that car hit us. We were so close that you couldn't have refused me.'

Sol sprayed cracker crumbs. 'What the fuck are you talking about?'

Noise: front-door scrapes, a bottle breaking. Then KAAA-WHOOOOOOSH – fire eating sewing machines, garment racks, air.

Rushing at us, oxygen-fed—

Sol grabbed his Cheez Whiz and ran. Jane's knees went; I picked her up and stumbled toward the back exit. Big-time heat behind us – I caught an over-the-shoulder glimpse of mannequins sizzling.

Sol hit the exit door – cool air, sunshine. Jane moaned in my arms and actually smiled. I risked a look back – flames torched the Border Patrol cars.

BOOM – an air clap hit me. Jane and I went topsy-turvy airborne.

A dim voice:

'. . . yeah, and we held it back from the press. Right . . . we had an

58

eyeball witness on the last Whipcord snuffs. No, he only saw the killer's vehicle. No license numbers, but the guy got away in a '53 Buick Skylark, light in color. Yeah, needle-in-a-haystack stuff . . . There's probably six thousand of the fuckers registered in California. Yeah, right, I'll call you—'

Bench slats raked my back. Not so dim: a phone slammed receiver to cradle. My eyes fluttered open behind a huge headache – a police squadroom came into focus.

A cop said, 'You're supposed to say "Where am I?" '

Lightish '53 Skylark/Whipcord vehicle/Chrissy.

I said, 'Did the eyewitness say the car had a *temporary* license?'

Quick on the uptake: 'No, the witness didn't specify, and temp licenses only account for 8 percent of all registered vehicles, so I'd call it a long shot that's none of your business. *Now*, you're supposed to say, "How did I get here?" and "Where's the redhead that I was passed out with?" '

My head throbbed. My bones ached. My lungs belched up a smoky aftertaste. 'Okay, I'll bite.'

Fat Joe Plainclothes smiled. 'You're at the West Hollywood Sheriff's Substation. You may not recall it, but you refused medical help at the arson scene and signed autographs for the ambulance attendants. The driver asked you to play "Lady of Spain," and you passed out again walking to your car to get your accordion. Sol Slotnick is in stable condition in the cardiac ward at Queen of Angels, and the redhead's father picked her up and drove her home. There's an APB out for the spics that tossed the Molotov, and Mr. DePugh left you a note.'

I reached out woozy; the cop forked a memo slip over.

Dick – the bar at the Luau tonight at 8:00. There's some boys I want you to meet. PS – Slotnick got the script pages out, so we're still on schedule. PPS – what happened to Janie's tooth?

Woozy – weak legs, hand tremors. The cop said, 'Your car's in the back lot with the keys under the mat. Go home.'

I woozy-legged it outside. Clear, smogless, so bright my eyes stung. Soot hung in the eastbound air – RIP, Sol Slotnick Productions.

Leigh was waiting on the Fort Contino porch. Armed: a .45 in her belt, a black-and-white glossy held up.

Jane DePugh and I – passed out entwined behind Sol Slotnick's sweatshop.

'Marty Bendish from the *Times* brought this by. He owes Bob Yeakel a favor, so it won't be printed. Now, will you explain your behavior for the past week or so?'

I did.

Chrissy, Bud Brown, scalps, redskin fall guys – publicity kidnap extraordinaire. Dave DePugh and horny daughter extrication; the People's Collective/Sol Slotnick/*Border Patrol!* The off chance that the tail-car man and Whipcord were one; DePugh as the new kidnap mastermind.

Leigh said, 'When you get out of prison I'll be waiting.'

'That won't happen.'

'My mother said Italians were all suckers for big gestures, which is why they wrote such great operas.'

'Yeah?'

'Don't act disingenuous and don't look so handsome, or I'll try to talk you out of it. And don't let that chipped-toothed vixen French-kiss you during your love scenes, or I will fucking *kill* you both.'

Anchovy pizza on Leigh's breath – I kissed her long and hard anyway.

9

'This is my daughter's movie debut, so I want a good deal of publicity surrounding it. You need men with no police records to play the kidnappers, in case any eyewitnesses get called in to look at mug shots, but they've got to be real hard boys who can act the parts convincingly. Now, check these guys out. Are they not the stuff criminal nightmares are made of?'

Introducing:

Fritz Shoftel – blond, crew-cut, fireplug-thick Teamster thug. Wire-rimmed glasses, acne scars, six extra knuckles minimum per hand. Pop/pop/pop – he stretched a few digits to show me they worked. Loud – a man in the adjoining booth winced.

Pat Marichal – dark-skinned Paraguayan beanpole with a stark resemblance to the morgue pic of Chief Joe Running Car. A smiler – tiki table-torchlight made his too-bright dentures gleam.

I said, 'I'm impressed. But Slotnick's Border Patrol cars got fried, so I'm not entirely sure there's going to *be* a movie.'

DePugh sipped his mai tai. 'I have faith in Sol. Any man that can eat cheese dip in the middle of a heart attack is resourceful.'

Shoftel stretched his fingers. 'I studied acting under Stella Adler. My kidnapper's motivation is that he's a rape-o. I'll maul the Staples babe a little bit for verisimilitude's sake, you know, give her a few hickeys.'

Marichal chewed the fruit out of his zombie. Those teeth – fucking incandescent. 'I was a contract Indian at Universal until I got my Teamster card. My motivation's a hatred of the white man. I drop a load of redskin grievance shit on you and Chris while I get ready to scalp you. You grab my tomahawk and slice me, then make your getaway. When you bring the cops back to the shack, they'll see those scalps from those unsolved snuffs back in '46. See, Fritzie's the guy with the ransom-sex-perv motives, and I'm the out-of-control guy that fucks this genius plan up.'

I said, 'Who do you hit up for the ransom?'

DePugh: 'Sol, and Charlie Morrison, the owner of the Mocambo. You see, Dick, I'm a cop, and I know what all cops know: that kidnappers are brainless scum who don't know shit from Shinola. You and Chris are not exactly big-name kidnap bait, and Morrison and Sol wouldn't lift a finger to save you. This crime has to *reek* of vicious incompetence, and Fritz and Pat are two guys who know how to play the part.'

Shoftel said, 'My parents abused me when I was a kid, so that's why I'm a rapist.'

Marichal said, 'The white-eyes stole my people's land and got me hooked on firewater. I need scalps to sate my blood lust and the ransom money to set up an Indian curio shop outside Bisbee, Arizona.'

DePugh tiki-torched a cigar. 'We do the snatch in broad daylight outside your house. Pat and Fritz will haul you and Chris out to a mud-smeared Chevy, then transfer you to another car and drive you to Griffith Park. Fritz will call Sol with the first ransom demand, and Sol will haul ass to the Hollywood Police Station. You said that Getchell guy gets first crack at the story, and you said he hangs out at the Hollywood Station chasing tips. Okay, he'll be there and overhear Sol tell the cops about the ransom demand. These are solid embellishments, and we've got time to set things up right, because we can't move until Sol gets financing for the movie and it's ready to shoot.'

Fiends by torchlight: rape-o/scalper/stage-door dad/rogue accordionist. We shook hands all around – Shoftel's knuckles popped castenet-loud.

I went by Queen of Angels to see Sol.

A clerk told me he'd checked out against doctor's advice. His forwarding address: Pink's Hot Dogs, Melrose and La Brea.

I doubled back west. Pink's was SRO – feed lines counter to curb. Sol hogged a pay phone and table at the rear – spritzing with one eye on a row of half-gnawed wienies.

Spritzing: 'I'm not wedded to *Border Patrol!* at the expense of your script, and I can get you Contino for an even grand!'

Spraying: sauerkraut strands, French-fry morsels.

His color rose and fell; his medic-alert bracelet, jangled. 'Elmer, all right, your girlfriend can co-star. Yes, Elmer, I'll relinquish my producer's credit for a profit percentage! Listen, there's a publicity angle rigged to Contino's participation that I can't reveal the details of, but believe me, it's a doozie!'

Hot-dog meat flew.

A pickle chunk hit a babe in a low-backed sweater; the mid-spine bull's-eye made her go, 'EEEK!'

Sol saw me and smothered the phone to his chest. '*Border Patrol!* is now *Daddy-O.*'

10

Genealogies:

Wetback! into *Border Patrol!* into *Daddy-O*. Pedro into Big Pete into Phil 'Daddy-O' Sandifer: truck driver/singer/romantic lead. Maria Martinez to Maggie Martell to Jana Ryan; Jane DePugh to Sandra Giles – pitch-girl for Mark C. Bloome Tires, semi-regular on Tom Duggan's TV gabfest.

Jane gave up her 'Movie Star' option and switched her major to pre-law – 'So I can be more like my Dad.' She sent me a farewell gift: her chipped tooth enshrined in a locket.

Dave DePugh continued to boss the kidnap plot – 'Hollywood publicist might be a shrewd career switch.'

Pat Marichal and Fritz Shoftel stayed on-board – Sol Slotnick promised them SAG cards if the scheme succeeded.

Ten days raced by.

Chris, Kay, and Nancy continued to bunk at Fort Contino.

Bob Yeakel sent Pizza De-Luxe over with daily injections of grease.

Chrissy seduced pizza-boy Ramon.

Ramon renounced his homosexuality.

Ramon told Kay he had to pretend Chris was a man.

Yeakel double delivered: some DMV flunky was collating license slips. Leigh was helping him out – she wanted the Chrissy problem resolved and the Fort Contino red alert suspended.

No more 'Fuck You to Death' notes arrived.

No cars tailed Chris on her out-of-fort journeys. My journeys ditto – no suspicious vehicles, period.

I spilled my insider lead to Nancy and Chris: the West Hollywood Whipcord drove a light-colored '53 Skylark. Crime Queen Nancy cut me off short: the Whipcord only snuffed couples; single-o women and hate notes weren't his MO.

'Sex killers never change their modus operandi. I've been intimate with enough of them to know that's true.'

Sol Slotnick found a pad down the street from Pink's and secured his *Daddy-O* financing via a high-interest loan from Johnny Stompanato. Stomp said he'd use his payback cash to market a new woman's tonic – a Spanish-fly compound guaranteed to induce instant and permanent nymphomania.

Chris and I joined Pat and Fritz for acting practice. Both men were 'Motivation' obsessed. Fritz picked up a lightweight case of paranoia – sometimes he imagined a primer-gray sports car tailing him. Practice, dress rehearsals – waiting for a *Daddy-O* GO date.

Schizo days.

I rehearsed with the Scalper and the Rapist; I rehearsed with the *Daddy-O* director, Lou Place. David Moessinger's *Daddy-O* script replaced *Border Patrol!* – it was tighter, but lacked political punch. Sol rescued his nightclub set from sweatshop rubble – it would serve as both the 'Rainbow Gardens' and 'Sidney Chillis's Hi-Note' – major *Daddy-O* venues. The new screenplay called for me to sing – I learned 'Rock Candy Baby', 'Angel Act' and 'Wait'll I Get You Home' pronto. My *Daddy-O* costars – Sandra Giles, Bruno VeSota, Ron McNeil, Jack McClure, Sonia Torgesen – were swell, but Scalp Man and Rape Man claimed my soul.

We'd hike up into the Griffith Park hills and bullshit. Pat Marichal brought firewater – he was working the 'Method' on his Chief Joe Running Car persona. A few shots, a few yuks. Then the inevitable segue to the topic of courage.

My best take: you never knew when it was real or just moonshine to impress other people.

Pat's best take: *you* know when you're scared, but do what you're scared of anyway – nobody else can ever know.

Fritzie's best take: give the world what it respects to get you what you want, and keep close watch on your balls when nobody's looking.

Time schizzing by – this fine L.A. winter fading out breezy.

Sol called and hit the brakes: *Daddy-O* was set to go four days hence. The word flashed:

Mastermind/Scalper/Rapist to Victims – forty-eight hours until kidnap morning.

11

Tick tick tick tick tick tick tick tick tick.

Leigh left for the DMV early.

Nancy and Kay left with her – baby Merri ditto.

Tick tick tick tick tick.

Chris and I watched the door.

Tick tick tick – my pulse worked triple-digit overtime. Chrissy's neck veins pop-pop-popped – every cigarette drag made them throb.

8:00 even – the doorbell.

'Hello? Is anyone home? My car's broken down and I need to call the Auto Club.'

Good neighbor Dick opens up.

Two men in stocking masks sap him prone. He's grabbed and hauled outside, good neighbor Chris likewise – she gets off her muffled scream right on cue.

Manhandled across the street – Stanislavsky Method tough. Weird: no mud-smeared Chevy in view.

More weird:

I made Pat Marichal through his mask. Nix on the other man – he was half a foot taller than Fritz Shoftel.

Slammed into a copper-colored sports coupe. Skewed glimpses: 'Skylark' in longhand chrome, a spanking new metal license plate. My shoulder rubbed the door – paint smeared – a primer-gray spot showed through.

The car MOVED – Chris and I backseat-tangled – Pat driving.

The other man held a cocked roscoe on us.

Down into Hollywood, speed limit cautious. Pat spoke out of character. 'This is Duane. Fritz had an appendicitis, and sent him in as a sub. He says he's solid.'

Blip: Fritz said *he'd* been tailed by a primer-gray car.

Blip: Skylark/fresh paint/new permanent license.

Blip: tails on Chrissy.

Blip: light-colored and primer-gray = similar.

Chris shook from plain tension – she didn't waft hink. The other man spoke in character. 'Baby, you look so gooooooooooood. Baby, it's gonna be so gooooooooooood.'

Talking stretched his mask. I recognized him: the scarf-trick geek from the *Rocket to Stardom* tryouts.

Silk sashes – fashioned into hangman's knots.

Blip: the WHIPCORD.

Fountain and Virgil looming – THE car switch – our only chance.

Chris, improvising nice: 'You're a filthy degenerate shitbird.'

Whipcord/sash man: 'Baby, I want to fuck you to death.'

Neon-bright hink – Chris flashed me this big HOLY SHIT!

On cue – Pat pulled into the deserted Richfield station.

Off cue – I kicked the Whipcord's seat and slammed him against the dashboard.

Go—

Whipcord – stunned. Pat, stunned – this wasn't in the script. A '51 Ford by some gas pumps – the transfer/getaway car.

Very very fast:

I kicked the seat again.

Chris tumbled out the passenger door. I got one leg out – and kicked Whipcord with the other.

Chrissy stumbled and fell.

Whipcord shot Pat in the face – brains spattered the windshield.

I tripped and fell out of the car. Whipcord kicked me – I rolled into a ball and dervish-spun toward Chris. Shots zinged the pavement – asphalt exploded shrapnel-like.

Chrissy got to her feet.

Whipcord grabbed her.

I stood up, charged, and tripped over a pump hose. Whipcord pistol-whipped Chris into the Ford and peeled out eastbound.

'I Want to Fuck You to—'

DEATH.

I pulled Pat out of the car and wiped his brains off the windshield with my sports coat. Keys in the ignition – *I* peeled eastbound.

25, 40, 60, 70 – double the speed limit. Blood streaks on my windshield – I hit the wipers and thinned it red to pink. No sight of the Ford; sirens behind me.

Sticky hands – I wiped them on the seat to grip the wheel better. Sirens in front of me, sirens wailing from both sides, earsplitter loud.

Black-and-white police cars – a four-point press descending. Bullhorn roar – garbled – something like, 'Buick Skylark pull over!'

I obeyed – very very slow.

I got out of the car and raised my brain-crusted hands.

Cop cars fishtailed up and boxed me in. Somebody yelled, 'That's Contino, not the Whipcord!' Harness bull stampede – gun-wielding fuzz surrounded me.

A plainclothesman got up to my face. 'Your wife called us from the DMV. She got a make on that 1116 temp license and traced it to the Skylark, which just got a paint job and some permanent plates. She told us how the car was tailing your friend the Staples woman, and Sheriff's Homicide just got a second eyewitness who tagged this as the West Hollywood Whipcord's very own—'

I cut in. 'I'll explain all this later, but right now you've got to be looking for a light blue '51 Ford. The Whipcord's got Chris Staples, and he's heading east with her in that car.'

The cop shrieked orders; black-and-whites shrieked eastbound *rapidamente*. My brain shrieked.

Spill on the kidnap caper? No, don't implicate Chrissy. Dead certain – the Whipcord killed Fritzie – don't reveal that either. Would Whipcord take Chris to the Griffith Park shack – NO – he wouldn't go near it.

'Fuck You to Death' implied slow torture implied Chris with a chance to survive.

The plainclothesman said, 'The Whipcord's got an apartment near here. Follow me in the Skylark, maybe you'll see something that will help us.'

I saw:

Plastic dolls sash-cord strangled, dripping nail-polish blood.

Stuffed dolls ripped open, spilling kapok.

Polaroids of bumper-jack-bludgeoned lovers.

Thousands of silk scarves tossed helter-skelter.

Chris Staples publicity pix, semen-crusted.

Chrissy's *Nugget* foldout defaced with swastikas.

Barbie and Ken dolls going 69. Crudely glued-on photograph faces: Chris Staples, Dick Contino.

A photo-faced pincushion voodoo doll: Dick Contino with a hatpin stuck in his crotch.

It hit me:

He thinks Chris and I are lovers. He wants to kill us both. This fixation will make him indecisive – he'll keep Chrissy alive for a while.

The plainclothesman said, 'His name's Duane Frank Yarnell, and I don't think he takes too kindly to you and Miss Staples.'

Those dolls – Jesus fuck. 'Can I go now? Can I take the Skylark and drop it off later?'

'Yeah, you can. I yanked the APB on it, but the Sheriff's have a want on it, so you'll have to get it back by tonight. And *I* want to see you downtown at LAPD Homicide tonight, no later than 6:00. There's a dead man with a stocking on his face and a bullet in his head that you have to explain, and I'm just dying to hear your story.'

I said, 'Just find Chris and save her.'

He said, 'We will make every effort. Are you sure there's nothing you can tell us *now* that will help us?'

I lied: 'No.'

Tears in my eyes, a blood-smeared windshield – luck got me to Fritz Shoftel's pad intact. I laid some jive and a tensky on his landlady – she unlocked his apartment and bugged out.

The living room and kitchen – nothing amiss. The bedroom – Fritzie hung from a ceiling beam – cinched up by at least fifty neckties. Eviscerated: entrails oozing from deep torso rips. Viscera piles on the floor – shaped into a swastika.

I ran for the bathroom and hurled just short of the door. Towels atop a hamper – I soaked one in cold water, swabbed my face and got up the juice for a search.

The bedroom, first glance:

A bookshelf crammed with acting texts. Knife wounds on Fritzie's arms – figure Whipcord tortured him for kidnap info. A dresser and closet – be thorough, now.

Work clothes. Teamster T-shirts. A photo of Fritz and Jimmy Hoffa – someone drew devil's horns on the big man. Rubbers, women's undies – Fritz admitted he was a longtime panty-sniffer. Rolls of dimes, *Playboy* Magazines, a *Playboy* rabbit key chain. A group picture: Fritzie's World War II outfit. More panties, more rubbers, more

*Playboy*s, an *L.A. Parks and Recreation Field Guide* dog-eared to a Griffith Park page.

I examined it. The kidnap-shack location was X-marked; pencil-press indentation lines grew out of it. I found a magnifying glass and traced them to their terminus: a cave area a half-mile southwest of the shack.

I rechecked the map. Tilt – dirt roads marked off – Observatory to cave turf access.

Somebody charted escape routes and other hideouts on tracing paper. They weren't part of the initial kidnap plan – I would have known. Double tilt: Whipcord gets us to the shack and kills Marichal *there*. It's just a short hop to the caves – where he can kill Contino and Staples at leisure.

Leisure = time = go NOW, don't buzz the fuzz.

I hauled up to Griffith Park. Danny Getchell lurked by the Greek Theater, backstopped by some movie-camera schmuck. Oblivious shitbird – he didn't know the whole scheme had gone blooey.

I ditched the Skylark in the Observatory lot. Access roads would take me straight to the caves – but I couldn't risk car noise that close to Whipcord. Sprint time – I ran straight up to the kidnap shack.

Empty – scalps on the table, biz as usual. I followed tracing-paper lines southwest; adrenaline jacked my heart up to my pompadour.

There – a clearing offset by cave-dotted hills. Tire marks on the road; a '51 Ford covered with camouflage shrubs.

Four cave openings.

I crept up and reconned, ears cocked for horror. One, two – silent. Three – squelched screams and insane ramblings.

'I have worshipped the Great Fire God for lo these years, and I have heeded the teachings of His only son, Adolf Hitler. He has asked me for silk-scarf sacrifices, and I have given them to Him. Now the Great Fire God wishes me to take a wife, and first consecrate her with the markings of His son.'

I crept in. Pitch-dark, twisty, damp – I hugged the cave wall. Motor hum, then light – Whipcord had an arc lamp set up.

Shadows, shapes half visible. Shadow bounces, full light on pale skin: Chrissy's back, marked with a red swastika.

Trickling blood – not a gouge – still TIME.

I tiptoed outside to the Ford. Adrenaline: one good yank ripped the backseat out clean. I found a siphon tube in the trunk, popped the gas cap and sucked.

Lip traction caught – I soaked the seat cushion with ethyl. Springs and a baseboard to grip – I hoisted the hundred pounds of vinyl and foam up easy.

Unwieldy – but I got a match lit. WHOOOOOOOOOSH – the Fire God stormed the cave.

Smoke, screams up ahead. Flames snaking sideways – my arm hair sizzled. Godawful heat, shots – I felt foam rip close to my heart.

Chris screamed.

Whipcord screamed gobbledygook. Bullets smashed my shield of fire and exploded.

Heat, smoke, wind sucking flames *away* from me.

Whipcord kept firing – two guns – very close range. The top of the seat cushion blew off – I held on to red-hot springs and kept coming.

A blue halo behind Whipcord: clear sky.

I piled into him.

His hair caught fire.

I kept pushing toward the blue.

Whipcord ran backwards, screaming.

I chased him.

He hit thin air – I hurled the cushion at him.

Flaming pinwheels off a hundred-foot cliff.

I grabbed Chris, ran her out to the Ford, tucked her low in the passenger seat. Fire God fast: down dirt roads, through the lot, Vermont south. Roadblocks by the Greek Theater; Danny Getchell, camera ready. Cops yelled, 'Stop!' – I got the notion this Fire God Buggy could fly. I worked the clutch/gas/shifter just right – the fucker went airborne. Shots behind me, residual shouts – magically audible. I heard 'CONTINO', but no one yelled, 'COWARD'.

That was thirty-five years ago.

History in ellipses: the cops covered all of it up.

I skated on kidnap-plot charges – a police bullet meant for the Ford killed an old lady. Shoftel, Marichal and the Whipcord – stonewalled.

Chris Staples healed up nicely – and avoids low-cut gowns that expose her faint scarring. She married a right-wing nut who digs swastikas – they're big in born-again Christian TV fraud.

Sol Slotnick has survived nineteen heart attacks on an all-junk-food diet.

Spade Cooley beat Ella Hue to death in 1961.

Jane DePugh had an affair with President John F. Kennedy.

Dave DePugh is a major JFK snuff suspect.

Leigh died of cancer in '82. Our three kids are grown up now.

Daddy-O bombed critically and nosedived at the box office. My career never regained its early momentum. Lounge gigs, dago banquets – I earn a decent living playing music I love.

'Draft Dodger', 'Coward' – every once in a while I still hear it.

It's only mildly annoying.

LAPD goons muscled Danny Getchell for his flying-car footage.

He dumped it on the *Daddy-O* cinematographer. It was spliced into the movie – not too convincingly.

People who've seen the raw film stock deem my driving feat miraculous. The word has spread in a limited fashion: one day in 1958 I touched God or something equally powerful. I believe it – but only to an ambiguous point. The truth is that at any given moment anything is possible.

Every word of this memoir is true.

High Darktown

From my office windows I watched L.A. celebrate the end of World War II. Central Division Warrants took up the entire north side of City Hall's eleventh floor, so my vantage point was high and wide. I saw clerks drinking straight from the bottle in the Hall of Records parking lot across the street and harness bulls forming a riot squad and heading for Little Tokyo a few blocks away, bent on holding back a conga line of youths with two-by-fours who looked bent on going the atom bomb one better. Craning my neck, I glimpsed tall black plumes of smoke on Bunker Hill – a sure sign that patriotic Belmont High students were stripping cars and setting the tires on fire. Over on Sunset and Figueroa, knots of zooters were assembling in violation of the Zoot Suit Ordinance, no doubt figuring that today it was anything goes.

The tiny window above my desk had an eastern exposure, and it offered up nothing but smog and a giant traffic jam inching toward Boyle Heights. I stared into the brown haze, imagining shitloads of Code 2s and 3s thwarted by noxious fumes and bumper-to-bumper revelry. My daydreams got more and more vivid, and when I had a whole skyful of A-bombs descending on the offices of the LAPD Detective Bureau, I slammed my desk and picked up the two pieces of paper I had been avoiding all morning.

The first sheet was a scrawled memo from the Day-watch Robbery boss down the hall: 'Lee – Wallace Simpkins paroled from Quentin last week – to our jurisidiction. Thought you should know. Be careful. G.C.'

Cheery V-J Day tidings.

The second page was an interdepartmental teletype issued from University Division, and, when combined with Georgie Caulkin's warning, it spelled out the beginning of a new one-front war.

Over the past five days there had been four heavy-muscle stickups in the West Adams district, perpetrated by a two-man heist team, one

73

white, one Negro. The MO was identical in all four cases: liquor stores catering to upper-crust Negroes were hit at night, half an hour before closing, when the cash registers were full. A well-dressed male Caucasian would walk in and beat the clerk to the floor with the barrel of a .45 automatic, while the Negro heister stuffed the till cash into a paper bag. Twice customers had been present when the robberies occurred; they had also been beaten senseless – one elderly woman was still in critical condition at Queen of Angels.

It was as simple and straightforward as a neon sign. I picked up the phone and called Al Van Patten's personal number at the County Parole Bureau.

'Speak, it's your nickel.'

'Lee Blanchard, Al.'

'Big Lee! You working today? The war's over!'

'No, it's not. Listen, I need the disposition on a parolee. Came out of Quentin last week. If he reported in, I need an address; if he hasn't, just tell me.'

'Name? Charge?'

'Wallace Simpkins, 655 PC. I sent him up myself in '39.'

Al whistled. 'Light jolt. He got juice?'

'Probably kept his nose clean and worked a war-industries job inside; his partner got released to the army after Pearl Harbor. Hurry it up, will you?'

'Off and running.'

Al dropped the receiver to his desk, and I suffered through long minutes of static-filtered party noise – male and female giggles, bottles clinking together, happy county flunkies turning radio dials trying to find dance music but getting only jubilant accounts of the big news. Through Edward R. Murrow's uncharacteristically cheerful drone I pictured Wild Wally Simpkins, flush with cash and armed for bear, looking for *me*. I was shivering when Al came back on the line and said, 'He's hot, Lee.'

'Bench warrant issued?'

'Not yet.'

'Then don't waste your time.'

'What are you talking about?'

'Small potatoes. Call Lieutenant Holland at University dicks and tell him Simpkins is half of the heist team he's looking for. Tell him to put out an APB and add, "armed and extremely dangerous" and "apprehend with all force deemed necessary".'

Al whistled again. 'That bad?'

I said, 'Yeah,' and hung up. 'Apprehend with all force deemed necessary' was the LAPD euphemism for 'shoot on sight'. I felt my fear decelerate just a notch. Finding fugitive felons was my job. Slipping an extra piece into my back waistband, I set out to find the man who had vowed to kill me.

After picking up standing mugs of Simpkins and a carbon of the robbery report from Georgie Caulkins, I drove toward the West Adam district. The day was hot and humid, and sidewalk mobs spilled into the street, passing victory bottles to horn-honking motorists. Traffic was bottlenecked at every stoplight, and paper debris floated down from office windows – a makeshift ticker-tape parade. The scene made me itchy, so I attached the roof light and hit my siren, weaving around stalled cars until downtown was a blur in my rearview mirror. When I slowed, I was all the way to Alvarado and the city I had sworn to protect looked normal again. Slowing to a crawl in the right-hand lane, I thought of Wallace Simpkins and knew the itch wouldn't stop until the bastard was bought and paid for.

We went back six years, to the fall of '39, when I was a vice officer in University Division and a regular light-heavyweight attraction at the Hollywood Legion Stadium. A black-white stickup gang had been clouting markets and juke joints on West Adams, the white guy passing himself off as a member of Mickey Cohen's mob, coercing the proprietor into opening up the safe for the monthly protection payment while the Negro guy looked around innocently, then hit the cash registers. When the white guy got to the safe, he took all the money, then pistol-whipped the proprietor senseless. The heisters would then drive slowly north into the respectable Wilshire district, the white guy at the wheel, the Negro guy huddled down in the back seat.

I got involved in the investigation on a fluke.

After the fifth job, the gang stopped cold. A stoolie of mine told me that Mickey Cohen found out that the white muscle was an ex-enforcer of his and had him snuffed. Rumor had it that the colored guy – a cowboy known only as Wild Wallace – was looking for a new partner and a new territory. I passed the information along to the dicks and thought nothing more of it. Then, a week later, it all hit the fan.

As a reward for my tip, I got a choice moonlight assignment: bodyguarding a high-stakes poker game frequented by LAPD brass and navy bigwigs up from San Diego. The game was held in the back room at Minnie Roberts's Casbah, the swankiest police-sanctioned whorehouse on the south side. All I had to do was look big, mean, and servile and be willing to share boxing anecdotes. It was a major step toward sergeant's stripes and a transfer to the Detective Division.

It went well – all smiles and backslaps and recountings of my split-decision loss to Jimmy Bivins – until a Negro guy in a chauffeur's outfit and an olive-skinned youth in a navy officer's uniform walked in the door. I saw a gun bulge under the chauffeur's left arm, and chandelier light fluttering over the navy man's face revealed pale Negro skin and processed hair.

And I knew.

I walked up to Wallace Simpkins, my right hand extended. When he grasped it, I sent a knee into his balls and a hard left hook at his neck. When he hit the floor, I pinned him there with a foot on his gun bulge, drew my own piece, and leveled it at his partner. 'Bon voyage, Admiral,' I said.

The admiral was named William Boyle, an apprentice armed robber from a bourgeois black family fallen on hard times. He turned state's evidence on Wild Wallace, drew a reduced three-to-five jolt at Chino as part of the deal, and was paroled to the war effort early in '42. Simpkins was convicted of five counts of robbery, one with aggravated assault, got five-to-life at Big Q, and voodoo-hexed Billy Boyle and me at his trial, vowing on the soul of Baron Samedi to kill both of us, chop us into stew meat, and feed it to his dog. I more than half believed his vow, and for the first few years he was away, every time I got an unexplainable ache or pain I thought of him in his cell, sticking pins into a bluesuited Lee Blanchard voodoo doll.

I checked the robbery report lying on the seat beside me. The addresses of the four new black-white stickups covered 26th and Gramercy to La Brea and Adams. Hitting the racial demarcation line, I watched the topography change from negligent middle-class white to proud colored. East of St. Andrews, the houses were unkempt, with peeling paint and ratty front lawns. On the west the homes took on an air of elegance: small dwellings were encircled by stone fencing and well-tended greenery. The mansions that had earned West Adams the sobriquet High Darktown put Beverly Hills pads to shame – they were older, larger, and less architecturally pretentious, as if the owners knew that the only way to be rich and black was to downplay the performance with the quiet noblesse oblige of old white money.

I knew High Darktown only from the scores of conflicting legends about it. When I worked University Division, it was never on my beat. It was the lowest per capita crime area in L.A. The University brass followed an implicit edict of letting rich black police wear black, as if they figured bluesuits couldn't speak the language there at all. And the High Darktown citizens did a good job. Burglars foolish enough to trek across giant front lawns and punch in Tiffany windows were dispatched by volleys from thousand-dollar skeet guns held by Negro financiers with an aristocratic panache to rival that of *anyone* white and big-moneyed. High Darktown did a damn good job of being inviolate.

But the legends were something else, and when I worked University, I wondered if they had been started and repeatedly embellished only because squarejohn white cops couldn't take the fact that there were 'niggers', 'shines', 'spooks', and 'jigs' who were capable of buying their low-rent lives outright. The stories ran from the relatively prosaic: Negro bootleggers with mob connections taking their loot and buying liquor stores in Watts and wetback-staffed garment mills in San Pedro, to exotic: the same thugs flooding low darktowns with cut-rate heroin and pimping out their most beautiful high-yellow sweethearts to L.A.'s powers-that-be in order to circumvent licensing and real-estate statutes enforcing racial exclusivity. There was only one common denominator to all the legends: it was agreed that although High Darktown money started out dirty, it was now squeaky-clean and snow white.

Pulling up in front of the liquor store on Gramercy, I quickly scanned the dick's report on the robbery there, learning that the clerk was alone when it went down and saw both robbers up close before the white man pistol-whipped him unconscious. Wanting an eyeball witness to back up Lieutenant Holland's APB, I entered the immaculate little shop and walked up to the counter.

A Negro man with his head swathed in bandages walked in from the back. Eyeing me top to bottom, he said, 'Yes, Officer?'

I liked his brevity and reciprocated it. Holding up the mug shot of Wallace Simpkins, I said, 'Is this one of the guys?'

Flinching backward, he said, 'Yes. Get him.'

'Bought and paid for,' I said.

An hour later I had three more eyeball confirmations and turned my mind to strategy. With the all-points out on Simpkins, he'd probably get juked by the first bluesuit who crossed his path, a thought only partly comforting. Artie Holland probably had stakeout teams stationed in the back rooms of other liquor stores in the area, and a prowl of Simpkins's known haunts was a ridiculous play for a solo white man. Parking on an elm-lined street, I watched Japanese gardeners tend football-field-sized lawns and started to sense that Wild Wallace's affinity for High Darktown and white partners was the lever I needed. I set out to trawl for pale-skinned intruders like myself.

South on La Brea to Jefferson, then up to Western and back over to Adams. Runs down 1st Avenue, 2nd Avenue, 3rd, 4th, and 5th. The only white men I saw were other cops, mailmen, store owners, and poontang prowlers. A circuit of the bars on Washington yielded no white faces and no known criminal types I could shake down for information.

Dusk found me hungry, angry, and still itchy, imagining Simpkins poking pins in a brand-new, plainclothes Blanchard doll. I stopped at a barbecue joint and wolfed down a beef sandwich, slaw, and fries. I was on my second cup of coffee when the mixed couple came in.

The girl was a pretty high yellow – soft angularity in a pink summer dress that tried to downplay her curves, and failed. The man was squat and muscular, wearing a rumpled Hawaiian shirt and pressed khaki trousers that looked like army issue. From my table I heard them place their order: jumbo chicken dinners for six with extra gravy and biscuits. 'Lots of big appetites,' the guy said to the counterman. When the line got him a deadpan, he goosed the girl with his knee. She moved away, clenching her fists and twisting her head as if trying to avoid an unwanted kiss. Catching her face full view, I saw loathing etched into every feature.

They registered as trouble, and I walked out to my car in order to tail them when they left the restaurant. Five minutes later they appeared, the girl walking ahead, the man a few paces behind her, tracing hourglass figures in the air and flicking his tongue like a lizard. They got into a prewar Packard sedan parked in front of me, Lizard Man taking the wheel. When they accelerated, I counted to ten and pursued.

The Packard was an easy surveillance. It had a long radio antenna topped with a foxtail, so I was able to remain several car lengths in back and use the tail as a sighting device. We moved out of High Darktown on Western, and within minutes mansions and proudly tended homes were replaced by tenements and tarpaper shacks encircled by chicken wire. The farther south we drove the worst it got; when the Packard hung a left on 94th and headed east, past auto graveyards, storefront voodoo mosques and hair-straightening parlors, it felt like entering White Man's Hell.

At 94th and Normandie, the Packard pulled to the curb and parked; I continued on to the corner. From my rearview I watched Lizard Man and the girl cross the street and enter the only decent-looking house on the block, a whitewashed adobe job shaped like a miniature Alamo. Parking myself, I grabbed a flashlight from under the seat and walked over.

Right away I could tell the scene was way off. The block was nothing but welfare cribs, vacant lots, and gutted jalopies, but six beautiful '40–'41 vintage cars were stationed at curbside. Hunkering down, I flashed my light at their license plates, memorized the numbers, and ran back to my unmarked cruiser. Whispering hoarsely into the two-way, I gave R&I the figures and settled back to await the readout.

I got the kickback ten minutes later, and the scene went from way off to way, *way* off.

Cupping the radio mike to my ear and clamping my spare hand over it to hold the noise down, I took in the clerk's spiel. The Packard was registered to Leotis McCarver, male Negro, age forty-one, of 1348 West 94th Street, L.A. – which had to be the cut-rate Alamo. His occupation was on file as union officer in the Brotherhood of Sleeping Car Porters. The other vehicles were registered to Negro and white thugs with strong-arm convictions dating back to 1922. When the clerk read off the last name – Ralph 'Big Tuna' De Santis, a known Mickey Cohen trigger – I decided to give the Alamo a thorough crawling.

Armed with my flashlight and two pieces, I cut diagonally across vacant lots toward my target's backyard. In the far distance I could see fireworks lighting up the sky, but down here no one seemed to be celebrating – their war of just plain living was still dragging on. When I got to the Alamo's yard wall, I took it at a run and kneed and elbowed my way over the top, coming down onto soft grass.

The back of the house was dark and quiet, so I risked flashing my light. Seeing a service porch fronted by a flimsy wooden door, I tiptoed over and tried it – and found it unlocked.

I walked in flashlight first, my beam picking up dusty walls and floors, discarded lounge chairs, and a broom-closet door standing half open. Opening it all the way, I saw army officers' uniforms on hangers, replete with campaign ribbons and embroidered insignias.

Shouted voices jerked my attention toward the house proper. Straining my ears, I discerned both white- and Negro-accented insults being hurled. There was a connecting door in front of me, with darkness beyond it. The shouting had to be issuing from a front room, so I nudged the door open a crack, then squatted down to listen as best I could.

'. . . and I'm just tellin' you we gots to find a place and get us off the streets,' a Negro voice was yelling, ''cause even if we splits up, colored with colored and the whites with the whites, there is still gonna be roadblocks!'

A babble rose in response, then a shrill whistle silenced it, and a white voice dominated: 'We'll be stopping the train way out in the country. Farmland. We'll destroy the signaling gear, and if the passengers take off looking for help, the nearest farmhouse is ten fucking miles away – and those dogfaces are gonna be on foot.'

A black voice tittered, 'They gonna be mad, them soldiers.'

Another black voice: 'They gonna fought the whole fucking war for free.'

Laughter, then a powerful Negro baritone took over: 'Enough clowning around, this is money we're talking about and nothing else!'

''Cepting revenge, mister union big shot. Don't you forget I got me other business on that train.'

I knew that voice by heart – it had voodoo-cursed my soul in court. I was on my way out the back for reinforcements when my legs went out from under me and I fell headfirst into darkness.

The darkness was soft and rippling, and I felt like I was swimming in a velvet ocean. Angry shouts reverberated far away, but I knew they were harmless; they were coming from another planet. Every so often I felt little stabs in my arms and saw pinpoints of light that made the voices louder, but then everything would go even softer, the velvet waves caressing me, smothering all my hurt.

Until the velvet turned to ice and the friendly little stabs became wrenching thuds up and down my back. I tried to draw myself into a ball, but an angry voice from this planet wouldn't let me. 'Wake up, shitbird! We ain't wastin' no more pharmacy morph on you! Wake up! Wake up, goddamnit!'

Dimly I remembered that I was a police officer went for the .38 on my hip. My arms and hands wouldn't move, and when I tried to lurch my whole body, I knew they were tied to my sides and that the thuds were kicks to my legs and rib cage. Trying to move away, I felt head-to-toe muscle cramps and opened my eyes. Walls and a ceiling came into hazy focus, and it all came back. I screamed something that was drowned out by laughter, and the Lizard Man's face hovered only inches above mine. 'Lee Blanchard,' he said, waving my badge and ID holder in front of my eyes. 'You got sucker-punched again, shitbird. I saw Jimmy Bivins put you down at the Legion. Left hook outta nowhere, and you hit your knees, then worthless-shine muscle puts you down on your face. I got no respect for a man who gets sucker-punched by niggers.'

At 'niggers' I heard a gasp and twisted around to see the Negro girl in the pink dress sitting in a chair a few feet away. Listening for background noises and hearing nothing, I knew the three of us were alone in the house. My eyes cleared a little more, and I saw that the velvet ocean was a plushly furnished living room. Feeling started to return to my limbs, sharp pain that cleared my fuzzy head. When I felt a grinding in my lower back, I winced; the extra .38 snub I had tucked into my waistband at City Hall was still there, slipped down into my skivvies. Reassured by it, I looked up at Lizard Face and said, 'Robbed any liquor stores lately?'

He laughed. 'A few. Chump change compared to the big one this after—'

The girl shrieked, 'Don't tell him nothin'!'

Lizard Man flicked his tongue. 'He's dead meat, so who cares? It's a train hijack, canvasback. Some army brass chartered the Super Chief, L.A. to Frisco. Poker games, hookers in the sleeping cars, smut movies in the lounge. Ain't you heard? The war's over, time to celebrate. We got hardware on board – shines playing porters, white guys in army suits. They all got scatterguns, and sweetie pie's boyfriend Voodoo, he's got himself a Tommy. They're gonna take the train down tonight around Salinas, when the brass is smashed to the gills, just achin' to throw away all that good separation pay. Then Voodoo's gonna come back here and perform some religious rites on you. He told me about it, said he's got this mean old pit bull named Revenge. A friend kept him while he was in Quentin. The buddy was white, and he tormented the dog so he hates white men worse than poison. The dog only gets fed about twice a week, and you can just bet he'd love a nice big bowl of canvasback stew. Which is you, white boy. Voodoo's gonna cut you up alive, turn you into dog food out of the can. Wanna take a bet on what he cuts off first?'

'That's not true! That's not what—'

'Shut up, Cora!'

Twisting on my side to see the girl better, I played a wild hunch. 'Are you Cora Downey?'

Cora's jaw dropped, but Lizard spoke first. 'Smart boy. Billy Boyle's ex, Voodoo's current. These high-yellow coozes get around. You know canvasback here, don't you, sweet? He sent both your boyfriends up, and if you're real nice, maybe Voodoo'll let you do some cutting on him.'

Cora walked over and spat in my face. She hissed 'Mother' and kicked me with a spiked toe. I tried to roll away, and she sent another kick at my back.

Then my ace in the hole hit me right between the eyes, harder than any of the blows I had absorbed so far. Last night I had heard Wallace Simpkins's voice through the door: ''Cepting revenge, mister union big shot . . . I got me other business on that train.' In my mind that 'business' buzzed as snuffing Lieutenant Billy Boyle, and I was laying five-to-one that Cora wouldn't like the idea.

Lizard took Cora by the arm and led her to the couch, then squatted next to me. 'You're a sucker for a spitball,' he said.

I smiled up at him. 'Your mother bats cleanup at a two-dollar whorehouse.'

He slapped my face. I spat blood at him and said, 'And you're ugly.'

He slapped me again; when his arm followed through I saw the handle of an automatic sticking out of his right pants pocket. I made my voice drip with contempt: 'You hit like a girl. Cora could take you easy.'

His next shot was full force. I sneered through bloody lips and said, 'You queer? Only nancy boys slap like that.'

A one-two set hit me in the jaw and neck, and I knew it was now or never. Slurring my words like a punch-drunk pug, I said, 'Let me up. Let me up and I'll fight you man-to-man. Let me up.'

Lizard took a penknife from his pocket and cut the rope that bound my arms to my sides. I tried to move my hands, but they were jelly. My battered legs had some feeling in them, so I rolled over and up onto my knees. Lizard had backed off into a chump's idea of a boxing stance and was firing roundhouse lefts and rights at the living-room air. Cora was sitting on the couch, wiping angry tears from her cheeks. Deep breathing and lolling my torso like a hophead, I stalled for time, waiting for feeling to return to my hands.

'Get up, shitbird!'

My fingers still wouldn't move.

'I said get up!'

Still no movement.

Lizard came forward on the balls of his feet, feinting and shadowboxing. My wrists started to buzz with blood, and I began to get unprofessionally angry, like I was a rookie heavy, not a thirty-one-year-old cop. Lizard hit me twice, left, right, open-handed. In a split second he became Jimmy Bivins, and I zoomed back to the ninth round at the Legion in '37. Dropping my left shoulder, I sent out a right lead, then pulled it and left-hooked him to the breadbasket. Bivins gasped and bent forward; I stepped backward for swinging room. Then Bivins was Lizard going for his piece, and I snapped to where I really was.

We drew at the same time. Lizard's first shot went above my head, shattering a window behind me; mine, slowed by my awkward rear pull, slammed into the far wall. Recoil spun us both around, and before Lizard had time to aim I threw myself to the floor and rolled to the side like a carpet-eating dervish. Three shots cut the air where I had been standing a second before, and I extended my gun arm upward, braced my wrist, and emptied my snubnose at Lizard's chest. He was blasted backward, and through the shots' echoes I heard Cora scream long and shrill.

I stumbled over to Lizard. He was on his way out, bleeding from three holes, unable to work the trigger of the .45. He got up the juice to give me a feeble middle-finger farewell, and when the bird was in midair I stepped on his heart and pushed down, squeezing the rest of his life out in a big arterial burst. When he finished twitching, I turned my attention to Cora, who was standing by the couch, putting out another shriek.

I stifled the noise by pinning her neck to the wall and hissing, 'Questions and answers. Tell me what I want to know and you walk, fuck with me and I find dope in your purse and tell the DA you've been selling it to white nursery-school kids.' I let up on my grip. 'First question. Where's my car?'

Cora rubbed her neck. I could feel the obscenities stacking up on her tongue, itching to be hurled. All her rage went into her eyes as she said, 'Out back. The garage.'

'Have Simpkins and the stiff been clouting the liquor stores in West Adams?'

Cora stared at the floor and nodded, 'Yes.' Looking up, her eyes were filled with the self-disgust of the freshly turned stoolie. I said, 'McCarver the union guy thought up the train heist?'

Another affirmative nod.

Deciding not to mention Billy Boyle's probable presence on the train, I said, 'Who's bankrolling? Buying the guns and uniforms?'

'The liquor-store money was for that, and there was this rich guy fronting money.'

Now the big question. 'When does the train leave Union Station?'

Cora looked at her watch. 'In half an hour.'

I found a phone in the hallway and called the Central Division squad room, telling Georgie Caulkins to send all his available plainclothes and uniformed officers to Union Station, that an army-chartered Super Chief about to leave for Frisco was going to be hit by a white–Negro gang in army and porter outfits. Lowering my voice so Cora wouldn't hear, I told him to detain a Negro quartermaster lieutenant named William Boyle as a material witness, then hung up before he could say anything but 'Jesus Christ'.

Cora was smoking a cigarette when I reentered the living room. I picked my badge holder up off the floor and heard sirens approaching. 'Come on,' I said. 'You don't want to get stuck here when the bulls show up.'

Cora flipped her cigarette at the stiff, then kicked him one for good measure. We took off.

I ran Code 3 all the way downtown. Adrenaline smothered the dregs of the morph still in my system, and anger held down the lid on the aches all over my body. Cora sat as far away from me as she could without hanging out the window and never blinked at the siren noise. I started to like her and decided to doctor my arresting officer's report to keep her out of the shithouse.

Nearing Union Station, I said, 'Want to sulk or want to survive?'

Cora spat out the window and balled her fists.

'Want to get skin-searched by some dyke matrons over at City Jail or you want to go home?'

Cora's fist balls tightened up; the knuckles were as white as my skin.

'Want Voodoo to snuff Billy Boyle?'

That got her attention. 'What!'

I looked sidelong at Cora's face gone pale. 'He's on the train. You think about that when we get to the station and a lot of cops start asking you to snitch off your pals.'

Pulling herself in from the window, Cora asked me the question that hoods have been asking cops since they patrolled on dinosaurs: 'Why you do this shitty kind of work?'

I ignored it and said, 'Snitch. It's in your best interest.'

'That's for me to decide. Tell me.'

'Tell you what?'

'Why you do—'

I interrupted, 'You've got it all figured out, you tell me.'

Cora started ticking off points on her fingers, leaning toward me so I could hear her over the siren. 'One, you yourself figured your boxin' days would be over when you was thirty, so you got yourself a nice civil-service-pension job; two, the bigwig cops loves to have ball players and fighters around to suck up to them – so's you gets the first crack at the cushy 'signments. Three, you likes to hit people, and *po*-lice work be full of that; four, your ID card said Warrants Division, and I knows that Warrants cops all serves process and does repos on the side, so I knows you pickin' up lots of extra change. Five—'

I held up my hands in mock surrender, feeling like I had just taken four hard jabs from Billy Conn and didn't want to go for sloppy fifths. 'Smart girl, but you forgot to mention that I work goon squad for Firestone Tire and get a kickback for fingering wetbacks to Border Patrol.'

Cora straightened the knot in my disreputable necktie. 'Hey, baby, a gig's a gig, you gots to take it where you finds it. I done things I ain't particularly proud of, and I—'

I shouted, 'That's not it!'

Cora moved back to the window and smiled. 'It certainly is, Mr. *Po*-liceman.'

Angry now, angry at losing, I did what I always did when I smelled defeat: attack. 'Shitcan it. Shitcan it now, before I forget I was starting to like you.'

Cora gripped the dashboard with two white-knuckled hands and stared through the windshield. Union Station came into view, and pulling into the parking lot I saw a dozen black-and-whites and unmarked cruisers near the front entrance. Bullhorn-barked commands echoed unintelligibly as I killed my siren, and behind the police cars I glimpsed plainclothesmen aiming riot guns at the ground.

I pinned my badge to my jacket front and said, 'Out.' Cora stumbled from the car and stood rubber-kneed on the pavement. I got out, grabbed her arm, and shoved-pulled her all the way over to the pandemonium. As we approached, a harness bull leveled his .38 at us, then hesitated and said, 'Sergeant Blanchard?'

I said 'Yeah' and handed Cora over to him, adding, 'She's a material witness, be nice to her.' The youth nodded, and I walked past two bumper-to-bumper black-and-whites into the most incredible shakedown scene I had ever witnessed:

Negro men in porter uniforms and white men in army khakis were lying facedown on the pavement, their jackets and shirts pulled up to their shoulders, their trousers and undershorts pulled down to their knees. Uniformed cops were spread-searching them while plainclothesmen held the muzzles of twelve-gauge pumps to their heads. A pile of confiscated pistols and sawed-off shotguns lay a safe distance away. The men on the ground were all babbling their innocence or shouting epithets, and every cop trigger finger looked itchy.

Voodoo Simpkins and Billy Boyle were not among the six suspects. I looked around for familiar cop faces and saw Georgie Caulkins by the station's front entrance, standing over a sheet-covered stretcher. I ran up to him and said, 'What have you got, Skipper?'

Caulkins toed the sheet aside, revealing the remains of a fortyish Negro man. 'The shine's Leotis McCarver,' Georgie said. 'Upstanding colored citizen, Brotherhood of Sleeping Car Porters big shot, a credit to his race. Put a .38 to his head and blew his brains out when the black-and-whites showed up.'

Catching a twinkle in the old lieutenant's eyes, I said, 'Really?'

Georgie smiled. 'I can't shit a shitter. McCarver came out waving a white handkerchief, and some punk-kid rookie cancelled his ticket. Deserves a commendation, don't you think?'

I looked down at the stiff and saw that the entry wound was right between the eyes. 'Give him a sharpshooter's medal and a desk job before he plugs some innocent civilian. What about Simpkins and Boyle?'

'Gone,' Georgie said. 'When we first got here, we didn't know the real soldiers and porters from the heisters, so we threw a net over the whole place and shook everybody down. We held every legit shine lieutenant, which was two guys, then cut them loose when they weren't your boy. Simpkins and Boyle probably got away in the shuffle. A car got stolen from the other end of the lot – citizen said she saw a nigger in a porter's suit breaking the window. That was probably Simpkins. The license number's on the air along with an all-points. That shine is dead meat.'

I thought of Simpkins invoking protective voodoo gods and said, 'I'm going after him myself.'

'You owe me a report on this thing!'

'Later.'

'*Now!*'

I said, 'Later, *sir*,' and ran back to Cora, Georgie's 'now' echoing behind me. When I got to where I had left her, she was gone. Looking around, I saw her a few yards away on her knees, handcuffed to the bumper of a black-and-white. A cluster of bluesuits were hooting at her, and I got very angry.

I walked over. A particularly callow-looking rookie was regaling the others with his account of Leotis McCarver's demise. All four snapped to when they saw me coming. I grabbed the storyteller by his necktie and yanked him toward the back of the car. 'Uncuff her,' I said.

The rookie tried to pull away. I yanked at his tie until we were face-to-face and I could smell Sen-Sen on his breath. 'And apologize.'

The kid flushed, and I walked back to my unmarked cruiser. I heard muttering behind me, and then I felt a tap on my shoulder. Cora was there, smiling. 'I owe you one,' she said.

I pointed to the passenger seat. 'Get in. I'm collecting.'

The ride back to West Adams was fueled by equal parts of my nervous energy and Cora's nonstop spiel on her loves and criminal escapades. I had seen it dozens of times before. A cop stands up for a prisoner against another cop, on general principles or because the other cop is a turd, and the prisoner takes it as a sign of affection and respect and proceeds to lay out a road map of their life, justifying every wrong turn because he wants to be the cop's moral equal. Cora's tale of her love for Billy Boyle back in his heister days, her slide into call-house service when he went to prison, and her lingering crush on Wallace Simpkins was predictable and mawkishly rendered. I got more and more embarrassed by her 'you dig?' punctuations and taps on the arm, and if I didn't need her as a High Darktown tour guide I would have kicked her out of the car and back to her old life. But then the monologue got interesting.

When Billy Boyle was cut loose from Chino, he had a free week in L.A. before his army induction and went looking for Cora. He found her hooked on ether at Minnie Roberts's Casbah, seeing voodoo visions, servicing customers as Coroloa, the African Slave Queen. He got her out of there, eased her off the dope with steam baths and vitamin B_{12} shots, then ditched her to fight for Uncle Sam. Something snapped in her brain when Billy left, and, still vamped on Wallace Simpkins, she started writing him at Quentin. Knowing his affinity for voodoo, she smuggled in some slave-queen smut pictures taken of her at the Casbah, and they got a juicy correspondence going. Meanwhile, Cora went to work at Mickey Cohen's Southside numbers mill, and everything looked peachy. Then Simpkins came out of Big Q, the voodoo sex fantasy stuff became tepid reality, and the Voodoo Man himself went back to stickups, exploiting her connections to the white criminal world.

When Cora finished her story, we were skirting the edge of High Darktown. It was dusk; the temperature was easing off; the neon signs of the Western Avenue juke joints had just started flashing. Cora lit a cigarette and said, 'All Billy's people is from around here. If he's lookin' for a hideout or a travelin' stake, he'd hit the clubs on West Jeff. Wallace wouldn't show his evil face around here, 'less he's lookin' for Billy, which I figure he undoubtedly is. I—'

I interrupted, 'I thought Billy came from a squarejohn family. Wouldn't he go to them?'

Cora's look said I was a lily-white fool. 'Ain't no squarejohn families around here, 'ceptin' those who work domestic. West Adams was built on bootlegging, sweetie. Black sellin' white lightnin' to black, gettin' fat, then investin' white. Billy's folks was runnin' shine when I was in pigtails. They're respectable now, and they hates him for takin' a jolt. He'll be callin' in favors at the clubs, don't you worry.'

I hung a left on Western, heading for Jefferson Boulevard. 'How do you know all this?'

'I am from High, *High* Darktown, sweet.'

'Then why do you hold on to that Aunt Jemima accent?'

Cora laughed. 'And I thought I sounded like Lena Horne. Here's why, sweetcakes. Black woman with a law degree they call "nigger".

Black girl with three-inch heels and a shiv in her purse they call "baby". You dig?'

'I dig.'

'No, you don't. Stop the car, Tommy Tucker's club is on the next block.'

I said, 'Yes, ma'am,' and pulled to the curb. Cora got out ahead of me and swayed around the corner on her three-inch heels, calling, 'I'll go in,' over her shoulder. I waited underneath a purple neon sign heralding 'Tommy Tucker's Playroom.' Cora come out five minutes later, saying, 'Billy was in here 'bout half an hour ago. Touched the barman for a double saw.'

'Simpkins?'

Cora shook her head. 'Ain't been seen.'

I hooked a finger in the direction of the car. 'Let's catch him.'

For the next two hours we followed Billy Boyle's trail through High Darktown's nightspots. Cora went in and got the information, while I stood outside like a white wallflower, my gun unholstered and pressed to my leg, waiting for a voodoo killer with a Tommy gun to aim and fire. Her info was always the same: Boyle had been in, had made a quick impression with his army threads, had gotten a quick touch based on his rep, and had practically run out the door. And no one had seen Wallace Simpkins.

11:00 P.M. found me standing under the awning of Hank's Swank Spot, feeling pinpricks all over my exhausted body. Squarejohn Negro kids cruised by waving little American flags out of backseat windows, still hopped up that the war was over. Male and female, they all had mug-shot faces that kept my trigger finger at half-pull even though I knew damn well they couldn't be *him.* Cora's sojourn inside was running three times as long as her previous ones, and when a car backfired and I aimed at the old lady behind the wheel, I figured High Darktown was safer with me off the street and went in to see what was keeping Cora.

The Swank Spot's interior was Egyptian: silk wallpaper embossed with pharaohs and mummies, papier-mâché pyramids surrounding the dance floor, and a long bar shaped like a crypt lying sideways. The patrons were more contemporary: Negro men in double-breasted suits and women in evening gowns who looked disapprovingly at my rumpled clothes and two-and-a-half-day beard.

Ignoring them, I eyeballed in vain for Cora. Her soiled pink dress would have stood out like a beacon amid the surrounding hauteur, but all the women were dressed in pale white and sequined black. Panic was rising inside me when I heard her voice, distorted by bebop, pleading behind the dance floor.

I pushed my way through minglers, dancers, and three pyramids to get to her. She was standing next to a phonograph setup, gesturing at a black man in slacks and a camel-hair jacket. The man was sitting in a folding chair, alternately admiring his manicure and looking at Cora like she was dirt.

The music was reaching a crescendo; the man smiled at me; Cora's pleas were engulfed by saxes, horns, and drums going wild. I flashed back to my Legion days – rabbit punches and elbows and scrubbing my laces into cuts during clinches. The past two days went topsy-turvy, and I kicked over the phonograph. The Benny Goodman sextet exploded into silence, and I aimed my piece at the man and said, '*Tell me now.*'

Shouts rose from the dance floor, and Cora pressed herself into a toppled pyramid. The man smoothed the pleats in his trousers and said, 'Cora's old flame was in about half an hour ago, begging. I turned him down, because I respect my origins and hate snitches. But I told him about an old mutual friend – a soft touch. Another Cora flame was in about ten minutes ago, asking after flame number one. Seems he has a grudge against him. I sent him the same place.'

I croaked, 'Where?' and my voice sounded disembodied to my own ears. The man said, 'No. You can apologize now, Officer. Do it, and I won't tell my good friends Mickey Cohen and Inspector Waters about your behavior.'

I stuck my gun in my waistband and pulled out an old Zippo I used to light suspects' cigarettes. Sparking a flame, I held it inches from a stack of brocade curtains. 'Remember the Coconut Grove?'

The man said, 'You wouldn't,' and I touched the flame to the fabric. It ignited immediately, and smoke rose to the ceiling. Patrons were screaming 'Fire!' in the club proper. The brocade was fried to a crisp when the man shrieked, 'John Downey,' ripped off his camel-hair and flung it at the flames. I grabbed Cora and pulled her through the club, elbowing and rabbit-punching panicky revelers to clear a path. When we hit the sidewalk, I saw that Cora was sobbing. Smoothing her hair, I whispered hoarsely, 'What, babe, what?'

It took a moment for Cora to find a voice, but when she spoke, she sounded like a college professor. 'John Downey's my father. He's very big around here, and he hates Billy because he thinks Billy made me a whore.'

'Where does he li–'

'Arlington and Country Club.'

We were there within five minutes. This was High, *High* Darktown – Tudor estates, French chateaux, and Moorish villas with terraced front lawns. Cora pointed out a plantation-style mansion and said, 'Go to the side door. Thursday's the maid's night off, and nobody'll hear you if you knock at the front.'

I stopped the car across the street and looked for other out-of-place vehicles. Seeing nothing but Packards, Caddys, and Lincolns nestled in driveways, I said, 'Stay put. Don't move, no matter what you see or hear.'

Cora nodded mutely. I got out and ran over to the plantation, hurdling a low iron fence guarded by a white iron jockey, then treading down a long driveway. Laughter and applause issued from the adjoining mansion, separated from the Downey place by a high hedgerow. The happy sounds covered my approach, and I started looking in windows.

Standing on my toes and moving slowly toward the back of the house, I saw rooms festooned with crewel-work wall hangings and hunting prints. Holding my face up to within a few inches of the glass, I looked for shadow movement and listened for voices, wondering why all the lights were on at close to midnight.

Then faceless voices assailed me from the next window down. Pressing my back to the wall, I saw that the window was cracked for air. Cocking an ear toward the open space, I listened.

'. . . and after all the setup money I put in, you still had to knock down those liquor stores?'

The tone reminded me of a mildly outraged Negro minister rebuking his flock, and I braced myself for the voice that I knew would reply.

'I gots cowboy blood, Mister Downey, like you musta had when you was a young man runnin' shine. That cop musta got loose, got Cora and Whitey to snitch. Blew a sweet piece of work, but we can still get off clean. McCarver was the only one 'sides me knew you was bankrollin', and he be dead. Billy be the one *you* wants dead, and he be showin' up soon. Then I cuts him and dumps him somewhere, and nobody knows he was even here.'

91

'You want money, don't you?'

'Five big get me lost somewheres nice, then maybe when he starts feelin' safe again, I comes back and cuts that cop. That sound about—'

Applause from the big house next door cut Simpkins off. I pulled out my piece and got up some guts, knowing my only safe bet was to backshoot the son of a bitch right where he was. I heard more clapping and joyous shouts that Mayor Bowron's reign was over, and then Johnny Downey's preacher baritone was back in force: 'I want him dead. My daughter is a white-trash consort and a whore, and he's—'

A scream went off behind me, and I hit the ground just as machine-gun fire blew the window to bits. Another burst took out the hedgerow and the next-door window. I pinned myself back first to the wall and drew myself upright as the snout of a Tommy gun was rested against the ledge a few inches away. When muzzle flame and another volley exploded from it, I stuck my .38 in blind and fired six times at stomach level. The Tommy strafed a reflex burst upward, and when I hit the ground again, the only sound was chaotic shrieks from the other house.

I reloaded from a crouch, then stood up and surveyed the carnage through both mansion windows. Wallace Simpkins lay dead on John Downey's Persian carpet, and across the way I saw a banner for the West Adams Democratic Club streaked with blood. When I saw a dead woman spread-eagled on top of an antique table, I screamed myself, elbowed my way into Downey's den, and picked up the machine gun. The grips burned my hands, but I didn't care; I saw the faces of every boxer who had ever defeated me and didn't care; I heard grenades going off in my brain and was glad they were there to kill all the innocent screaming. With the Tommy's muzzle as my directional device, I walked through the house.

All my senses went into my eyes and trigger finger. Wind ruffled a window curtain, and I blew the wall apart; I caught my own image in a gilt-edged mirror and blasted myself into glass shrapnel. Then I heard a woman moaning, 'Daddy, Daddy, Daddy,' dropped the Tommy, and ran to her.

Cora was on her knees on the entry-hall floor, plunging a shiv into a man who had to be her father. The man moaned baritone low and tried to reach up, almost as if to embrace her. Cora's 'Daddy's' got lower and lower, until the two seemed to be working toward harmony. When she let the dying man hold her, I gave them a moment together, then pulled Cora off of him and dragged her outside. She went limp in my arms, and with lights going on everywhere and sirens converging from all directions, I carried her to my car.

Dial Axminster 6-400

Ellis Loew rapped on the pebbled-glass door that separated LAPD Warrants from the Office of the District Attorney. Davis Evans, dozing in his chair, muttered 'Mother dog.' I said, 'That's his college-ring knock. It's a personal favor or a reprimand.'

Davis nodded and got to his feet slowly, befitting a man with twenty years and two days on the job – and an ironclad civil-service pension as soon as he said the words, 'Fuck you, Ellis. I retire.' He smoothed his plaid shirt, adjusted the knot in his Hawaiian tie, hitched up the waistband of his shiny black pants, and patted the lapels of the camel-hair jacket he stole from a black pimp at the Lincoln Heights drunk tank. 'That boy wants a favor, he gonna pay like a mother dog.'

'Blanchard! Evans! I'm waiting!'

We walked into the Deputy DA's office and found him smiling, which meant that he was either practicing for the press or getting ready to kiss some ass. Davis nudged me as we took seats, then said, 'Hey, Mr. Loew. What did the leper say to the prostitute?'

Loew's smile stayed glued on; it was obviously a big favor he wanted. 'I don't know, Sergeant. What?'

'Keep the tip. Ain't that a mother dog?'

Loew put out his hail-fellow-well-met chuckle. 'Yes, it's so simple that it has a certain charm. Now, the reason I—'

'What do you call an elephant that moonlights as a prostitute?'

Loew's smile spread into nasty little facial tics. 'I . . . don't . . . know. What?'

'A two-ton pickup that lays for peanuts. Woooo! Mother dog!'

The Ted Mack Amateur Hour had gone far enough. I said, 'Did you want something, Boss?'

Davis laughed uproariously, like my question was the real punch line; Loew wiped the smile remnants off his face with a handkerchief.

94

'Yes, I do. Did you know that there was a kidnapping in L.A. four days ago? Monday afternoon on the USC campus?'

Davis kiboshed his stage chuckles; snatch jobs were meat and potatoes to him – the kind of cases he loved to work. I said, 'You've got Fred Allen's interest. Keep going.'

Loew twirled his Phi Beta Kappa key as he spoke. 'The victim's name is Jane Mackenzie Viertel. She's nineteen, a USC frosh. Her father is Redmond Viertel, an oil man with a big string of wells down on Signal Hill. Three men in USC letter jackets grabbed her Monday, about two o'clock. It's rush week, so all the witnesses thought it was some sort of fraternity stunt. The men called the girl's father late that night and made their demand: a hundred thousand dollars in fifties. Viertel got the money together, then got frightened and called the FBI. The kidnappers called back and set up a trade for the following day in an irrigation field up near Ventura.

'Two agents from the Ventura office set up a trap, one hiding, one posing as Viertel. The kidnappers showed up, then it all went haywire.'

Davis said, 'Wooooo,' and cracked his knuckles; Loew grimaced at the sound and continued. 'One of the kidnappers found the agent who was hiding. They were both afraid of disturbing the transaction with gunfire, so they had a little hand-to-hand combat. The kidnapper beat the agent up with a shovel, then hacked off six of his fingers with the blade. The other agent sensed something was wrong and started to act fidgety. He grabbed one of the men and put a gun to his head, and the other man did the same to the girl. A real Mexican standoff, until the Fed grabbed the moneybag and a windstorm played hell with all that cash. The man with the girl grabbed the bag and took off, and the Fed took his captive in. You see what I mean by haywire?'

I said, 'So two snatchers and the girl are still at large?'

'Yes. The third man is in custody in Ventura, and the other agent is very angry.'

Davis laced his fingers together and cracked a total of eight knuckles. 'Wooooo. These boys got names, Mr. Loew? And what's this got to do with me and Lee?'

Now Loew's smile was genuine – that of a fiend who loves his work. Consulting some rap sheets on his desk, he said, 'The man in custody is Harwell Jackson Treadwell, white male, age thirty-one. He's from Gila Bend, Oklahoma; your neck of the woods, Evans. He's got three strong-arm convictions running back to 1934 and has two outstanding warrants here in L.A. – robbery charges filed in '44 and '45. Treadwell also has two charming brothers, Miller and Leroy. Both are registered sex offenders and do not seem to care much about the gender of their conquests. In fact, Leroy rather likes those of a four-footed persuasion. He was arrested for aggravated assault on an animal and served thirty days for it in '42.'

Davis picked at his teeth with his tie clip. 'Any old port in a storm. Miller and Leroy got the girl and part of the money?'

'That's right.'

'And you want me and Lee to—'

I interrupted, seeing my Friday night go up in smoke. 'This is Ventura County's business. Not ours.'

Loew held up an extradition warrant and carbons of two bench summonses. 'The kidnapping took place in Los Angeles, in my judicial district. I would very much like to prosecute Mr. Treadwell along with his brothers when they are apprehended. So I want you two to drive up to Ventura and return Mr. Treadwell to City Jail before the notoriously ill-mannered Ventura sheriffs beat him to death.'

I groaned; Davis Evans made an elaborate show of standing up and smoothing out the various tucks and folds of his outfit. 'I'll be a mother dog, but I was thinkin' about retiring this afternoon.'

Winking at me, Loew said, 'You won't retire when you hear what the other two brothers escaped in.'

'Wooooo. Keep talkin', boy.'

'A 1936 Auburn speedster. Two-tone, maroon and forest green. When they get captured, and you know they will, the car will go to City Impound until claimed or bid on. Davis, I expect to send those Okie shitheads to the gas chamber. It's very hard to claim a vehicle from death row, and the duty officer at the impound is a close friend of mine. Still want to retire?'

Davis exclaimed, 'Wooooooo!', grabbed the warrants and hustled his two-thirty-five toward the door. I was right behind him – reluctantly – the junior partner all the way. With his hand on the knob, the senior man got in a parting shot: 'What do you call a gal who's got the syph, the clap, and the crabs? An incurable romantic! Wooooo! Mother dog!'

We took the Ridge Road north, Davis at the wheel of his showroom-fresh '47 Buick ragtop, me staring out at the L.A. suburbs dwindling into scrub-covered hills, then farmland worked by Japs out of the relocation camps and transplanted Okies. The Okie sitting beside me never spoke when he drove; he stayed lost in a man-car reverie. I thought about our brief Warrants partnership, how our differences made it work.

I was the prototypical athlete-cop the high brass loved, the ex-boxer one L.A. scribe labeled 'the Southland's good but not great white hope.' No one knew the 'but not' better than me, and plain 'good' meant flash rolls, steak, and nightlife until you were thirty, then permanently scrambled brains. The department was the one safe place where my fight juice could see me through to security – with muted glory along the way – and I went for it like Davis's mother dog, cultivating all the right people, most notably boxing fanatic Ellis Loew.

Davis Evans was another opportunist, out for plain loot, out to shut down Norman, Oklahoma, fourteen siblings, family inbreeding, the proximity to oil money you could breathe but never quite touch. He took what he could and reveled in it, and he made up for being on the take by exercising the best set of cop faces I had ever seen – Mr. Courtly to those who deserved it, Mr. Grief to the bad ones, Mr. Civil to whoever was left over. That a man could be so self-seeking and lacking in mean-spiritedness astonished me, and I deferred to him on the job – senior man aside – because I knew my own selfishness ran twice as deep as his did. And I realized that the hard-nosed buffoon probably would retire soon, leaving me to break in a replacement cut out of my own cloth: young, edgy, eager for the glory the assignment offered. And that made me sad.

Warrants was plainclothes LAPD under the aegis of the Criminal Division, District Attorney's Office. Two detectives to every Superior Court judiciary. We went after the bad guys the felony DAs were drooling to prosecute. If things were slow, there was money to be made serving summonses for the downtown shysters, and – Davis Evans's raison d'être – repossessions.

Davis lived, ate, drank, yearned, and breathed for beautiful cars. His Warrants cubicle was wallpapered with pictures of Duesenbergs and Pierce Arrows and Cords, Caddys, and Packards, and sleek foreign jobs. Since he stole all his clothes from arrestees, shook down hookers for free poon, ate on the cuff, and lived in the spare room of a county boarding house for recently paroled convicts, he had plenty of money to spend on them. The storage garage he rented held a '39 Packard cabriolet, a Mercedes rumored to have once been driven by Hitler, a purple Lincoln convertible that Davis called his 'Jig Rig', and a sapphire-blue Model T dubbed the 'Li'l Shitpeeler'.

He acquired all of them through repos. There was a twenty-four-hour-a-day phone number issuing recorded information on delinquent cars, and every greedy L.A. cop had it memorized. All you had to do was dial Axminster 6-400 to get the dope on wanteds – who they belonged to, what dealer or credit agency was paying what amount of money for their return. Davis only moved on cars that he craved, and only on delinquent owners with outstanding warrants. It was a parlay that frequently occurred, on-the-lam punks not being known for sending in their monthly auto payments. Once the warrantee was arrested, Davis would locate the car, let it molder in his garage, do some minor defacing of it, then report to the dealer that the mother dog was in bad, bad shape. The dealer would believe him; being a soft-hearted misanthrope, Davis would offer a decent amount to keep the vehicle. The dealer would agree, thinking he'd taken advantage of a dust-bowl refugee with a leaky seabag – and Sergeant Davis Evans would have himself another true love.

We were cruising through truck-farm country now – flat acres of furrowed land that looked dry, used up, like this was brutal August, not mild October. All the farmers were the sunburned poor-white prototype that Davis narrowly escaped being one of. Off to our right, nestled at the edge of a scrub valley, was Wayside Honor Rancho – a new county facility to house misdemeanor offenders. It had housed Japs during the war, Okie farmers their keepers on the temporary War Relocation Board payroll. But now the war was over – and it was back to dry dirt.

I nudged Davis and pointed to a group of farmers uprooting cabbages. 'There but for the grace of God go you, partner.'

Davis saluted the assembly, then flipped them his middle finger. 'You can lead a dog to gravy, but you can't make him a lapper.'

It was shortly past noon when we pulled up in front of the Ventura courthouse-jail. For a hick-town county seat, the joint had aspirations to class, all of them low – Greek pillars, a Tudor roof, and Spanish-style canvas awnings came together to produce a building that gave you the feeling of DT's without the benefit of booze. Davis groaned as we pushed open a door etched with Egyptian hieroglyphics; I said, 'Be grateful it goes with your clothes.'

The interior was divided into two wings, and bars at the far end of the left corridor showed us where to go. There was a deputy seated just outside the enclosure, a fat youth done up in khaki that enclosed his blubbery body like a sausage casing. Looking up from his comic book, he said, 'Ah . . . yessirs?'

Davis whipped out our three warrants and held them up for the kid to scrutinize. 'LAPD, son. We've got an extradition warrant for Harwell Treadwell, plus two others on old beefs of his. You wanna go get him for us?'

The kid thumbed through the papers, probably looking for the pictures. When he couldn't figure the words out, he unlocked the barred door and led us down a long hallway inset with cells on both sides. Nearing the end, I heard muffled obscenities and thudding sounds. The deputy announced our presence by clearing his throat and saying, 'Ah . . . Sheriff? I got two men here need to talk to you.'

I stepped in front of the open cell door and looked in. A tall, beefy man in a ribbon-festooned version of the deputy's getup was standing next to an even taller guy dressed like the archetypal G-man: gray suit, gray tie, gray hair, gray expression on his face. Handcuffed to a chair was our warrantee – white-trash defiance with a duck's-ass haircut, purple and puke-green bruises covering his face, brass-knuck marks dotting his bare torso.

The kid took off before the two hardcases could reprimand him for disturbing their third degree; Davis flashed our papers. The sheriff looked at them silently, and the fed buttoned his jacket over the knuckle dusters sticking out of his waistband. 'I'm Special Agent Stensland,' he said. 'Ventura Office, FBI. What—'

Harwell Treadwell laughed and spat blood on the floor. I said, 'We're taking him back to L.A. Did he cough up any dope on the other two?'

The sheriff shoved the papers at Davis. 'He might have, you didn't interrupt our interrogation.'

'You've had him for three days,' I said. 'He should have blabbed by now.'

Treadwell spat blood on the sheriff's spit-shined cowboy boots; when the man balled his fist to retaliate, Davis stationed himself between the two. 'He's my prisoner now. Signed, sealed, and deeeelivered.'

Stensland said, 'This won't wash. Treadwell's a Federal prisoner.'

I shook my head. 'He's got city warrants predating the extradition one, and the extradition warrant is countersigned by a Federal judge. He's ours.'

Stensland bored in on me with beady gray eyes. I stood there, deadpan, and he tried to smile and cop-to-cop empathy. 'Listen, Officer—'

'It's Sergeant.'

'All right, *Sergeant*, listen: the Viertel girl and the other two men are still at large, and this filth was responsible for one of my agents losing six fingers. Don't you want to go back to Los Angeles with a confession? Don't you want his filthy brothers captured? Don't you want to let us try it our way just a little bit longer?'

Davis said, 'Your way don't work, so we try mine,' walked over, and unlocked Harwell Treadwell's cuffs. Standing up, the Okie snatch artist almost collapsed, and bile crept from the corners of his mouth. Davis eased him out to the catwalk, and I said to Stensland, 'That warrant has an evidence clause. I need everything you found at the crime scene, including the ransom money you recovered.'

The Fed flinched, then shook his head. 'Not until Monday. It's locked up in a safe at the courthouse, and the courthouse is closed until then.'

'How much was there?'

'Twenty-one hundred something.'

I said, 'Send it down with an itemized receipt,' and walked out of the cell with the two minions of the law staring razor blades at me. I caught up with Davis and Treadwell at the barred enclosure, and the deputy snickered at the doubled-over prisoner. Treadwell shot a blood cocktail onto his shirtfront, and when fat boy stood up, shot him a pointy-toe boot to the balls. Davis whooped, 'You a mother dog!' and the deputy nosedived onto his well-thumbed issue of *Batman*.

Davis's 'way' consisted of our taking Harwell Treadwell to a jig joint on Ventura's south side and plying him with fried chicken, gravy-drenched biscuits, and yams while I held my gun on him and my car-crazed partner fired questions about the '36 Auburn speedster. Treadwell obliged between wolfish mouthfuls, and Davis expressed worry that the Auburn would get shot up when the remaining Treadwell brothers got taken down by the law. 'You worry about that girl,' Harwell told us over and over. 'Them partners of mine got hound blood.' Then I interjected, 'You mean your brothers?' and Treadwell always countered with, 'I ain't no snitch, son.'

It was midafternoon when we finally headed south on Pacific Coast Highway, me at the wheel, Davis and the extraditee in the backseat, Treadwell's wrists cuffed behind his back, ankles manacled to the front-seat housing. The ragtop was down and sunlight and sea breeze had me thinking that this wasn't such a bad assignment after all. Behind me, the two Okies jawed, sparred, rattled each other's cages.

'Who's got the pink slip on the speedster, boy?'

'Who's your haberdasher? I never seen so many divergent angles on a set of threads in my life.'

'I got Hollywood in me, boy.'

'Nigger blood more like it. Where you from in Oklahoma?'

'Outside Norman. You from Gila Bend?'

'Yeah.'

'What's to do there?'

'Set dog's tails on fire and watch flies fuck, drink, fight, and chase your sister.'

'I heard your brothers go for anything white and on the hoof.'

'Plain anything, boss. If I'm lyin', I'm flyin'.'

'You think they'll hurt the Viertel girl?'

'That girl can take care of herself, and I ain't sayin' my brothers got her.'

'How'd you find out about her?'

'Miller read the society page and fell in love.'

'I thought you said your brothers weren't in on this.'

'I ain't sayin' they are, I ain't sayin they isn't.'

'Kidnappin's Oklahoma stuff from way back. The Barkers, Pretty Boy. How you account for that?'

'Well . . . I think maybe fellas comin' from hunger are real curious about the ante on loved ones. How high can you go before they say, "No sir, you keep the son of a bitch"?'

'Let's get back to the Auburn, boy.'

'Let's not. I need somethin' to keep you tantalized with.'

'Tantalize me now.'

'How's this: tan leather upholstery that Miller spilled liquor on, radio that picks up the San Dago stations real good, a little grind on the gearbox when you go into third. Hey!'

I saw it then, too: an overturned motorcycle on fire smack in the middle of the highway. No cops were at the scene, but a sawhorse detour sign had been placed in the middle lane, directing southbound traffic to a road running inland. Reflexively, I hung a hard left turn onto it, the flames lapping at the car's rear bumper.

Davis whooped, 'Whooo! Mother dog.' Harwell Treadwell laughed like a white-trash hyena. The two-lane blacktops took us up and over a series of short slopes, then down into a box canyon closed in by scrub-covered hills that pressed right up against the roadside. I cursed the hour or so the detour was going to cost us, then a loud 'Ka-raaack' sounded, and the windshield exploded in front of me.

Glass shrapnel filled the air; I shut my eyes and felt slashes on my cheeks and my hands grapping the steering wheel. Davis screeched 'MOTHERFUCK!' and started firing at the hill to the left of us. Opening my eyes and looking over, I saw nothing but greenery, then three more shots hit the side of the car, ricocheting ding-ding-ding.

I floored the gas; Davis fired at the muzzle bursts on the hillside; Harwell Treadwell made strange noises – like he couldn't decide whether to laugh or weep. Head on the wheel, I kept one eye on the rearview, and through it I saw Davis haul Treadwell off the seat to use as a bulletproof vest, his .38 in Treadwell's mouth as added insurance.

Ka-raack! Ka-raack! Ka-raack!

The last shot hit the radiator; steam covered my entire field of vision. I drove blind, picking up speed on a downslope, then there was another shot; the left front tire buckled, and the car fishtailed. I decelerated and aimed at the roadside shoulder away from the gunfire, sightless, trying to bank us in just right. Scrub bushes, green and huge, jumped out of nowhere, and then everything went topsy-turvy – and I was eating blacktop and steam.

More 'ka-raacks' pulsated through me – and I didn't know if they were gunshots or parts of my brains going blooey. Enveloped by dust and vapor fumes, I heard, 'Legs! Legs, boy! Run!' I obeyed, stumble-running full out.

The vapor dissipated, and I saw that I was sprinting toward a patch of furrowed farm dirt. Davis was running in front of me, half hauling, half shoving Harwell Treadwell, gun at his head. I caught up with them, realizing the shots had ended, and at the far side of the dirt patch I saw trees and buildings – maybe a sharecropper shantytown.

We ran toward it – two cops and the kidnapper in handcuffs who was our bulletproof vest, life insurance and hole card, kicking dried-up cabbages and carrots and beanstalks out of the ground as we speedballed for sanctuary. Nearing the town, I saw that it was composed of one street with ramshackle wood structures on either side, a packed dirt road the only throughway. Slowing to a trot, I grabbed Davis's arm and gasped, 'We can't risk taking a car out. We've gotta call the Ventura bulls.'

Davis jerked Treadwell's bracelet chain, sending him face first to the ground. Catching his breath, he kicked him hard in the ass. 'That's for my car and in case I die.' Wiping dusty sweat off his brow, he pointed his .38 at the hick-town main street like he was imploring me to feast my eyes. I did, and a second later I saw what he was getting at: the phone lines were crumpled in a heap beside the base of the terminal pole that stood just inside the edge of the town proper.

I looked back at hardscrabble land and the roadway that held the remains of my partner's car; I looked ahead at Tobacco Road, California style. 'Let's go.'

We entered the town, and I gave it a long eyeballing while Davis walked in a side-by-side drape with Harwell Treadwell, .38 snub dangling by a thumb and forefinger, business end aimed at his *cojones*. The left-hand side of the street featured a grain store, a market, the front window filled with stacks of Tokay and muscatel short dogs, and a clapboard farm-machinery repair shop with rusted parts strewn in front of it. On the right, the facades were all boarded up, with a string of prewar jalopies parked up against them, including a strange-looking Model T hybrid that seemed made out of mismatched parts. The only strollers about were a couple of grizzled men dressed in sun-faded War Relocation Authority khakis – and they shot us a cursory fish-eye and kept on walking.

When we reached the end of the street, Davis spotted a flimsy-looking unboarded door, kicked it in, and shoved Treadwell inside. Turning to face me, he said, 'We got what them boys want. You run into them you tell them Harwell is chewing on the end of my .38, and the first shot I hear he gets a hot lead cocktail. *And you get us a car, boy.*'

I nodded, then backtracked to the stand of heaps, looking for a likely one to commandeer. All six of them had at least one dead tire, and I started wondering about the lack of people, and why the two I'd seen so far didn't seem alarmed at raggedy-assed armed strangers in their midst. Noticing a bolted-on fire ladder attached to the grain building across the street, I made for it, hoisting myself up the rungs.

At the top, I had a good view of the surrounding area. Shacks were nestled in little green pockets bordered by fenced-off crop acreage, with dirt access roads connecting them to each other and the town. No one seemed to be working in the fields, but there were a few people taking the breeze in front of their cribs, which struck me as eerie.

I descended the ladder, and when I was halfway down, saw an old man on one of the roads staring at me. I pretended not to notice, and he turned his back and ran – flat out – to the biggest shack in the community, a corrugated metal job with a white wood barn attached.

I hopped off the ladder and pursued, taking foot roads out of town and over an eighth of a mile or so to a stand of sycamore trees that formed a perimeter a few yards from the barn. The man was nowhere in sight, but the sliding barn door was open just a crack. I drew my .38 and sprinted over and in.

Sunlight through a side window illuminated a big empty space, and the smell of hay plus something medicinal hit my nostrils. In the center of the barn, the acid stench got stronger, and somehow familiar. I noticed a table covered with a tarpaulin wedged into a corner near the connecting door to the shack and saw dry ice hissing out of rips in the canvas. The shape underneath took form, and I pulled the tarp off.

A buck-naked dead man was lying on top of dry ice blocks, sachets oozing formaldehyde placed strategically on his body. He was a stone ringer for Harwell Treadwell, and you didn't have to be a medical examiner to figure the cause of death – his crotch was blown to bits, torn, blooded flesh laced with buckshot all that remained.

I redraped the stiff, then eased the connecting door into a test jiggle. It gave, and I very slowly pulled it open, just a tiny fraction of an inch, in order to look in. Then it flew open all the way, and a big double-barreled shotgun was sighting down, and I shoved both my hands at midpoint on the stock and pushed up.

A huge 'Ka-boom!' went off; the tin roof lurched under the force of the blast; pellets ricocheted. I threw myself at the shotgun-wielder just as he tried to slam me with the butt of his weapon, wrestled it away from him, then chopped down at his head with the flat side of my .38 – one blow, two blows, three. Finally the man went limp. I kicked the shotgun out of harm's way, then weaved on shaky, shaky legs.

It was the old man who'd rabbited when he saw me on the ladder. I looked around the room, saw a pail of water on the cracked wood floor by the front door, picked it up, and dumped it on my assailant. He stirred, then started sputtering, and I knelt down and placed my gun on his nose so he could get the picture up close. 'You admit you killed that man back there or you convince me somebody else did, and you live. You tell me where the other Treadwell brother is and I don't arrest you for assault on a police officer. You dick me around, you die.'

The geezer took it all in, his eyes getting clearer by the second, exhibiting the remarkable recuperative powers of the seasoned shat-upon. When he curled his lips to spit invective, I said, 'No banter, no wisecracks, no shit,' and cocked the hammer.

Now pops got the *whole* picture, in Technicolor. 'I ain't no killer,' he said with a Midwestern twang. 'I'm a truck farmer likes to dabble in the medical arts, but I sure ain't no killer.'

'I am. So you keep going and keep my interest, because I get bored easy, and when I get bored I get mad.'

Pops gulped, then spoke rapid-fire. 'People here put up Miller and Leroy, 'long with the girl, when they had that trouble up in Ventura. They—'

I interrupted. 'Did they pay you for it?'

Pops cackled. 'Where you think everbody is? Miller and Leroy got cousins up the wazoo here, they spread the money around, everbody went up to Oxnard and Big V to spend it. Like to put Miller and Leroy broke they spent so—'

'What?'

''Fore he died, Leroy told me they spent eight, nine thousand dollars, said this town of ours had hospitality like Hot Springs in the old days.'

I said, 'Mister, the ransom money came to a hundred thousand.'

Pops snorted. 'Big commotion back where it went bad. Police got most of it, Miller and Leroy got the dregs.'

My first thought was of the Ventura sheriffs holding back *big*. 'Keep going.'

'Well, everbody got happy here, and Miller and Leroy and the cooze holed up, and Miller and Leroy started schemin' another trade, and they started arguin' and feudin' over the girl, and she took to Miller 'cause Leroy was so nasty to her. Then Leroy tried to do her what you might call against her will, and she talked Miller into payin' back her virtue.'

'Miller killed his own brother?'

'That's right. And he felt so bad about it he paid me just about his last two hundred dollars to fix that boy up for burial, then put him in the ground when all the cousins got back after spendin' their money.'

'Then Miller and the girl took off?'

'That's right. Headed south, brand-new black paint on that pretty car of Harwell's.'

'When?'

'Yesterday. 'Bout noon.'

'Did they cut the phone lines before they went?'

Pops shrugged. 'Don't think so. Seems to me they was up this mornin'.'

I got the pins and needles tingling up the spine I always got when something was real wrong. Stensland the Fed had said that there was 'twenty-one hundred something' locked up as evidence, and Miller and Leroy dished out 'eight or nine' grand for shelter. That left almost ninety thousand missing. Figure a few thousand blown away during the Mexican standoff, and the rest sucked up – probably by the Feds and/or the Ventura sheriffs. And the scary part: if Miller Treadwell took off with Jane Viertel yesterday, it was the law that ambushed us – to make sure Harwell Treadwell didn't squawk about his brother's whereabouts – so *they* couldn't tell *us* about their paltry take of the ransom pie.

I put my gun away, said 'Bury the degenerate bastard,' and walked out the front door mad – like I'd been sucker-punched.

When I got back to the dump where I'd left Davis and our prisoner, they were gone. A fresh wave of panic hit me; then I heard grunts and metal-on-metal noises coming from the other side of the building. I walked around, and there was Harwell Treadwell chained to a fence and my forty-six-year-old partner embarking on a new career as a hot-rod engineer.

He was working on a jerry-built heap I'd noticed earlier, which now resembled a cross between Buck Rogers's spaceship and a collection of spare parts some trash-can dog dragged in. It was a Model T chassis with two motorcycle tires on the front, two tractor tires on the back, what looked like a half-dozen hooked-together lawn-mower engines, and an undercarriage made up of chicken wire and friction tape. The man himself was on the ground toiling on the drive shaft, and when I reached into the driver's seat and beeped the horn, he came up gun first, laughing when he saw who it was.

'Woooo, boy! You almost died!'

I walked over and whispered in Davis's ear. 'Miller killed Leroy and took off with the girl in the Auburn yesterday. The Ventura bulls are holding back on the ransom money, and I think it was them shooting at us. Let's roll *now*. On foot if this thing won't go.'

Davis smiled. 'She's got a name, boy. "Li'l Assdragger". And she'll *fly*.'

I heard engines in the distance and stood on the contraption's running board to grab a look. A three-vehicle caravan was thumping across the hardscrabble that bordered the town, sending up clouds of dust. Squinting hard, I saw black-and-white paint on one car, cherry lights on another.

Davis said, 'Them?' I nodded. Suddenly he was a nut-tightening, screw-fastening, wire-connecting dervish, and Harwell Treadwell was shouting, 'Come to big brother! Home cookin' tonight! Come and get me!'

I ran over and fumbled at Treadwell's bracelets with my handcuff key. I'd just gotten the left one off when he shot me a short right uppercut. Stunned, I started to duck into a crouch; then the free cuff lashed my face, the open ratchet ripping loose a chunk of my brows, blood in my eyes blinding me.

The black-and-white noise drew closer; I heard Davis frantically trying to start Li'l Assdragger. I wiped the blood from my eyes and got my balance just in time to see Harwell Treadwell hotfoot it around the edge of the building. I started to run after him, then the Okie jalopy lurched forward, cutting me off. Davis jelled, 'I can't brake too good. Jump in!'

I did. Davis popped the two foot pedals simultaneously, and the thing crept forward. I shouted 'Treadwell!' above the engine noise. Davis shouted 'He'll pay!' twice as loud. On the street, I turned around and looked back, and there was our extraditee running headlong into the three-car dust storm, whooping and waving his arms. A second later I heard shotgun blasts and machine-gun fire, and parts of Treadwell flew in all directions before the storm clouds ate him up. Then I just held on.

We lurched, we bumped, we hit potholes and jumped three feet off the ground. We brodied through dirt and skidded over the connecting roads that led out of town. We fishtailed when we hit gravel, and we turned doughnuts when we hit wet spots. Davis leadfooted, double-

and triple-clutched, honked stray dogs out of our way, and did everything else but hit the brakes. Dusk started coming on, and then we were on the big, broad Ridge Road southbound, blacktop under our mismatched wheels, a skinny yellow line separating us from collisions with real, live, normal cars. Davis hooted, 'Ain't got no lights!' and a moment later I saw the Wayside Honor Rancho turnoff sign. Davis saw it too, decelerated, pumped the floorboard and hooted 'Ain't got no brakes!' I shut my eyes and felt Li'l Assdragger shimmy. Then it was a triple fishtail-doughnut combo, and we were stone-cold still in the northbound lane, staring down the headlights of death.

We got out and ran. Tire screeches and thud-crunch-cracks behind us told me that Li'l Assdragger was fond recent history. Hugging the shoulder, we trudged over to the turnoff and up a road to the barbed-wire-enclosed guard hut that separated squarejohn citizens from county inmates. A light flashed on as we approached; I had my badge out and the word *Peace* on my lips. Then my legs turned to Jell-O, and I passed out thinking I should have more wind than a fat Okie fifteen years my senior.

I woke up to see that fat Okie standing over me in a clean white shirt and sedate print necktie. My first thought was that we had to be dead – Davis Evans would never dress that square unless God himself forced him to.

'Wake up, boy. I been doin' police work while you been beauty sleepin'.'

In a split second it all came back. I groaned, felt the cot beneath me and looked around at the cramped interior of the guard hut. 'Oh shit.'

Davis handed me a wet towel. 'On a stick. I made me some phone calls. Pal of mine at the Ventura courthouse said he logged twenty-one hundred sixty-six beans of the ransom money into the evidence locker. What you think of that?'

I stood up and tried my legs. They wobbled, but held. 'Miller and Leroy spread eight or nine grand around the town,' I said. 'Leaving close to ninety out there. It's got to be the Ventura cops.'

Davis shook his head. 'Uh-uh. That was a legit dispatch that came into town and shot down Harwell. They saw that wreck of ours on the detour road and came lookin' for survivors. See, I called R&I and Robbery for a list of Miller's known associates from his old rousts. Got six names from his jacket, and the records clerk told me a Ventura Fed called in a few hours before, got the same information. You think that ain't sweet?'

I thought of Stensland, the all-gray Federal man with the big tax-free pension – if he could kibosh the fact that the snatchers glommed only chump change. 'Let's go get him.'

'That mother dog gonna pay for hurtin' my Buick.'

'Get a car from the duty officer. And this time I'll drive.'

Back in familiar, if not safe-and-sane L.A., we formed an itinerary out of the six names and last-known addresses from Miller Treadwell's KA file. Davis took the wheel again, and I picked and poked at my various cuts, lacerations, and bruises as we prowled the South-Central part of the city – home to our first three possibles.

Number one's wife told us her husband was back in Quentin; the apartment house of the number-two man had been torn down and was now an amusement arcade frequented by Mexican youths wearing zoot suits; number three had gotten religion and praised Jesus as we searched his pad. He told us he hadn't seen Miller Treadwell since their last job together in '41, damned him as a fornicating whore-monger, and handed us leaflets that cogently explained that Jesus Christ was an Aryan, not a Jew, and that *Mein Kampf* was the lost book of the Bible. Davis's response to the man was the longest 'Wooooooo' I'd ever heard him emit, and we drove across town to Hollywood and KA number four, debating the pros and cons of parole violation on grounds of mental bankruptcy.

Number four – 'Jungle' John Lembeck, white male, age thirty-four, two-time convicted strong-arm heister – lived in a bungalow court on Serrano just off the Boulevard. Giving the address a rolling once-over, Davis and I said 'Bingo' simultaneously, and I added, 'The Auburn with a bad black paint job. Right by that streetlight.'

Davis blurted, 'What?', slowed the car, and squinted out at the dark street. Noticing the dream-mobile, he said, 'Double bingo. There's a fed sled three cars down. If it's got Ventura tags, this is grief.'

I got out and walked back to check; Davis continued on to the corner and parked. Squatting down, I squinted at the steel-gray Plymouth's rear license plate. Triple bingo: five-digit federal vehicle designation, 1945 Ventura County tags. Grief on a Popsicle stick.

Davis trotted over, and we circled the bungalows in a flanking movement. They were individual stucco huts arranged around a cement courtyard, and John Lembeck's file placed him in unit three. Alleys separated the court from the adjoining apartment buildings, and I took the one on the left.

The night was deep blue and cloudless, and I crept through the alleyway helped by light from apartment windows. The first two huts had drawn curtains, but the third one back was cracked for air, the venetian blinds down to just above the narrow open space. I drew my gun, put my eyes to the slice of light, and looked in.

Quadruple bingo – and then some.

The man who had to be Miller Treadwell was sitting in an overstuffed chair, his pants down, moaning, 'Guddamn, guddamn.' I could see a woman's left hand bracing the chair arm, but nothing more of the woman herself. Agent Stensland was trussed up, lying on his side on the floor, next to the entranceway into the front room. He was working his wrist bonds against a wall grate, his breath expanding and contracting against the fabric tape crisscrossing his mouth.

Miller moaned with his eyes shut, then a pretty blonde head popped up and spoke to him: 'Sugar, let me talk to you for a sec.'

'Guddamn, girl, don't stop.'

'Miller, you have to make him tell you where he put the money.'

'We got ours, girl. He ain't gonna tell us; he knows I'll kill him if he does. We got ours, and we can trade you again.'

'Daddy's too cheap to pay more. We could have twice as much, Sugar. We could go away and be together and just forget about Daddy.'

'Sugar, don't talk nonsense. We got plenty, your papa's got plenty more, and I ain't able to talk so good in this state you got me in. You wanta . . .'

The head disappeared again; Miller went back to moaning. I wondered where Evans was and watched Stensland move his bound wrists against the grate. The kidnapper-killer's ecstasy was reaching a crescendo when I saw my partner, inside the pad, tiptoeing over to the entranceway. He was just a few feet in back of Stensland when the G-man got his hands free and ripped the tape from his mouth. He went flush at the pain, and I followed his eyes to a .45 automatic on the armrest beside Miller's right hand.

Pawing at his leg restraints, racing against the Okie's release, Stensland banged his elbow on the grate. Miller jerked out of heaven and aimed the .45 at him just as I wedged my gun through the window

110

crack. He fired at the Fed; I fired at him; Davis emptied his piece at the chair. There must have been a dozen explosions, and then it was all over except for Jane Mackenzie Viertel's record-length scream.

A shitload of Hollywood Division black-and-whites showed up, and the meat wagon removed Miller Treadwell and Special Agent Norris Stensland, DOA. A detective lieutenant told Davis and me he wanted a full report before he contacted the Feds. We kept the Viertel girl in handcuffs on general principles, and when the commotion wound down and the crowd of rubbernecks dispersed, we braced her on the front lawn of the courtyard.

Unlocking her cuffs, I said, 'Come clean on the money. What happened? Where's the dough Miller was talking about?'

Jane Viertel, backlit by a streetlamp, rubbed her wrists. 'The money was in two packages. When it got crazy, they were dropped. Miller and Leroy got one, and it ripped open. The FBI man dropped his and Leroy ran with me, then Miller took off. The FBI man took Harwell to his car, then came back and grabbed the last package so Harwell wouldn't know he had it. But Miller saw him. He had some loose bills he picked up, and he hid the rest of the money from Leroy. Miller and Leroy gave the loose money to these dreadful slobs to hide us out, and Leroy thought that was all there was. Then Miller and I got cozy, and he told me there was forty thousand for us.'

I looked at the girl, nineteen-year-old pulchritude with whorehouse smarts. 'Where's Miller's money?'

Jane watched Davis lovingly eye the Auburn speedster. 'Why should I tell you? You'd just give it back to that cheapskate father of mine.'

'He paid a hundred grand to save your life.'

The girl shrugged and lit a cigarette. 'He probably used the interest from Mother's trust fund. What's wrong with fatso? Is he queer for cars or something?'

Davis walked over to us. 'She needs a complete paint strip, new paint job, new upholstery and some whitewalls. Then she's a peach.' Winking at Jane Viertel, he said, 'What's your goal in life, Sweetheart? Pussy-whipping killers?'

Jane smiled, walked to the car, and unscrewed the gas cap. She dropped in her cigarette and started running. Davis and I hit the ground and ate grass. The gas tank exploded and the car went up in flames. The girl stood up and curtsied, then walked to us and said,

'Miller's money was in the trunk. Too bad, Daddy. Maybe you can tell Mother it's a tax write-off.'

I recuffed Jane Viertel; the flames sent flickers of light over Davis Evans's bereaved face. He stuck his hands in his pockets, pulled them out empty, and said to me, 'You got a couple dimes, partner? AX6-400's a toll call. I need me a peach like a mother dog.'

Since I Don't Have You

During the postwar years I served two masters – running interference and hauling dirty laundry for the two men who defined L.A. at that time better than anyone else. To Howard Hughes I was security boss at his aircraft plant, pimp, and troubleshooter for RKO Pictures – the ex-cop who could kibosh blackmail squeezes, fix drunk drivings, and arrange abortions and dope cures. To Mickey Cohen – rackets overlord and would-be nightclub shtickster – I was a bagman to the LAPD, the former Narco detective who skimmed junk off Niggertown dope rousts, allowing his Southside boys to sell it back to the hordes of shvartzes eager to fly White Powder Airlines. Big Howard: always in the news for crashing an airplane someplace inappropriate, stubbing his face on the control panel in some hick-town beanfield, then showing up at Romanoff's bandaged like the Mummy with Ava Gardner on his arm; Mickey C.: also a pussy hound par excellence, pub crawling with an entourage of psychopathic killers, press agents, gag writers, and his bulldog Mickey Cohen, Jr. – a flatulent beast with a schlong so large that the Mick's stooges strapped it to a roller skate so it wouldn't drag on the ground.

Howard Hughes. Mickey Cohen. And me, Turner 'Buzz' Meeks, Lizard Ridge, Oklahoma, armadillo poacher, strikebreaker goon, cop, fixer, and keeper of the secret key to his masters' psyches: they were both cowards *mano a mano*; airplanes and lunatic factotums their go-betweens, while I would go anywhere, anyplace, gun or billy club first, courting a front-page death to avenge my second-banana life. And the two of them courted me because I put their lack of balls in perspective: it was irrational, meshuga, bad business – a Forest Lawn crypt years before my time. But I got the last laugh there: I always knew that when faced with the grave I'd pull a smart segue to keep kicking – and I write this memoir as an old, old man – while Howard and Mickey stuff caskets, bullshit biographies their only legacy.

Howard. Mickey. Me.

Sooner or later, my work for the two of them had to produce what the yuppie lawyer kids today call 'conflict of interest'. Of course, it was over a woman – and, of course, being a suicidal Okie shitkicker, forty-one years old and getting tired, I decided to play both ends against the middle. A thought just hit me: that I'm writing this story because I miss Howard and Mickey, and telling it gives me a chance to be with them again. Keep that in mind – that I loved them – even though they were both world-class shitheels.

January 15, 1949.

It was cold and clear in Los Angeles, and the papers were playing up the two-year anniversary of the Black Dahlia murder case – still unsolved, still speculated on. Mickey was still mourning Hooky Rothman's death – he French-kissed a sawed-off shotgun held by an unknown perpetrator – and Howard was still pissed at me over the Bob Mitchum reefer roust: he figured that my connections with Narco Division were still so solid that I should have seen it coming. I'd been shuttling back and forth between Howard and Mickey since New Year's. The Mick's signature fruit baskets stuffed with C-notes had to be distributed to cops, judges, and City Council members he wanted to grease, and the pilot-mogul had me out bird-dogging quiff: prowling bus depots and train stations for buxom young girls who'd fall prey to RKO contracts in exchange for frequent nighttime visits. I'd been having a good run: a half-dozen Midwestern farm maidens were now ensconced in Howard's fuck pads – strategically located apartments tucked all over L.A. And I was deep in hock to a Darktown bookie named Leotis Dineen, a six-foot-six jungle bunny who hated people of the Oklahoma persuasion worse than poison. I was sitting in my Quonset-hut office at Hughes Aircraft when the phone rang.

'That you, Howard?'

Howard Hughes sighed. 'What happened to "Security, may I help you"?'

'You're the only one calls this early, Boss.'

'And you're alone?'

'Right. Per your instructions to call you Mr. Hughes in the presence of others. What's up?'

'Breakfast is up. Meet me at the corner of Melrose and La Brea in half an hour.'

114

'Right, Boss.'

'Two or three, Buzz? I'm hungry and having four.'

Howard was on his all-chilli-dog diet; Pink's Dogs at Melrose and La Brea was his current in spot. I knew for a fact that their chilli was made from horsemeat air-freighted up daily from Tijuana. 'One kraut, no chilli.'

'Heathen. Pink's chilli is better than Chasen's.'

'I had a pony when I was a boy.'

'So? I had a governess. You think I wouldn't eat—'

I said, 'Half an hour,' and hung up. I figured if I got there five minutes late I wouldn't have to watch the fourth richest man in America eat.

Howard was picking strands of sauerkraut off his chin when I climbed in the backseat of his limousine. He said, 'You didn't really want it, did you?'

I pressed the button that sent up the screen that shielded us from the driver. 'No, coffee and doughnuts are more my style.'

Howard gave me a long, slow eyeballing – a bit ill at ease because sitting down we were the same height, while standing I came up to his shoulders. 'Do you need money, Buzz?'

I thought of Leotis Dineen. 'Can niggers dance?'

'They certainly can. But call them colored, you never know when one might be listening.'

Larry the chauffeur was Chinese; Howard's comment made me wonder if his last plane crash had dented his cabeza. I tried my standard opening line. 'Getting any, Boss?'

Hughes smiled and burped; horse grease wafted through the backseat. He dug into a pile of papers beside him – blueprints, graphs, and scraps covered with airplane doodles – pulling out a snapshot of a blonde girl naked from the waist up. He handed it to me and said, 'Gretchen Rae Shoftel, age nineteen. Born in Prairie du Chien, Wisconsin, July 26, 1929. She was staying at the place on South Lucerne – the screening house. This is the woman, Buzz. I think I want to marry her. And she's gone – she flew the coop on the contract, me, all of it.'

I examined the picture. Gretchen Rae Shoftel was prodigiously lunged – no surprise – with a blonde pageboy and smarts in her eyes, like she knew Mr. Hughes's two-second screen test was strictly an audition for the sack and an occasional one-liner in some RKO turkey. 'Who found her for you, Boss? It wasn't me – I'd have remembered.'

Howard belched again – my hijacked sauerkraut this time. 'I got the picture in the mail at the studio, along with an offer – a thousand dollars cash to a PO box in exchange for the girl's address. I did it, and met Gretchen Rae at her hotel downtown. She told me she posed for some dirty old man back in Milwaukee, that he must have pulled the routine for the thousand. Gretchen Rae and I got to be friends, and, well . . .'

'And you'll give me a bonus to find her?'

'A thousand, Buzz. Cash, off the payroll.'

My debt to Leotis Dineen was eight hundred and change; I could get clean and get even on minor-league baseball – the San Diego Seals were starting their pre-season games next week. 'It's a deal. What else have you got on the girl?'

'She was carhopping at Scrivner's Drive-In. I know that.'

'Friends, known associates, relatives here in L.A.?'

'Not to my knowledge.'

I took a deep breath to let Howard know a tricky question was coming. 'Boss, you think maybe this girl is working an angle on you? I mean, the picture out of nowhere, the thousand to a PO box?'

Howard Hughes harrumphed. 'It had to be that piece in *Confidential*, the one that alleged my talent scouts take topless photographs and that I like my women endowed.'

'*Alleged*, Boss?'

'I'm practicing coming off as irate in case I sue *Confidential* somewhere down the line. You'll get on this right away?'

'*Rapidamente.*'

'Outstanding. And don't forget Sid Weinberg's party tomorrow night. He's got a new horror picture coming out from the studio, and I need you there to keep the autograph hounds from going crazy. Eight, Sid's house.'

'I'll be there.'

'Find Gretchen Rae, Buzz. She's special.'

Howard's one saving grace with females is that he keeps falling in love with them – albeit only after viewing Brownie snaps of their lungs. It more or less keeps him busy between crashing airplanes and designing airplanes that don't fly.

'Right, Boss.'

116

The limousine's phone rang. Howard picked it up, listened and murmured, 'Yes. Yes, I'll tell him.' Hanging up, he said, 'The switchboard at the plant. Mickey Cohen wants to see you. Make it brief, you're on my time now.'

'Yes, sir.'

It was Howard who introduced me to Mickey, right before I got wounded in a dope shootout and took my LAPD pension. I still give him a hand with his drug dealings – unofficial liaison to Narcotics Division, point man for the Narco dicks who skim X number of grams off every ounce of junk confiscated. The LAPD has got an unofficial heroin policy: it is to be sold only to coloreds, only east of Alvarado and south of Jefferson. I don't think it should be sold anywhere, but as long as it is, I want the 5 percent. I test the shit with a chem kit I stole from the crime lab – no poor hophead is going to croak from a Mickey Cohen bindle bootjacked by Turner 'Buzz' Meeks. Dubious morality: I sleep well 90 percent of the time and lay my bet action off with shine bookies, the old exploiter washing the hand that feeds him. Money was right at the top of my brain as I drove to Mickey's haberdashery on the Strip. I always need cash, and the Mick never calls unless it is in the offing.

I found the man in his back room, surrounded by sycophants and muscle: Johnny Stompanato, guinea spit curl dangling over his handsome face – he of the long-term crush on Lana Turner; Davey Goldman, Mickey's chief yes-man and the author of his nightclub shticks; and a diffident-looking little guy I recognized as Morris Hornbeck – an accountant and former trigger for Jerry Katzenbach's mob in Milwaukee. Shaking hands and pulling up a chair, I got ready to make my pitch: you pay me now; I do my job after I run a hot little errand for Howard. I opened my mouth to speak, but Mickey beat me to it. 'I want you to find a woman for me.'

I was about to say 'What a coincidence,' when Johnny Stomp handed me a snapshot. 'Nice gash. Not Lana Turner quality, but USDA choice tail nonetheless.'

Of course, you see it coming. The photo was a nightspot job, compliments of Preston Sturges's Players Club: Gretchen Rae Shoftel blinking against flashbulb glare, dairy-state pulchritude in a tight black dress. Mickey Cohen was draping an arm around her shoulders, aglow with love. I swallowed to keep my voice steady. 'Where was the wife, Mick? Off on one of her Hadassah junkets?'

117

Mickey grunted. ' "Israel, the New Homeland." Ten-day tour with her mah-jongg club. While the cat is away, the mice will play. Va va va voom. Find her, Buzzchik. A grand.'

I got obstreperous, my usual reaction to being scared. 'Two grand, or go take a flying fuck at a rolling doughnut.'

Mickey scowled and went into a slow burn; I watched Johnny Stomp savor my bravado, Davey Goldman write down the line for his boss's shticks, and Morris Hornbeck do queasy double takes like he wasn't copacetic with the play. When the Mick's burn stretched to close to a minute, I said, 'Silence implies consent. Tell me all you know about the girl, and I'll take it from there.'

Mickey Cohen smiled at me – his coming-from-hunger minion. 'Goyishe shitheel. For a twosky I want satisfaction guaranteed within forty-eight hours.'

I already had the money laid off on baseball, the fights, and three horse parlays. 'Forty-seven and change. Go.'

Mickey eyed his boys as he spoke – probably because he was pissed at me and needed a quick intimidation fix. Davey and Johnny Stomp looked away; Morris Hornbeck just twitched, like he was trying to quash a bad case of the heebie-jeebies. 'Gretchen Rae Shoftel. I met her at Scrivner's Drive-In two weeks ago. She told me she's fresh out of the Minnesota sticks, someplace like that. She—'

I interrupted. 'She said "Minnesota" specifically, Mick?'

'Right. Moosebreath, Dogturd, some boonies town – but definitely Minnesota.'

Morris Hornbeck was sweating now; I had myself a hot lead. 'Keep going, Mick.'

'Well, we hit it off; I convince Lavonne to see Israel before them dune coons take it back; Gretchen Rae and I get together; we va va va voom; it's terrific. She plays cagey with me, won't tell me where she's staying, and she keeps taking off – says she's looking for a man, some friend of her father's back in Antelope Ass or wherever the fuck she comes from. Once she's gassed on vodka collinses and gets misty about some hideaway she says she's got. That—'

I said, 'Wrap it up.'

Mickey slammed his knees so hard that Mickey Cohen, Jr., asleep in the doorway twenty feet away, woke up and tried to stand on all fours – until the roller skate attached to his wang pulled him back down. 'I'll fucking wrap you up if you don't find her for me! That's it! I want her! Find her for me! *Do it now!*'

I got to my feet wondering how I was going to pull this one off – with the doorman gig at Sid Weinberg's party thrown smack in the middle of it. I said, 'Forty-seven, fifty-five and rolling,' and winked at Morris Hornbeck – who just happened to hail from Milwaukee, where Howard told me Gretchen Rae Shoftel told him a dirty old man had snapped her lung shots. Hornbeck tried to wink back; it looked like his eyeball was having a grand mal seizure. Mickey said, 'Find her for me. And you gonna be at Sid's tomorrow night?'

'Keeping autograph hounds at bay. You?'

'Yeah, I've got points in Sid's new picture. I want hot dope by then, Buzzchik. *Hot*.'

I said, 'Scalding,' and took off, almost tripping over Mickey Cohen, Jr.'s appendage as I went out the door.

A potential three grand in my kick; Morris Hornbeck's hinkyness doing a slow simmer in my gourd; an instinct that Gretchen Rae Shoftel's 'hideaway' was Howard Hughes's fuck pad on South Lucerne – the place where he kept the stash of specially cantilevered bras he designed to spotlight his favorite starlet's tits, cleavage gowns for his one-night inamoratas, and the stag-film collection he showed to visiting defense contractors – some of them rumored to costar Mickey Cohen, Jr., and a bimbo made up to resemble Howard's personal heroine: Amelia Earhart. But first there was Scrivner's Drive-In and a routine questioning of Gretchen Rae's recent coworkers. Fear adrenaline was scorching my soul as I drove there – maybe I'd played my shtick too tight to come out intact.

Scrivner was on Sunset three blocks east of Hollywood High School, an eat-in-your-car joint featuring a rocket-ship motif – chromium scoops, dips, and portholes abounding – Jules Verne as seen by a fag set designer scraping the stars on marijuana. The carhops – all zoftig numbers – wore tight space-cadet outfits; the fry cooks wore plastic rocket helmets with clear face shields to protect them from spattering grease. Questioning a half-dozen of them was like enjoying the DT's without benefit of booze. After an hour of talk and chump-change handouts, I knew the following:

That Gretchen Rae Shoftel carhopped there for a month, was often tardy, and during midafternoon lulls tended to abandon her shift. This was tolerated because she was an atom-powered magnet that attracted men by the shitload. She could tote up tabs in her head, deftly computing sales tax – but had a marked tendency toward spilling milkshakes and French fries. When the banana-split-loving Mickey Cohen started snouting around after her, the manager gave her the go-by, no doubt leery of attracting the criminal elements who had made careers out of killing innocent bystanders while trying to kill the Mick. Aside from that I glommed one hard lead plus suppositions to hang it on: Gretchen Rae had persistently questioned the Scrivner's crew about a recent regular customer – a man with a long German surname who'd been eating at the counter, doing arithmetic tricks with meal tabs and astounding the locals with five-minute killings of the L.A. *Times* crossword. He was an old geez with a European accent – and he stopped chowing at Scrivner's right before Gretchen Rae Shoftel hired on. Mickey told me the quail had spoken of looking for a friend of her father's; Howard had said she was from Wisconsin; German accents pointed to the dairy state in a big way. And Morris Hornbeck, Mr. Shakes just a few hours before, had been a Milwaukee mob trigger and money man. And the lovely Gretchen Rae had continued carhopping after becoming the consort of two of the richest, most powerful men in Los Angeles – an eyeopener if ever there was one.

I drove to a pay phone and made some calls, straight and collect. An old LAPD pal gave me the lowdown on Morris Hornbeck – he had two California convictions for felony statch rape, both complainants thirteen-year-old girls. A guy on the Milwaukee force that I'd worked liaison with supplied Midwestern skinny: Little Mo was a glorified bookkeeper for Jerry Katzenbach's mob, run out of town by his boss in '47, when he was given excess gambling skim to invest as he saw best and opened a call house specializing in underaged poon dressed up as movie stars – greenhorn girls, coiffed, cosmeticked, and gowned to resemble Rita Hayworth, Ann Sheridan, Veronica Lake and the like. The operation was a success, but Jerry Katzenbach, Knights of Columbus family man, considered it bum PR. Adios, Morris – who obviously found an amenable home in L.A.

On Gretchen Rae Shoftel, I got bupkis; ditto on the geezer with the arithmetic tricks similar to the carhop/vamp. The girl had no criminal record in either California or Wisconsin – but I was willing to bet she'd learned her seduction techniques at Mo Hornbeck's whorehouse.

I drove to Howard Hughes's South Lucerne Street fuck pad and let myself in with a key from my fourteen-pound Hughes Enterprises key ring. The house was furnished with leftovers from the RKO prop department, complete with appropriate female accoutrements for each of the six bedrooms. The Moroccan Room featured hammocks and settees from *Casbah Nocturne* and a rainbow array of low-cut silk lounging pajamas; the *Billy the Kid* Room – where Howard brought his Jane Russell look-alikes – was four walls of mock-saloon bars with halter-top cowgirl getups and a mattress covered by a Navajo blanket. My favorite was the Zoo Room: taxidermied cougar, bison, moose, and bobcats – shot by Ernest Hemingway – mounted with their eyes leering down on a narrow strip of sheet-covered floor. Big Ernie told me he decimated the critter population of two Montana counties in order to achieve the effect. There was a kitchen stocked with plenty of fresh milk, peanut butter, and jelly to sate teenage tastebuds, a room to screen stag movies, and the master bedroom – my bet for where Howard installed Gretchen Rae Shoftel.

I took the back staircase up, walked down the hall, and pushed the door open, expecting the room's usual state: big white bed and plain white walls, the ironic accompaniment to snatched virginity. I was wrong; what I saw was some sort of testament to squarejohn American home life.

Mixmasters, cookie sheets, toasters, and matched cutlery sets rested on the bed; the walls were festooned with Currier & Ives calendars and framed *Saturday Evening Post* covers drawn by Norman Rockwell. A menagerie of stuffed animals was admiring the artwork – pandas and tigers and Disney characters placed against the bed, heads tilted upward. There was a bentwood rocker in a corner next to the room's one window. The seat held a stack of catalogs. I leafed through them: Motorola radios, Hamilton Beach kitchen goodies, bed quilts from a mail-order place in New Hampshire. In all of them the less expensive items were checkmarked. Strange, since Howard let his master-bedroom poon have anything they wanted – top-of-the-line charge accounts, the magilla.

I checked the closet. It held the standard Hughes wardrobe – low-cut gowns and tight cashmere sweaters, plus a half-dozen Scrivner's carhop outfits, replete with built-in uplift breastplates, which

121

Gretchen Rae Shoftel didn't need. Seeing a row of empty hangers, I checked for more catalogs and found a Bullocks Wilshire job under the bed. Flipping through it, I saw tweedy skirts and suits, flannel blazers, and prim and proper wool dresses circled; Howard's charge-account number was scribbled at the top of the back page. Gretchen Rae Shoftel, math whiz, searching for another math whiz, was contemplating making herself over as Miss Upper-Middle-Class Rectitude.

I checked out the rest of the fuck pad – quick eyeball prowls of the other bedrooms, a toss of the downstairs closets. Empty Bullocks boxes were everywhere – Gretchen Rae had accomplished her transformation. Howard liked to keep his girls cash-strapped to ensure their obedience, but I was willing to guess he stretched the rules for this one. Impersonating a police officer, I called the dispatcher's office at the Yellow and Beacon cab companies. Paydirt at Beacon: three days ago at 3:10 P.M., a cab was dispatched to 436 South Lucerne; its destination: 2281 South Mariposa.

Big pay dirt.

2281 South Mariposa was a Mickey Cohen hideout, an armed fortress where the Mick's triggers holed up during their many skirmishes with the Jack Dragna gang. It was steel-reinforced concrete; shitloads of canned goods in the bomb shelter/basement; racks of Tommys and pump shotguns behind fake walls covered by cheesecake pics. Only Mickey's boys knew about the place – making it conclusive proof that Morris Hornbeck was connected to Gretchen Rae Shoftel. I drove to Jefferson and Mariposa – quicksville.

It was a block of wood-frame houses, small, neatly tended, mostly owned by Japs sprung from the relocation camps, anxious to stick together and assert their independence in new territory. 2281 was as innocuous and sanitary as any pad on the block: Mickey had the best Jap gardener in the area. No cars were in the driveway; the cars parked curbside looked harmless enough, and the nearest local taking the sun was a guy sitting on a porch swing four houses down. I walked up to the front door, punched in a window, reached around to the latch and let myself in.

The living room – furnished by Mickey's wife, Lavonne, with sofas and chairs from the Hadassah thrift shop – was tidy and totally silent. I was half expecting a killer hound to pounce on me before I snapped that Lavonne had forbid the Mick to get a dog because it might wizz on the carpeting. Then I caught the smell.

Decomposition hits you in the tear ducks and gut about simultaneously. I tied my handkerchief over my mouth and nose, grabbed a lamp for a weapon, and walked toward the stink. It was in the right front bedroom, and it was a doozie.

There were two stiffs – a dead man on the floor and another on the bed. The floor man was lying facedown, with a white nightgown still pinned with a Bullocks price tag knotted around his neck. Congealed beef stew covered his face, the flesh cracked and red from scalding. A saucepan was upended a few feet away, holding the caked remains of the goo. Somebody was cooking when the altercation came down.

I laid down the lamp and gave the floor stiff a detailed eyeing. He was fortyish, blond and fat; whoever killed him had tried to burn off his fingerprints – the tips on both hands were scorched black, which meant that the killer was an amateur: the only way to eliminate prints is to do some chopping. A hot plate was tossed in a corner near the bed; I checked it out and saw seared skin stuck to the coils. The bed stiff was right there, so I took a deep breath, tightened my mask and examined him. He was an old guy, skinny, dressed in clothes too heavy for winter L.A. There was not one mark of any kind on him; his singed-fingered hands had been folded neatly on his chest, rest in peace, like a mortician had done the job. I checked his coat and trouser pockets – goose egg – and gave him a few probes for broken bones. Double gooser. Just then a maggot crawled out of his gaping mouth, doing a spastic little lindy hop on the tip of his tongue.

I walked back into the living room, picked up the phone and called a man who owes me a big, big favor pertaining to his wife's association with a Negro nun and a junior congressman from Whittier. The man is a crime-scene technician with the Sheriff's Department; a med-school dropout adept at spot-checking cadavers and guessing causes of death. He promised to be at 2281 South Mariposa within the hour in an unmarked car – ten minutes of forensic expertise in exchange for my erasure of his debt.

I went back to the bedroom, carrying a pot of Lavonne Cohen's geraniums to help kill the stink. The floor stiff's pockets had been picked clean; the bed stiff had no bruises on his head, and there were now two maggots doing a tango across his nose. Morris Hornbeck, a pro, probably packed a silencered heater like most Mickey muscle – he looked too scrawny to be a hand-to-hand killer. I was starting to make Gretchen Rae Shoftel for the snuffs – and I was starting to like her.

123

Lieutenant Kirby Falwell showed up a few minutes later, tap-tap-tap on the window I broke. I let him in, and he lugged his evidence kit into the bedroom, pinching his nose. I left him there to be scientific, staying in the living room so as not to bruise his ego with my inside scoop on his wife. After half an hour he came out and greeted me:

'We're even, Meeks. The clown on the floor was hit on the head with a flat, blunt object, maybe a frying pan. It probably knocked him silly. Then somebody threw their dinner in his face and gave him second-degree burns. Then they strangled him with that negligee. I'll give you asphyxiation as cause of death. On Pops, I'd say heart attack – natural causes. I mighta said poison, but his liver isn't distended. Heart attack, fifty-fifty odds. Both dead about two days. I picked the scabs off both sets of fingers and rolled their prints. I suppose you want a forty-eight-state teletype on them?'

I shook my head. 'California and Wisconsin – but quick.'

'Inside four hours. We're even, Meeks.'

'Take the nightgown home to the wife, Kirby. She'll find a use for it.'

'Fuck you, Meeks.'

'Adios, Lieutenant.'

I settled in, the lights off, figuring if Mo Hornbeck and Gretchen Rae were some kind of partners, he would be by to dump the stiffs, or she would be, or someone would drop in to say hello. I sat in a chair by the front door, the lamp in my hand ready to swing if it came to that kind of play. Danger juice was keeping me edgy; my brain fluids were roiling, trying to figure a way out of the parlay – my two benefactors hiring me to glom one woman for their exclusive use, two corpses thrown in. As hard as I brainstormed, I couldn't think up squat. With half an hour to kill before I called Kirby Falwell, I gave up and tried the Other Guy Routine.

The Other Guy Routine dates back to my days as a youth in Oklahoma, when my old man would beat the shit out of my old lady, and I'd haul a mattress out into the scrub woods so I wouldn't have to listen. I'd set my armadillo traps down, and every once in a while I'd hear a snap-squeak as some stupid 'dillo ate my bait and got his spine crunched for his trouble. When I finally fell asleep, I'd usually wake up to screeches – men hurting women – always just wind playing havoc with the scrub pines. I'd start thinking then: ways to get the old man off the old lady's back without consulting my brother Fud, in the Texas Pen for armed robbery and grievous aggravated assault. I knew I didn't have the guts to confront Pop myself, so I started thinking about other people just to get them off my mind. And that always let me develop a play: some church woman conned into dropping off a pie and religious tracts to calm the old man down; steering some local slick who thought Mom was a beauty in her direction, knowing Pop was a coward with other men and would love up the old girl for weeks and weeks just to keep her. That last play stood all of us good at the end – it was right before the old lady caught typhus. She took to bed with a fever, and the old man got in with her to keep her warm. He caught it himself – and died – sixteen days after she did. Under the circumstances, you have to believe there was nothing but love between them – right up to curtains.

So the Other Guy Routine gets you out of the hole and makes some other poor fuck feel good in the process. I worked it in Niggertown as a cop: let some pathetic grasshopper slide, send him a Mickey fruit basket at Christmas, get him to snitch a horse pusher and skim five percent full of yuletide cheer. The only trouble with it this time is that I was locked on the horns of a jumbo dilemma: Mickey, Howard – two patrons, only one woman. And claiming failure with either man was against my religion.

I gave up thinking and called Kirby Falwell at the Sheriff's Bureau. His two-state teletype yielded heat:

The floor stiff was Fritz Steinkamp, Chicago-Milwaukee gunsel, one conviction for attempted murder, currently on parole and believed to be a Jerry Katzenbach torpedo. Mr. Heart Attack was Voyteck Kirnipaski, three-time loser, also a known Katzenbach associate, his falls for extortion and grand larceny – specifically stock swindles. The picture getting a little less hazy, I called Howard Hughes at his flop at the Bel Air Hotel. Two rings, hang up, three rings – so he'd know it's not some gossip columnist.

'Yes?'

'Howard, you been in Milwaukee the past few years?'

'I was in Milwaukee in the spring of '47. Why?'

'Any chance you went to a whorehouse that specialized in girls made up like movie stars?'

Howard sighed. 'Buzz, you know my alleged propensity in that department. Is this about Gretchen Rae?'

'Yeah. Did you?'

'Yes. I was entertaining some colleagues from the Pentagon. We had a party with several young women. My date looked just like Jean Arthur, only a bit more . . . endowed. Jean broke my heart, Buzz. You know that.'

'Yeah. Did the high brass get looped and start talking shop around the girls?'

'Yes, I suppose so. What does this—'

'Howard, what did you and Gretchen Rae talk about – besides your sex fantasies?'

'Well, Gretchy seemed to be interested in business – stock mergers, the little companies I've been buying up, that sort of thing. Also politics. My Pentagon chums have told me about Korea heating up, implying lots of aircraft business. Gretchy seemed interested in that, too. A smart girl always interests herself in her lovers' endeavors, Buzz. You know that. Have you got leads on her?'

'I surely have. Boss, how have you managed to stay alive and rich so long?'

'I trust the right people, Buzz. Do you believe that?'

'I surely do.'

I gave my sitting-in-the-dark stakeout another three hours, then raided the icebox for energy and took the Other Guy Routine on the road, a *mitzvah* for Mickey in case I had to play an angle to shoot Gretchen Rae to Howard – his very own teenage murderess. First I wrapped up Fritz Steinkamp in three windows' worth of chintz curtains and hauled him out to my car; next I mummified Voyteck Kirnipaski in a bedspread and wedged him into the trunk between Fritz and my spare tire. Then it was a routine wipe of my own possible prints, lights off, and a drive out to Topanga Canyon, to the chemical debris dump operated by the Hughes Tool Company: a reservoir bubbling with caustic agents adjacent to a day camp for under-privileged kids – a Howard tax dodge. I dumped Fritz and Voyteck into the cauldron and listened to them snap, crackle, and pop like Kellogg's Rice Krispies. Then, just after midnight, I drove to the Strip to look for Mickey and his minions.

They weren't at the Trocadero, the Mocambo, or the La Rue; they weren't at Sherry's or Dave's Blue Room. I called the DMV night information line, played cop, and got a read on Mo Hornbeck's wheels – 1946 tan Dodge coupe, CAL–4986–J, 896¼ Moonglow Vista, South

Pasadena – then took the Arroyo Seco over the hill to the address, a block of bungalow courts.

At the left-side tail end of a stucco streamline job was 896¼ – rounded handrails and oblong louvers fronting tiny windows strictly for show. No lights were burning; Hornbeck's Dodge was not in the carport at the rear. Maybe Gretchen Rae was inside, armed with stuffed animals, negligee garrotes, stew pots, and frying pans – and that suddenly made me not give a fuck whether the world laid, prayed, stayed, or strayed. I kicked the door in, flipped on a wall light, and got knocked flat on my ass by a big furry mother with big, shiny, razor-white teeth.

It was a Doberman, sleek black muscle out for blood – mine. The dog snapped at my shoulder and got a snootful of Hart, Schaffner & Marx worsted; he snapped at my face and got an awkwardly thrown Meeks right jab that caused him to flinch momentarily. I dug in my pocket for my Arkansas toad-stabber, popped the button, and flailed with it; I grazed the beast's paws and snout – and he still kept snapping and snarling.

Giving the fucker a stationary target was the only way. I put my left arm over my eyes and tried to stay prone; Rex the Wonder Dog went for my big, fat, juicy elbow. I hooked my shiv up at his gut, jammed it in and yanked forward. Entrails dropped all over me; Rex vomited blood in my face and died with a snap-gurgle.

I kicked the day's third corpse off of me, stumbled to the bathroom, rummaged through the medicine cabinet, and found witch hazel. I doused my elbow bite and the blood-oozing teeth marks on my knuckles. Deep breathing, I splashed sink water on my face, looked in the mirror, and saw a middle-aged fat man, terrified and pissed to his drawers, in deep, deep shit without a depth gauge. I held the gaze, thinking it wasn't me for long seconds. Then I smashed the image with the witch-hazel bottle and eyeballed the rest of the bungalow.

The larger of the two bedrooms had to be Gretchen Rae's. It was all girlish gewgaws: pandas and arcade Kewpie dolls, pinups of matinee idols and college pennants on the walls. Kitchen appliances still in their boxes were stacked on the dresser; publicity glossies of RKO pretty boys littered the bedspread.

The other bedroom reeked of VapoRub and liniment and sweat and flatulence – bare walls, the floor space almost completely taken up by a sagging Murphy bed. There was a medicine bottle on the night-stand

– Dr. Revelle prescribing Demerol for Mr. Jamelka – and checking under the pillow got me a .38 police special. I flipped the cylinder, extracted four of the shells and stuck the gun in my waistband, then went back to the living room and picked up the dog, gingerly, so as not to drench myself in his gore. I noticed that it was a female; that a tag on its collar read 'Janet'. That hit me as the funniest thing since vaudeville, and I started laughing wildly, shock coming on. I spotted an Abercrombie & Fitch dog bed in the corner, dumped Janet in it, doused the lights in the room, found a couch, and collapsed. I was heading into some sort of weird heebie-jeebie haze when wood creaking, a choked 'Oh, my god!' and hot yellow glare jolted me to my feet.

'Oh Janet no!'

Mo Hornbeck beelined for the dead dog, not even noticing me. I stuck out my leg and tripped him; he hit the floor almost snout to snout with Janet. And I was right there, gun at his head, snarling like the psycho Okie killer I could have been. 'Boy, you're gonna blab on you, Gretchen Rae, and them bodies on Mariposa. You're gonna spill on her and Howard Hughes, and I mean *now*.'

Hornbeck found some balls quicksville, averting his eyes from the dog, latching them onto me. 'Fuck you, Meeks.'

'Fuck you' was acceptable from a ranking Sheriff's dick in my debt, but not from a statch-raper hoodlum. I opened the .38's cylinder and showed Hornbeck the two rounds, then spun it, and put the muzzle to his head. 'Talk. *Now*.'

Hornbeck said, 'Fuck you, Meeks'; I pulled the trigger; he gasped and looked at the dog, turning purple at the temples, red at the cheeks. Seeing myself in a cell next to Fud, the Meeks boys playing pinochle sideways through the bars, I popped off another shot, the hammer clicking on an empty chamber. Hornbeck bit at the carpet to staunch his tremors, going deep purple, then subsiding into shades of crimson, pink, death's-head white. Finally he spat dust and dog hair and gasped, 'The pills by my bed and the bottle in the cupboard.'

I obeyed, and the two of us sat on the porch like good buddies and killed the remains of the jug – Old Overholt Bonded. Hornbeck blasted Demerol pills along with the juice, flew to cloud nine, and told me the saddest goddamn story I'd ever heard.

Gretchen Rae Shoftel was his daughter. Mom hit the road shortly after she was born, hightailing it to parts unknown with a Schlitz Brewery driver rumored to be double-digit hung, like the human equivalent of Mickey Cohen, Jr. He raised Gretch as best he could, nursing a bad case of the hots for her, ashamed of it until he picked up scads of unrelated skinny: that his wife was servicing the entire Schlitz night shift during the time his little girl was conceived. On general principles he stayed hands off, taking his lust out on girls from the greenhorn hooker camps up in Green Bay and Saint Paul.

Gretchy grew up strange, ashamed of her old man – a gang stooge and occasional killer. She took her old lady's maiden name and buried her head in books, loving arithmetic tricks, figures, calculations – stuff that proved she was smart. She also took up with a rough South Milwaukee crowd. One crazy Polack boyfriend beat her silly every night for a week straight when she was fifteen. Mo found out, put the kid in cement skates, and dumped him in Lake Michigan. Father and daughter were happily reunited by the revenge.

Mo moved up in Jerry Katzenbach's organization; Gretch got a bundle together tricking the hotel bars in Chicago. Mo installed Gretchen Rae as sixteen-year-old pit boss of a swank whorehouse: movie star surrogates, the rooms bugged to pick up gangland and political skinny that might prove valuable to Jerry K. Gretch got friendly with stock swindler Voyteck Kirnipaski; she just happened to be listening through a vent one night when Howard Hughes and a cadre of army three-stars were cavorting with Jean Arthur, Lupe Velez, and Carole Lombard, greenhorn versions. Gretch picked up lots of juicy Wall Street gossip, and realized that this could be the start of something big. Mo contracted stomach cancer about that time and got the word: half a decade tops – enjoy life while you can. Cash skimmed off Jerry Katzenbach's books provided class A treatment. Mo held his own against the Big C. Jerry K. got bum press for his whorehouse, kiboshed it, and banished Mo to the Coast, where Mickey Cohen welcomed him with open arms, using his juice to get Mo's two statch-rape indiscretions plea-bargained to bubbkis.

Back in Milwaukee, Gretchen Rae audited business classes at Marquette, and hauled Voyteck Kirnpaski's ashes for free when she learned he was working for Jerry K. and was dissatisfied with the pay. Then Mo had a relapse and came back to Milwaukee on a visit; Voyteck Kirnipaski skipped town with a bundle of Katzenbach's money so he could bankroll stock swindles in L.A.; Gretchen Rae, always reading the papers with an eye toward political repercussions, put her overhead dope from Howard and the high brass together with whispers on the Korea situation and decided to get more info from the man himself. Mo took some lung shots of his little girl and mailed them to Big How; he bit; Gretchy glommed leads that the on-the-lam and hotly pursued Voyteck was hanging out at Scrivner's Drive-In, and, wanting to enlist his aid in possible squeeze plays, got a job there. Mickey Cohen's crush on her put a monkey wrench into things – but she thought, somehow, that the little big man could be tapped for juice. She became his consort concurrent with Howard, father and daughter pretending to be strangers at Mickey's nightclub get-togethers. Then, at a Santa Monica motel, she located Voyteck, terrified that Katzenbach triggers were right behind him. Mo gave her the key to Mickey's Mariposa Street hideout; she ensconced Voyteck there, moving back and forth between Howard's fuck pad, pumping information subtly and pumping Kirnipaski blatantly – attempting to lure him into her web of schemes. She was making progress when Fritz Steinkamp made the scene. And damned if Gretchy didn't rise to the occasion and throttle, scald, and frying-pan him to death. She attempted to soothe the terrified Voyteck after-ward, but he went into cardiac arrest: the volatile combo of a murder attempt, a murder, and a murderess's tongue. Gretchen Rae panicked and took off with Voyteck's pilfered cash – and was currently trying to unload 'secret insider' prospectuses on Hughes stock to a list of potential customers Kirnipaski had compiled. The girl was holed up someplace – Mo didn't know where – and tomorrow she would be calling at the homes and offices of her last wave of potential 'clients'.

Somewhere in the course of the story I started liking Mo almost as much as I liked Gretchen Rae. I still couldn't see any way out of the mess, but I was curious about one thing: the girly gewgaws, the appliances, all the squarejohn homey stuff Gretchy had glommed. When Mo finished his tale, I said, 'What's with all the clothes and gadgets and stuffed animals?'

Morris Hornbeck, worm bait inside six months, just sighed. 'Lost time, Meeks. The father and daughter act someplace safe, the shtick we shoulda played years ago. But that's tap city, now.'

I pointed to the dead dog, its paws starting to curl with rigor mortis like it was going to be begging biscuits for eternity. 'Maybe not. You sure ain't gonna have a trusty mascot, but you might get a little taste of the rest.'

Morris went to his bedroom and passed out. I laid down on the homey dreambed, holding a stuffed panda, the lights off to ensure some good brainwork. Straight manipulation of Mickey and Howard fell by the wayside quick, so I shifted to the Other Guy Routine and made a snag.

Sid Weinberg.

RKO Line Producer.

Filthy rich purveyor of monster cheapies, drive-in-circuit turkeys that raked in the cash.

A valuable RKO mainstay – his pictures never flopped. Howard kissed his ass, worshipped his dollars and cents approach to movie-making and gave him carte blanche at the studio.

'I'd rather lose my you-know-what than lose Sid Weinberg.'

Mickey Cohen was indebted to Sid Weinberg, the owner of the Blue Lagoon Saloon, where Mickey was allowed to perform his atrocious comedy routines without cops hanging around – Sid had LAPD connections.

The Mick: 'I'd be without a pot to piss in without Sid. I'd have to buy my own nightclub, and that's no fun – it's like buying your own baseball team so you can play yourself.'

Sid Weinberg was a widower, a man with two grown daughters who patronized him as a buffoon. He often spoke of his desire to find himself a live-in housekeeper to do light dusting and toss him a little on the side. About fifteen years ago, he was known to be in love with a dazzling blonde starlet named Glenda Jensen, who hotfooted it off into the sunset one day, never to be seen again. I'd seen pictures of Glenda: she looked suspiciously like my favorite teenage killer. At eight tomorrow night Sid Weinberg was throwing a party to ballyhoo *Bride of the Surf Monster*. I was to provide security. Mickey Cohen and Howard Hughes would be guests.

I fell asleep on the thought, and dreamed that benevolent dead dogs were riding me up to heaven, my pockets full of other guys' money.

In the morning we took off after the prodigal daughter. I drove, Mo Hornbeck gave directions – where he figured Gretchen Rae would be, based on their last conversation, a panicky talk two days ago, the girl afraid of phone taps, Mo saying he would let the evidence chill, then dispose of it.

131

Which, of course, he didn't. According to Mo, Gretch told him Voyteck Kirnipaski had given her a list of financial-district sharks who might be interested in her Hughes Enterprises graphs: when to buy and sell shares in Toolco, Hughes Aircraft and its myriad subsidiaries, based on her new knowledge of upcoming defense contracts and her assessment of probable stock price fluctuations. Mo stressed that that was why Gretchy raped the Bullocks catalog – she wanted to look like a businesswoman, not a seductress/killer.

So we slow-lane trawled downtown, circuiting the Spring Street financial district, hoping to catch a streetside glimpse of Gretchen Rae as she made her office calls. I'd won Mo partially over with kind words and a promise to plant Janet in a ritzy West L.A. pet cemetery, but I could still tell he didn't trust me – I was too close to Mickey for too long. He gave me a steady sidelong fisheye and only acknowledged my attempts at conversation with grunts.

The morning came and went; the afternoon followed. Mo had no leads on Gretchen Rae's home calls, so we kept circling Spring Street – Third to Sixth and back again – over and over, taking piss stops at the Pig & Whistle on Fourth and Broadway every two hours. Dusk came on, and I started getting scared: my Other Guy Routine would work to perfection only if I brought Gretchy to Sid Weinberg's party right on time.

6:00.

6:30.

7:00

7:09. I was turning the corner onto Sixth Street when Mo grabbed my arm and pointed out the window at a sharkskin-clad secretary type perusing papers by the newsstand. 'There. That's my baby.'

I pulled over; Mo stuck his head out the door and waved, then shouted, 'No! Gretchen!'

I was setting the hand brake when I saw the girl – Gretch with her hair in a bun – notice a man on the street and start running. Mo piled out of the car and headed toward the guy; he pulled a monster hand cannon, aimed, and fired twice. Mo fell dead on the sidewalk, half his face blown off; the man pursued Gretchen Rae; I pursued him.

The girl ran inside an office building, the gunman close behind. I caught up, peered in, and saw him at the top of the second-floor landing. I slammed the door and stepped back; the act coaxed two wasted shots out of the killer, glass and wood exploding all around me. Four rounds gone, two to go.

Screams on the street; two sets of footsteps scurrying upstairs; sirens in the distance. I ran to the landing and shouted, 'Police!' The word drew two ricocheting bang-bangs. I hauled my fat ass up to floor three like a flabby dervish.

The gunman was fumbling with a pocketful of loose shells; he saw me just as he flicked his piece's cylinder open. I was within three stairs of him. Not having time to load and fire, he kicked. I grabbed his ankle and pulled him down the stairs; we fell together in a tangle of arms and legs, hitting the landing next to an open window.

We swung at each other, two octopuses, blows and gouges that never really connected. Finally he got a choke hold on my neck; I reached up through his arms and jammed my thumbs hard in his eyes. The bastard let go just long enough for me to knee his balls, squirm away, and grab him by the scalp. Blinded now, he flailed for me. I yanked him out the window headfirst, pushing his feet after him. He hit the pavement spread-eagled, and even from three stories up I could hear his skull crack like a giant eggshell.

I got some more breath, hauled up to the roof and pushed the door open. Gretchen Rae Shoftel was sitting on a roll of tarpaper, smoking a cigarette, two long single tears rolling down her cheeks. She said, 'Did you come to take me back to Milwaukee?'

All I could think of to say was, 'No.'

Gretchen reached behind the tarpaper and picked up a briefcase – brand-new, Bullocks. Wilshire quality. The sirens downstairs were dying out; two bodies gave lots of cops lots to do. I said, 'Mickey or Howard, Miss Shoftel? You got a choice.'

Gretch stubbed out her cigarette. 'They both stink.' She hooked a thumb over the roof in the direction of the dead gunman. 'I'll take my chances with Jerry Katzenbach and his friends. Daddy went down tough. So will I.'

I said, 'You're not that stupid.'

Gretchen Rae said, 'You play the market?'

I said, 'Want to meet a nice rich man who needs a friend?'

Gretchen Rae pointed to a ladder that connected the roof to the fire escape of the adjoining building. 'If it's now, I'll take it.'

In the cab to Beverly Hills I filled Gretchy in on the play, promising all kinds of bonuses I couldn't deliver, like the Morris Hornbeck scholarship for impoverished Marquette University Business School students. Pulling up to Sid Weinberg's Tudor mansion, the girl had her hair down, makeup on, and was ready to do the save-my-ass tango.

At 8:03 the manse was lit up like a Christmas tree – extras in green-rubber monster costumes handing out drinks on the front lawn and loudspeakers on the roof blasting the love theme from a previous Weinberg tuna, *Attack of the Atomic Gargoyles*. Mickey and Howard always arrived at parties late in order not to appear too eager, so I figured there was time to set things up.

I led Gretchen Rae inside, into an incredible scene: Hollywood's great, near-great, and non-great boogie-woogieing with scads of chorus boys and chorus girls dressed like surf monsters, atomic gargoyles, and giant rodents from Mars; bartenders sucking punch out of punch bowls with ray-gun-like siphons; tables of cold cuts dyed surf-monster green passed up by the guests en masse in favor of good old booze, the line for which stood twenty deep. Beautiful gash was abounding, but Gretchen Rae, hair down like Sid Weinberg's old love Glenda Jensen, was getting the lion's share of the wolf stares. I stood with her by the open front door, and when Howard Hughes's limousine pulled up, I whispered, '*Now*.'

Gretchen slinked back to Sid Weinberg's glass-fronted private office in slow, slow motion; Howard, talk and handsome in a tailored tux, walked in the door, nodding to me, his loyal underling. I said, 'Good evening, Mr. Hughes,' out loud; under my breath, 'You owe me a grand.'

I pointed to Sid's office; Howard followed. We got there just as Gretchen Rae Shoftel/Glenda Jensen and Sid Weinberg went into a big open-mouthed clinch. I said, 'I'll lean on Sid, boss. Kosher is kosher. He'll listen to reason. Trust me.'

Inside of six seconds I saw the fourth richest man in America go from heartsick puppy dog to hardcase robber baron and back at least a dozen times. Finally he jammed his hands in his pockets, fished out a wad of C-notes, and handed them to me. He said, 'Find me another one just like her,' and walked back to his limo.

I worked the door for the next few hours, chasing crashers and autograph hounds away, watching Gretchen/Glenda and Sid Weinberg work the crowd, instant velvet for the girl, youth recaptured for the sad old man. Gretchy laughed, and I could tell she did it to hold back tears; when she squeezed Sid's hand I knew she didn't know who it belonged to. I kept wishing I could be there when her tears broke for real, when she became a real little girl for a while, before going back to being a stock maven and a whore. Mickey showed up just as the movie was starting. Davey Goldman told me he was pissed: Mo Hornbeck got himself bumped off by a Kraut trigger from Milwaukee who later nosedived out a window; the Mariposa Street hideout had been burglarized, and Lavonne Cohen was back from Israel three days early and henpecking the shit out of the Mick. I barely heard the words. Gretchy and Sid were cooing at each other by the cold-cut table – and Mickey was headed straight toward them.

I couldn't hear their words, but I could read the three faces. Mickey was taken aback, but paid gracious respect to his beaming host; Gretch was twitching with the aftershocks of her old man's death. L.A.'s #1 hoodlum bowed away, walked up to me, and flicked my necktie in my face. 'All you get is a grand, you hump. You shoulda found her quicker.'

So it worked out. Nobody made me for snuffing the Milwaukee shooter; Gretchy walked on the Steinkamp killing and her complicity in Voyteck Kirnipaski's demise – the chemical-sizzled stiffs, of course, were never discovered. Mo Hornbeck got a plot at Mount Sinai Cemetery, and Davey Goldman and I stuffed Janet into the casket with him at the mortuary – I gave the rabbi a hot tip on the trotters, and he left the room to call his bookie. I paid off Leotis Dineen and promptly went back into hock with him; Mickey took up with a stripper named Audrey Anders; Howard made a bundle off airplane parts for the Korean War and cavorted with the dozen or so Gretchen Rae Shoftel look-alikes I found him. Gretchy and Sid Weinberg fell in love, which just about broke the poor pilot-mogul's heart.

Gretchen Rae and Sid.

She did her light dusting – and must have thrown him a lot on the side. She also became Sid's personal investment banker, and made him a giant bundle, of which she took a substantial percentage cut, invested it in slum property, and watched it grow, grow, grow. Slumlord Gretch also starred in the only Sid Weinberg vehicle ever to lose money, a tearjerker called *Glenda* about a movie producer who falls in love with a starlet who disappears off the face of the earth. The critical consensus was that Gretchen Rae Shoftel was a lousy actress, but had great lungs. Howard Hughes was rumored to have seen the movie over a hundred times.

In 1950 I got involved in a grand jury investigation that went bad in an enormous way, and I ended up taking it on the road permanently, Mr. Anonymous in a thousand small towns. Mickey Cohen did a couple of Fed jolts for income-tax evasion, got paroled as an old man, and settled back into L.A. as a much-appreciated local character, a reminder of the colorful old days. Howard Hughes ultimately went squirrelshit with drugs and religion, and a biography that I read said that he carried a torch for a blonde whore straight off into the deep end. He'd spend hours at the Bel Air Hotel looking at her picture, playing a torchy rendition of 'Since I Don't Have You' over and over. I know better: It was probably scads of different pictures, lung shots all, the music a lament for a time when love came cheap. Gretchy was special to him, though. I still believe that.

I miss Howard and Mickey, and writing this story about them has only made it worse. It's tough being a dangerous old man by yourself – you've got nothing but memories and no one with the balls to understand them.

Gravy Train

Out of the Honor Farm and into the work force: managing the maintenance crew at a Toyota dealership in Koreatown. Jap run, a gook clientele, boogies for the shitwork and me, Stan 'The Man' Klein, to crack the whip and keep on-duty loafing at a minimum. My probation officer got me the gig: Liz Trent, skinny and stacked, four useless Masters degrees, a bum marriage to a guy on methadone maintenance and the hots for yours truly. She knew I got off easy: three convictions resulting from the scams I worked with Phil Turkel – a phone-sales racket that involved the deployment of hard-core loops synced to rock songs and Naugahyde Bibles embossed with glow-in-the-dark pictures of the Rev. Martin Luther King, Jr. – a hot item with the shvartzes. We ran a drug-recovery crash pad as a front, suborned teenyboppers into prostitution, coerced male patients into phone-sales duty and kept them motivated with Benzedrine-laced espresso – all of which peaked at twenty-four grand jury bills busted down to three indictments apiece. Phil had no prior record, was strung out on cocaine and got diverted to a drug rehab; I had two GTA convictions and no chemical rationalizations – bingo on a year County time, Wayside Honor Rancho, where my reputation as a lackluster heavyweight contender got me a dorm-boss job. My attorney, Miller Waxman, assured me a sentence reduction was in the works; he was wrong – counting 'good time' and 'work time' I did the whole nine and a half months. My consolation prize: Lizzie Trent, Waxman's ex-wife, for my PO – guaranteed to cut me a long leash, get me soft legitimate work and give me head before my probationary term was a month old. I took two out of three: Lizzie had sharp teeth and an overbite, so I didn't trust her on the trifecta. I was at my desk, watching my slaves wash cars, when the phone rang.

I picked up. 'Yellow Empire Imports, Klein speaking.'

'Miller Waxman here.'

'Wax, how's it hangin'?'

'A hard yard – and you still owe me money on my fee. Seriously, I need it. I lent Liz some heavy coin to get her teeth capped.'

The trifecta loomed. 'Are you dunning me?'

'No, I'm a Greek bearing gifts at 10 percent interest.'

'Such as?'

'Such as this: a grand a week cash and three hots and a cot at a Beverly Hills mansion, all legit. I take a tensky off the top to cover your bill. The clock's ticking, so yes or no?'

I said, 'Legit?'

'If I'm lyin', I'm flyin'. My office in an hour?'

'I'll be there.'

Wax worked out of a storefront on Beverly and Alvarado close to his clientele – dope dealers and wetbacks hot to bring the family up from Calexico. I double-parked, put a 'Clergyman on Call' sign on my windshield and walked in.

Miller was in his office, slipping envelopes to a couple of Immigration Service goons – big guys with that hinky look indigenous to bagmen worldwide. They walked out thumbing C-notes; Wax said, 'Do you like dogs?'

I took a chair uninvited. 'Well enough. Why?'

'Why? Because Phil feels bad about lounging around up at the Betty Ford Clinic while you went inside. He wants to play catch-up, and he asked me if I had ideas. A plum fell into my lap and I thought of you.'

Weird Phil: facial scars and a line of shit that could make the Pope go Protestant. 'How's Phil doing these days?'

'Not bad. Do you like dogs?'

'Like I said before, well enough. Why?'

Wax pointed to his clients' wall of fame – scads of framed mug shots. Included: Leroy Washington, the 'Crack King' of Watts; Chester Hardell, a TV preacher indicted for unnatural acts against cats; the murderous Sanchez family – scores of inbred cousins foisted on L.A. as the result of Waxie's green-card machinations. In a prominent spot: Richie 'The Sicko' Sicora and Chick Ottens, the 7–11 Slayers, still at large. Picaresque: Sicora and Ottens heisted a convenience store in Pacoima and hid the salesgirl behind an upended Slurpee machine to facilitate their escape. The machine disgorged its contents: ice, sugar and carcinogenic food coloring. The girl, a diabetic, passed out, sucked in the goo, went into sugar shock and kicked. Sicora and Ottens jumped bail for parts unknown – and Wax got a commendation letter from the ACLU, citing his tenacity in defending the L.A. underclass.

I said, 'You've been pointing for five minutes. Want to narrow it down?'

Wax brushed dandruff off his lapels. 'I was illustrating a point, the point being that my largest client is not on that wall because he was never arrested.'

I feigned shock. 'No shit, Dick Tracy?'

'No shit, Sherlock. I'm referring, of course, to Sol Bendish, entrepreneur, bail bondsman supreme, heir to the late great Mickey Cohen's vice kingdom. Sol passed on recently, and I'm handling his estate.'

I sighed. 'And the punch line?'

Wax tossed me a key ring. 'He left a twenty-five-million-dollar estate to his dog. It's legally inviolate and so well safeguarded that I can't contest it or scam it. You're the dog's new keeper.'

My list of duties ran seven pages. I drove to Beverly Hills wishing I'd been born canine.

'Basko' lived in a mansion north of Sunset; Basko wore cashmere sweaters and a custom-designed flea collar that emitted minute amounts of nuclear radiation guaranteed not to harm dogs – a physicist spent three years developing the product. Basko ate prime steak, Beluga caviar, Häagen-Dazs ice cream and Fritos soaked in ketchup. Rats were brought in to sate his blood lust: rodent mayhem every Tuesday morning, a hundred of them let loose in the backyard for Basko to hunt down and destroy. Basko suffered from insomnia and required a unique sedative: a slice of Velveeta cheese melted in a cup of hundred-year-old brandy.

I almost shit when I saw the pad; going in the door my knees went weak. Stan Klein enters the white-trash comfort zone to which he had so long aspired.

Deep-pile purple rugs everywhere.

A three-story amphitheater to accomodate a gigantic satellite dish that brought in four hundred TV channels.

Big-screen TVs in every room and a comprehensive library of porn flicks.

A huge kitchen featuring two walk-in refrigerators: one for Basko, one for me. Wax must have stocked mine – it was packed with the high-sodium, high-cholesterol stuff I thrive on. Rooms and rooms full of the swag of my dreams – I felt like Fulgencio Batista back from exile.

Then I met the dog.

I found him in the pool, floating on a cushion. He was munching a cat carcass, his rear paws in the water. I did not yet know that it was the pivotal moment of my life.

I observed the beast from a distance.

He was a white bull terrier – muscular, compact, deep in the chest, bow-legged. His short-haired coat gleamed in the sunlight; he was so heavily muscled that flea-nipping required a great effort. His head was perfect good-natured misanthropy: a sloping wedge of a snout, close-set beady eyes, sharp teeth and a furrowed brow that gave him the look of a teenaged kid scheming trouble. His left ear was brindled. I sighed as the realization hit me, an epiphany – like the time I figured out Annie 'Wild Thing' Behringer dyed her pubic hair.

Our eyes met.

Basko hit the water, swam and ran to me and rooted at my crotch. Looking back, I recall those moments in slow motion, gooey music on the soundtrack of my life, like those Frenchy films where the lovers never talk, just smoke cigarettes, gaze at each other and bang away.

Over the next week we established a routine.

Up early, roadwork by the Beverly Hills Hotel, Basko's A.M. dump on an Arab sheik's front lawn. Breakfast, Basko's morning nap; he kept his head on my lap while I watched porno films and read sci-fi novels. Lunch: blood-rare fillets, then a float in the pool on adjoining cushions. Another walk; an eyeball on the foxy redhead who strolled her Lab at the same time each day – I figured I'd bide my time and propose a double date: us, Basko and the bitch. Evenings went to Introspection: I screened films of my old fights, Stan 'The Man' Klein, feather-fisted, cannon fodder for hungry schmucks looking to pad their records. There I was: six-pointed star on my trunks, my back dusted with Clearasil to hide my zits. A film-editor buddy spliced me in with some stock footage of the greats; movie magic had me kicking the shit out of Ali, Marciano and Tyson. Wistful might-have-been stuff accompanied by Basko's beady browns darting from the screen to me. Soon I was telling the dog the secrets I always hid from women.

When I shifted into a confessional mode, Basko would scrunch up

140

his brow and cock his head; my cue to shut up was one of his gigantic mouth-stretching yawns. When he started dozing, I carried him upstairs and tucked him in. A little Velveeta and brandy, a little goodnight story – Basko seemed to enjoy accounts of my sexual exploits best. And he always fell asleep just as I began to exaggerate.

I could never sync my sleep to Basko's: his warm presence got me hopped up, thinking of all the good deals I'd blown, thinking that he was only good for another ten years on earth and then I'd be fifty-one with no good buddy to look after and no pot to piss in. Prowling the pad buttressed my sense that this incredible gravy train was tangible and would last – so I prowled with a vengeance.

Sol Bendish dressed antithetical to his Vegas-style crib: tweedy sports jackets, slacks with cuffs, Oxford cloth shirts, wingtips and white bucks. He left three closets stuffed with Ivy League threads just about my size. While my canine charge slept, I transformed myself into his sartorial image. Jewboy Klein became Jewboy Bendish, wealthy contributor to the UJA, the man with the class to love a dog of supreme blunt efficacy. I'd stand before the mirror in Bendish's clothes and my years as a pimp, burglar, car thief and scam artist would melt away – replaced by a thrilling and fatuous notion: finding *the* woman to complement my new personal . . .

I attacked the next day.

Primping formed my prelude to courtship: I gave Basko a flea dip, brushed his coat and dressed him in his best spiked collar; I put on a spiffy Bendish ensemble: navy blazer, gray flannels, pink shirt and penny loafers. Thus armed, we stood at Sunset and Linden and waited for the Labrador woman to show.

She showed right on time; the canine contingent sniffed each other hello. The woman deadpanned the action; I eyeballed her while Basko tugged at his leash.

She had the freckled look of a rare jungle cat – maybe a leopard/snow-tiger hybrid indigenous to some jungleland of love. Her red hair reflected sunlight and glistened gold – a lioness's mane. Her shape was both curvy and svelte; I remembered that some female felines actually stalked for mates. She said, 'Are you a professional dog walker?'

I checked my new persona for dents. My slacks were a tad too short; the ends of my necktie hung off kilter. I felt myself blushing and heard

Basko's paws scrabbling on the sidewalk. 'No, I'm what you might want to call an entrepreneur. Why do you ask?'

'Because I used to see an older man walking this dog. I think he's some sort of organized-crime figure.'

Basko and the Lab were into a mating dance – sniffing, licking, nipping. I got the feeling Cat Woman was stalking me – and not for love. I said, 'He's dead. I'm handling his estate.'

One eyebrow twitched and flickered. 'Oh? Are you an attorney?'

'No, I'm working for the man's attorney.'

'Sol Bendish was the man's name, wasn't it?'

My shit detector clicked into high gear – this bimbo was pumping me. 'That's right, Miss?'

'It's Ms. Gail Curtiz, that's with a T, I, Z. And it's Mr.?'

'Klein with an E, I, N. My dog likes your dog, don't you think?'

'Yes, a disposition of the glands.'

'I empathize. Want to have dinner some time?'

'I think not.'

'I'll try again then.'

'The answer won't change. Do you do other work for the Bendish estate? Besides walk the man's dog, I mean.'

'I look after the house. Come over some time. Bring your Lab, we'll double.'

'Do you thrive on rejections, Mr. Klein?'

Basko was trying to hump the Lab – but no go. 'Yeah, I do.'

'Well, until the next one, then. Good day.'

The brief encounter was Weirdsville, U.S.A. – especially Cat Woman's Strangeville take on Sol Bendish. I dropped Basko off at the pad, drove to the Beverly Hills library and had a clerk run my dead benefactor through their information computer. Half an hour later I was reading a lapful of scoop on the man.

An interesting dude emerged.

Bendish ran loan-sharking and union protection rackets inherited from Mickey Cohen; he was a gold-star contributor to Israel bonds and the UJA. He threw parties for underprivileged kids and operated his bail-bond business at a loss. He lost a bundle on a homicide bond forfeiture: Richie 'Sicko' Sicora and Chick Ottens, the 7–11 slayers, splitsvilled for Far Gonesville, sticking him with a two-million-dollar tab. Strange: the L.A. *Times* had Bendish waxing philosophical on the bug-out, like two mill down the toilet was everyday stuff to him.

On the personal front, Bendish seemed to love broads, and eschew birth control: no less than six paternity suits were filed against him. If the suit-filing mothers were to be believed, Sol had three grown sons and three grown daughters – and the complainants were bought off with chump-change settlements – weird for a man so given to charity for appearance's sake. The last clippings I scanned held another anomaly: Miller Waxman said Bendish's estate came to twenty-five mill, while the papers placed it at a cool forty. My scamster's brain kicked into very low overdrive . . .

I went back to my routine with Basko and settled into days of domestic bliss undercut with just the slightest touch of wariness. Wax paid my salary on time; Basko and I slept entwined and woke up simultaneously, in some kind of cross-species psychic sync. Gail Curtiz continued to give me the brush; I got her address from Information and walked Basko by every night, curious: a woman short of twenty-five living in a Beverly Hills mansion – a rental by all accounts – a sign on the lawn underlining it: 'For Sale. Contact Realtor. Please Do Not Disturb Renting Tenant.' One night the bimbo spotted me snooping; the next night I spotted her strolling by the Bendish/Klein residence. On impulse, I checked my horoscope in the paper: a bust, no mention of romance or intrigue coming my way.

Another week passed, business as usual, two late-night sightings of Gail Curtiz sniffing my turf. I reciprocated: late-night prowls by her place, looking for window lights to clarify my take on the woman. Basko accompanied me; the missions brought to mind my youth: heady nights as a burglar/panty raider. I was peeping with abandon, crouched with Basko behind a eucalyptus tree, when the shit hit the fan – a crap-o, non-Beverly Hills car pulled up.

Three shifty-looking shvartzes got out, burglar's tools gleamed in the moonlight. The unholy trio tiptoed up to Gail Curtiz's driveway.

I pulled a nonexistent gun and stepped out from hiding; I yelled, 'Police officer! Freeze!' and expected them to run. They froze instead; I got the shakes; Basko yanked at his leash and broke away from me. Then pandemonium.

Basko attacked; the schmucks ran for their car; one of them whipped out a cylindrical object and held it out to the hot-pursuing hound. A streetlamp illuminated the offering: a bucket of Kentucky Colonel ribs.

Basko hit the bucket and started snouting; I yelled 'No!' and chased. The boogies grabbed my beloved comrade and tossed him in the backseat of their car. The car took off – just as I made a last leap and hit the pavement memorizing plate numbers, a partial real: P-L-blank-0016. BASKO BASKO BASKO NO NO—

The next hour went by in a delirium. I called Liz Trent, had her shake down an ex-cop boyfriend for a DMV run-through on the plate and got a total of fourteen possible combinations. None of the cars were reported stolen; eleven were registered to Caucasians, three to Southside blacks. I got a list of addresses, drove to Hollywood and bought a .45 automatic off a fruit hustler known to deal good iron – then hit Darktown with a vengeance.

My first two addresses were losers: staid sedans that couldn't have been the kidnap car. Adrenaline scorched my blood vessels; I kept seeing Basko maimed, Basko's beady browns gazing at me. I pulled up to the last address seeing double: silhouettes in the pistol range of my mind. My trigger finger itched to dispense .45 caliber justice.

I saw the address, then smelled it: a wood-framed shack in the shadow of a freeway embankment, a big rear yard, the whole package reeking of dog. I parked and sneaked back to the driveway gun first.

Snarls, growls, howls, barks, yips – floodlights on the yard and two pit bills circling each other in a ring enclosed by fence pickets. Spectators yipping, yelling, howling, growling and laying down bets – and off to the side of the action my beloved Basko being primed for battle.

Two burly shvartzes were fitting black leather gloves fitted with razor blades to his paws; Basko was wearing a muzzle embroidered with swastikas. I padded back and got ready to kill; Basko sniffed the air and leaped at his closest defiler. A hot second for the gutting: Basko lashed out with his paws and disemboweled him clean. The other punk screamed; I ran up and bashed his face in with the butt of my Roscoe. Basko applied the coup de grâce: left-right paw shots that severed his throat down to the windpipe. Punk number two managed a death gurgle; the spectators by the ring heard the hubbub and ran over. I grabbed Basko and hauled ass.

We made it to my sled and peeled rubber; out of nowhere a car broadsided us, fender to fender. I saw a white face behind the wheel, downshifted, brodied, fishtailed and hit the freeway doing eighty. The attack car was gone – back to the nowhere it came from. I whipped off Basko's muzzle and paw weapons and threw them out the window; Basko licked my face all the way to Beverly Hills.

More destruction greeted us: the Bendish/Klein/Basko pad had been ransacked, the downstairs thoroughly trashed: shelves overturned, sections of the satellite dish ripped loose, velvet flocked Elvis paintings torn from the walls. I grabbed Basko again; we hotfooted it to Gail Curtiz's crib.

Lights were burning inside; the Lab was lounging on the lawn chomping on a nylabone. She noticed Basko and started demurely wagging her tail; I sensed romance in the air and unhooked my sidekick's leash. Basko ran to the Lab; the scene dissolved into horizontal nuzzling. I gave the lovebirds some privacy, sneaked around to the rear of the house and started peeping.

Va va va voom through a back window. Gail Curtiz, nude, was writhing with another woman on a tigerskin rug. The gorgeous brunette seemed reluctant: her face spelled shame and you could tell the perversity was getting to her. My beady eyes almost popped out of my skull; in the distance I could hear Basko and the Lab rutting like cougars. The brunette faked an orgasm and made her hips buckle – I could tell she was faking from twenty feet away. The window was cracked at the bottom; I put an ear to the sill and listened.

Gail got up and lit a cigarette; the brunette said, 'Could you turn off the lights, please?' – a dead giveaway – you could tell she wanted to blot out the dyke's nudity. Basko and the Lab, looking sated, trotted up and fell asleep at my feet. The room inside went black; I listened extra hard.

Smutty endearments from Gail; two cigarette tips glowing. The brunette, quietly persistent: 'But I don't understand why you spend your life savings renting such an extravagent house. You *never* spell things out for me, even though we're . . . And just who is this rich man who died?'

Gail laughing. 'My daddy, sweetie. Blood test validated. Momma was a carhop who died of a broken heart. Daddy stiffed her on the paternity suit, among many other stiffs, but he promised to take care of me – three million on my twenty-fifth birthday or his death, whichever

145

came first. Now, dear, would you care to hear the absurdist punch line? Daddy left the bulk of his fortune to his dog, to be overseen by a sharpie lawyer and this creep who looks after the dog. *But* – there has to be some money hidden somewhere. Daddy's estate was valued at twenty-five million, while the newspapers placed it as much higher. Oh, shit, isn't it all absurd?'

A pause, then the brunette. 'You know what you said when we got back a little while ago? Remember, you had this feeling the house had been searched?'

Gail: 'Yes. What are you getting at?'

'Well, maybe it *was* just your imagination, or maybe one of the other paternity-suit kids has got the same idea, maybe that explains it.'

'Linda, honey, I can't think of that just now. Right now I've got you on my mind.'

Small talk was over. Eclipsed by Gail's ardor, Linda's phony moans, I hitched Basko to his leash, drove us to a motel safe house and slept the sleep of the righteously pissed.

In the morning I did some brainwork. My conclusions: Gail Curtiz wanted to sink my gravy train and relegate Basko to a real dog's life. Paternity-suit intrigue was at the root of the Bendish house trashing and the 'searching' of Gail's place. The car that tried to broadside me was driven by a white man – a strange anomaly. Linda, in my eyes a non-dyke, seemed to be stringing the lust-blinded Gail along – could she also be a paternity-suit kid out for Basko's swag? Sleazy Miller Waxman was Sol Bendish's lawyer and a scam artist bent from the crib – how did he fit in? Were the shvoogies who tried to break into Gail's crib the ones who later searched it – and trashed my place? Were they in the employ of one of the paternity kids? *What was going on?*

I rented a suite at the Bel-Air Hotel and ensconced Basko there, leaving a grand deposit and detailed instructions on his care and feeding. Next I hit the Beverly Hills Library and reread Sol Bendish's clippings. I glommed the names of his paternity-suit complainants, called Liz Trent and had her give me DMV addresses. Two of Sol's playmates were dead; one was address unknown, two – Marguerita Montgomery and Jane Hawkshaw – were alive and living in Los Angeles. The Montgomery woman was out as a lead: a clipping I'd scanned two weeks ago quoted her on the occasion of Sol Bendish's death – she mentioned that the son he fathered had died in Vietnam. I already knew that Gail Curtiz's mother had died – and since none of the complainants bore the name Curtiz, I knew Gail was using it as an alias. That left Jane Hawkshaw: last known address 8902 Saticoy Street in Van Nuys.

I knocked on her door an hour later. An old woman holding a stack of *Watchtowers* opened up. She had the look of religious crackpots everywhere: bad skin, spaced-out eyes. She might have been hot stuff once – around the time man discovered the wheel. I said, 'I'm Brother Klein. I've been dispatched by the Church to ease your conscience in the Sol Bendish matter.'

The old girl pointed me inside and started babbling repentance. My eyes hit a framed photograph above the fireplace – two familiar faces smiling out. I walked over and squinted.

Ultra-pay dirt: Richie 'Sicko' Sicora and another familiar-looking dude. I'd seen pics of Sicora before – but in this photo he looked like someone *else* familiar. The resemblance seemed very vague – but niggling. The other man was easy – he'd tried to broadside me in Darktown last night.

The old girl said, 'My son Richard is a fugitive. He doesn't look like that now. He had his face changed when he went on the run. Sol was going to leave Richie money when he turned twenty-five, but Richie and Chuck got in trouble and Sol gave it out in bail money instead. I've got no complaint against Sol and I repent my unmarried fornication.'

I superimposed the other man's bone structure against photos I'd seen of Chick Ottens and got a close match. I tried, tried, tried to place Sicora's pre-surgery resemblance, but failed. Sicora pre-plastic, Ottens already sliced – a wicked brew that validated non-dyke Linda's theory straight down the line . . .

I gave the old woman a buck, grabbed a *Watchtower* and boogied Southside. The radio blared hype on the Watts homicides: the monster dog and his human accomplice. Fortunately for Basko and myself, eyewitnesses' accounts were dismissed and the deaths were attributed to dope intrigue. I cruised the bad boogaloo streets until I spotted the car that tried to ram me – parked behind a cinder-block dump circled by barbed wire.

I pulled up and jacked a shell into my piece. I heard yips emanating from the backyard, tiptoed around and scoped out the scene.

Pit Bull City: scores of them in pens. A picnic table and Chick

Ottens noshing bar-b-q'd chicken with his snazzy new face. I came up behind him; the dogs noticed me and sent out a cacophony of barks. Ottens stood up and wheeled around going for his waistband. I shot off his kneecaps – canine howls covered my gun blasts. Ottens flew backwards and hit the dirt screaming; I poured bar-b-q sauce on his kneeholes and dragged him over to the cage of the baddest-looking pit hound of the bunch. The dog snapped at the blood and soul sauce; his teeth tore the pen. I spoke slowly, like I had all the time in the world. 'I know you and Sicora got plastic jobs, I know Sol Bendish was Sicora's daddy and bailed you and Sicko out on the 7–11 job. You had your goons break into Gail Curtiz's place and the Bendish pad and all this shit relates to you trying to mess with my dog and screw me out of my gravy train. Now I'm beginning to think Wax Waxman set me up. I think you and Sicora have some plan going to get at Bendish's money, and Wax ties in. You got word that Curtiz was snouting around, so you checked out her crib. I'm a dupe, right? Wax's patsy? Wrap this up for me or I feed your kneecaps to Godzilla.'

Pit Godzilla snarled an incisor out of the mesh and nipped Ottens where it counts. Ottens screeched; going blue, he got out, 'Wax wanted . . . you . . . to . . . look after . . . dog . . . while him and . . . Phil . . . scammed a way to . . . discredit paternity . . . claims . . . I . . . I . . .'

Phil.

My old partner – I didn't know a thing about his life before our partnership.

Phil Turkel was Sicko Sicora, his weird facial scars derived from the plastic surgery that hid his real identity from the world.

'Freeze, suckah.'

I looked up. Three big shines were standing a few yards away, holding Uzis. I opened Godzilla's cage; Godzilla burst out and went for Chick's face. Ottens screamed; I tossed the bucket of chicken at the gunmen; shots sprayed the dirt. I ate crab grass and rolled, rolled, rolled, tripping cage levers, ducking, ducking, ducking. Pit bulls ran helter-skelter, then zeroed in: three soul brothers dripping with soul sauce.

The feast wasn't pretty. I grabbed a Uzi and got out quicksville.

Dusk.

I leadfooted it to Wax's office, the radio tuned to a classical station – I was hopped up on blood, but found some soothing Mozart to calm me down, and highballed it to Beverly Alvarado.

148

Waxman's office was stone silent; I picked the backdoor lock, walked in and made straight for the safe behind his playmate calendar – the place where I knew he kept his dope and bribery stash. Left-right-left: an hour of diddling the tumblers and the door creaked open. Four hours of studying memo slips, ledgers and little-black-book notations and I trusted myself on a reconstruction.

Labyrinthine, but workable:

Private-eye reports on Gail Curtiz and Linda Claire Woodruff – the two paternity-suit kids Wax considered most likely to contest the Bendish estate. Lists of stooges supplied by Wax contacts in the LAPD: criminal types to be used to file phony claims against the estate, whatever money gleaned to be kicked back to Wax himself. Address-book names circled: snuff artists I knew from jail, including the fearsome Angel 'Fritz' Trejo. A note from Phil Turkel to Waxman: 'Throw Stan a bone – he can babysit the dog until we get the money.' A diagram of the Betty Ford Clinic, followed by an ominous epiphany: Wax was going to have Phil and the real paternity kids clipped. Pages and pages of notes in legalese – levers to get at the extra fifteen million Sol Bendish had stuffed in Swiss bank accounts.

I turned off the lights and raged in the dark; I thought of escaping to a nice deserted island with Basko and some nice girl who wouldn't judge me for loving a bull terrier more than her. The phone rang – and I nearly jumped out of my hide.

I picked up and faked Wax's voice. 'Waxman here.'

'Ees Angel Fritz. You know your man Phil?'

'Yeah.'

'Ees history. You pay balance now?'

'My office in two hours, homeboy.'

'Ees bonaroo, homes.'

I hung up and called Waxman's pad; Miller answered on the second ring. 'Yes?'

'Wax, it's Klein.'

'Oh.'

His voice spelled it out plain: he'd heard about the Southside holocaust. 'Yeah, "Oh." Listen, shitbird, here's the drift. Turkel's dead, and I took out Angel Trejo. I'm at your office and I've been doing some reading. Be here in one hour with a cash settlement.'

Waxman's teeth chattered; I hung up and did some typing: Stan Klein's account of the whole Bendish/Waxman/Turkel/Ottens/

Trejo scam – a massive criminal conspiracy to bilk the dog I loved. I included everything but mention of myself and left a nice blank space for Wax to sign his name. Then I waited.

Fifty minutes later – a knock. I opened the door and let Wax in. His right hand was twitching and there was a bulge under his jacket. He said, 'Hello, Klein,' and twitched harder; I heard a truck rumble by and shot him point-blank in the face.

Wax keeled over dead, his right eyeball stuck to his law school diploma. I frisked him, relieved him of his piece and twenty large in cash. I found some papers in his desk, studied his signature and forged his name to his confession. I left him on the floor, walked outside and pulled over to the pay phone across the street.

A taco wagon pulled to the curb; I dropped my quarter, dialed 911 and called in a gunshot tip – anonymous citizen, a quick hang-up. Angel Fritz Trejo rang Wax's doorbell, waited, then let himself in. Seconds dragged; lights went on; two black-and-whites pulled up and four cops ran inside brandishing hardware. Multiple shots – and four cops walked out unharmed.

So in the end I made twenty grand and got the dog. The L.A. County Grand Jury bought the deposition, attributed my various dead to Ottens/Turkel/Trejo/Waxman et al. – all dead themselves, thus unindictable. A superior court judge invalidated Basko's twenty-five mill and divided the swag between Gail Curtiz and Linda Claire Woodruff. Gail got the Bendish mansion – rumor has it that she's turning it into a crash pad for radical lesbian feminists down on their luck. Linda Claire is going out with a famous rock star – androgynous, but more male then female. She admitted, elliptically, that she tried to 'hustle' Gail Curtiz – validating her dyke submissiveness as good old American fortune-hunting. Lizzie Trent got her teeth fixed, kicked me off probation and into her bed. I got a job selling cars in Glendale – and Basko comes to work with me every day. His steak and caviar diet has been replaced by Gravy Train – and he looks even groovier and healthier. Lizzie digs Basko and lets him sleep with us. We're talking about combining my twenty grand with her life savings and buying a house, which bodes marriage: my first, her fourth. Lizzie's a blast: she's smart, tender, funny and gives great skull. I love her almost as much as I love Basko.

Torch Number

Before Pearl Harbor and the Jap scare, my living-room window offered a great view: Hollywood Boulevard lit with neon, dark hillsides, movie spots crisscrossing the sky announcing the latest opening at Grauman's and the Pantages. Now, three months after the day of infamy – blackouts in effect and squadrons of Jap Zeros half expected any moment – all I could see were building shapes and the cherry lamps of occasional prowl cars. The 10.00 P.M. curfew kept night divorce work off my plate, and blowing my last assignment with Bill Malloy of the DA's Bureau made a special deputy's curfew waiver out of the question. Work was down, bills were up, and my botched surveillance of Maggie Cordova had me thinking of Lorna all the time, wearing the grooves on her recording of 'Prison of Love' down to sandpaper.

> *Prison of Love.*
> *Sky above.*
> *I feel your body like a velvet glove . . .*

I mixed another rye and soda and started the record over. Through a part in the curtains, I eyeballed the street; I thought of Lorna and Maggie Cordova until their stories melded.

Lorna Kafesjian.

Second-rate bistro chanteuse – first-rate lungs, third-rate club gigs because she insisted on performing her own tunes. I met her when she hired me to rebuff the persistent passes of a rich bull dagger who'd been voyeur perving on her out at Malibu Beach – Lorna with her swimsuit stripped to the waist, chest exposed for a deep cleavage tan to offset the white gowns she always wore on stage. The dyke was sending Lor a hundred long-stemmed red roses a day, along with mash notes bearing her nom de plume *d'amour*: 'Your Tongue of Fire'. I kiboshed the pursuit quicksville, glomming the Tongue's Vice jacket, shooting the dope to Louella Parsons – a socially connected, prominently married carpet-muncher with a yen for nightclub canaries was prime meat for the four-star *Herald*. I told Louella: she desists, you don't publish; she persists, you do. The Tongue and I had a little chat; I strong-armed her nigger bodyguard when *he* got persistent. Lorna was grateful, wrote me the torch number to torch all torch numbers – and *I* got persistent.

The flame burned both ways for about four months – from January to May of '38 I was Mr. Ringside Swain as Lorna gigged the Katydid Klub, Bido Lito's, Malloy's Nest, and a host of dives on the edge of Jigtown. Two A.M. closers, then back to her place; long mornings and afternoons in bed, my business neglected, clients left dangling while I lived the title of a Duke Ellington number: 'I Got It Bad, and That Ain't Good.' Lorna came out of the spell first; she saw that I was willing to trash my life to be with her. That scared her; she pushed me away; I played stage-door Johnny until I got disgusted with myself and she blew town for fuck knows where, leaving me a legacy of soft contralto warbles on hot black wax.

Lorna.

Lorna to Maggie.

Maggie happened this way:

Two weeks ago Malloy co-opted me to the DAs Bureau – the aftermath of the bank job was running helter-skelter, he needed a man good at rolling stakeouts, and a citizens' committee had posted extra reward gelt. The B of A on North Broadway and Alpine got knocked off; two shitbirds – Caucasians, one with outré facial scars – snuffed three armed guards and got away clean. A score of eyeball witnesses gave descriptions of the robbers, then – blam! – the next day a witness, a seventy-three-year-old Jap granny set for internment pickup, got plugged – double blam! – as she was walking her pooch to the corner market. LAPD Ballistics compared the slugs to the pills extracted from the stiffs at the bank scene: match-up, straight across.

Malloy was called in. He developed a theory: one of the eyewitnesses was in on the robbery; the heisters glommed the addresses of the other witnesses and decided to bump them to camouflage their guy. Malloy threw a net around the three remaining witnesses: two squarejohns named Dan Doherty and Bob Roscomere – working stiffs with no known criminal associates – and Maggie

Cordova, a nightclub singer who'd taken two falls for possession and sale of marijuana.

Maggie C. loomed as the prime suspect: she toked big H and maryjane, was rumored to have financed her way through music school by pulling gangbangs, and played it hardcase during her two-year jolt at Tehachapi. Doherty and Roscomere were put out as bait, not warned of the danger they were in, carrying DA's Bureau tails wherever they went. Malloy figured my still simmering torch for Lorna K. gave me added insight into the ways of errant songbirds and sent me out to keep loose track of Maggie, hoping she'd draw unfriendly fire if she wasn't the finger woman or lead me to the heisters if she was.

I found Maggie pronto – a call to a booking agent who owed me – and an hour later I was sipping rye and soda in the lounge of a Gardena pokerino parlor. The woman was a dumpy ash blonde in a spangly gown, long-sleeved, probably to hide her needle tracks. She looked vaguely familiar, like a stag-film actress you were hard for in your youth. Her eyes were flat and droopy and her microphone gestures were spastic. She looked like a hophead who'd spent her best years on cloud nine and would never adjust to life on earth.

I listened to Maggie butcher 'I Can't Get Started', 'The Way You Look Tonight', and 'Blue Moon'; she bumped the mike stand with her crotch and nobody whistled. She sang 'Serenade in Blue' off-key and a clown a couple of tables over threw a handful of martini olives at her. She flipped the audience the finger, got a round of applause, and belted the beginning of 'Prison of Love'.

I sat there, transfixed. I closed my eyes and pretended it was Lorna. I forced myself not to wonder how this pathetic no-talent dopester got hold of a song written exclusively for me. Maggie sang her way through all five verses, the material almost transforming her voice into something good. I was ripping off Lorna's snow-white gown and plunging myself into her when the music stopped and the lights went on.

And Maggie was ixnay, splitsville, off to Gone City. I tried her dressing room, the bar, the casino. I got her vehicle stats from the DMV and got nowhere with them. I slapped around a croupier with a junkie look, got Maggie's address, and found her dump cleaned out lock, stock, and barrel. I became a pistol-whipping, rabbit-punching, brass-knuckle-wielding dervish then, tearing up the Gardena Strip. I got a half-decent lead on a ginch Maggie used to whore with; the

153

woman got me jacked on laudanum, picked my pocket, and left me in Gone City, ripe prey for a set of strong-arm bulls from the Gardena PD. When I came off cloud ten in a puke-smelling drunk tank, Bill Malloy was standing over me with glad tidings: I'd been charged with six counts of aggravated assault, one count of felonious battery, and two counts of breaking and entering. Maggie Cordova was nowhere to be found; the other eyewitnesses were in protective custody. Bill himself was off the bank job, on temporary assignment to the Alien Squad, set to rustle Japs, the big cattle drive that wouldn't end until Uncle Sam gave Hirohito the big one where it hurt the most. My services were no longer required by the DA's office, and my night-curfew waiver was revoked until somebody figured a way to chill out the nine felony charges accumulated against me . . .

I heard a knock at the door, looked out the window and saw a prowl car at the curb, red lights blinking. I took my time turning on lamps, wondering if it was warrants and handcuffs or maybe somebody who wanted to talk dealsky. More knocks – a familiar cadence. Bill Malloy at midnight.

I opened the door. Malloy was backstopped by a muscle cop who looked like a refugee from the wrong side of a Mississippi chain gang: big ears, blond flattop, pig eyes, and a too-small suitcoat framing the kind of body you expect to see on convicts who haul cotton bales all day. Bill said, 'You want out of your grief, Hearns? I came to give you an out.'

I pointed to the man-monster. 'Expecting trouble you can't handle?'

'Policemen come in pairs. Easier to give trouble, easier to avoid it. Sergeant Jenks, Mr. Hearns.'

The big man nodded; an Adam's apple the size of a baseball bobbed up and down. Bill Malloy stepped inside and said, 'If you want those charges dropped and your curfew waiver back, raise your right hand.'

I did it. Sergeant Jenks closed the door behind him and read from a little card he'd pulled from his pocket. 'Do you, Spade Hearns, promise to uphold the laws of the United States Government pertaining to executive order number 9055 and obey all other Federal and municipal statutes while temporarily serving as an internment agent?'

I said 'Yeah.'

Bill handed me a fresh curfew pass and an LAPD rap sheet with a mug-shot strip attached. 'Robert no middle name Murikami. He's a lamster Jap, he's a youth-gang member, he did a deuce for B&E and when last seen he was passing out anti-American leaflets. We've got his known associates on this sheet, last known address, the magilla. We're swamped and taking in semipros like you to help. Usually we pay fifteen dollars a day, but you're in no position to demand a salary.'

I took the sheet and scanned the mug shots. Robert NMN Murikami was a stolid-looking youth – a samurai in a skivvy shirt and duck's-ass haircut. I said, 'If this kid's so wicked, why are you giving me the job?'

Jenks bored into me with his little pig eyes; Bill smiled. 'I trust you not to make the same mistake twice.'

I sighed. 'What's the punch line?'

'The punch line is that this punk is pals with Maggie Cordova – we got complete paper on him, including his bail reports. The Cordova cooze put up the jack for Tojo's last juvie beef. Get him, Hearns. All will be forgiven and maybe you'll get to roll in the gutter with another second-rate saloon girl.'

I settled in to read the junior kamikaze's rap sheet. There wasn't much: the names and addresses of a half-dozen Jap cohorts – tough boys probably doing the Manzanar shuffle by now – carbons of the kid's arrest reports, and letters to the judge who presided over the B&E trial that netted Murikami his two-spot at Preston. If you read between the lines, you could see a metamorphosis: little Tojo started out as a pad prowler out for cash and a few sniffs of ladies' undergarments and ended up a juvie gang honcho: zoot suits, chains and knives, boogie-woogie rituals with his fellow members of the 'Rising Sons'. At the bottom of the rap sheet there was a house key attached to the page with Scotch tape, an address printed beside it: 1746¼ North Avenue 46, Lincoln Heights. I pocketed the key and drove there, thinking of a Maggie-to-Lorna reunion parlay – cool silk sheets and a sleek tanned body soundtracked by the torch song supreme.

The address turned out to be a subdivided house on a terraced hillside overlooking the Lucky Lager Brewery. The drive over was eerie: streetlights and traffic signals were the only illumination and Lorna was all but there with me in the car, murmuring what she'd give me if I took down slant Bobby. I parked at the curb and climbed up the front steps, counting numbers embossed on doorways: 1744, 1744½, 1746,

1746½. 1746¼ materialized; I fumbled the key toward the lock. Then I saw a narrow strip of light through the adjoining window – the unmistakable glint of a pen flash probing. I pulled my gun, *eased* the key in the hole, watched the light flutter back toward the rear of the pad, and opened the door slower than slow.

No movement inside, no light coming toward me. 'Fuck, fuck, fuck,' echoed from a back room; a switch dropped and big light took over. And there was my target: a tall, skinny man bending over a chest of drawers, a pen flash clamped in his teeth.

I let him start rifling, then tiptoed over. When he had both hands braced on the dresser and his legs spread, I gave him the Big Fungoo.

I hooked his left leg back; Prowler collapsed on the dresser, pen flash cracking teeth as his head hit the wall. I swung him around, shot him a pistol-butt blow to the gut, caught a flailing right hand, jammed the fingers into the top-drawer space, slammed the drawer shut, and held it there with my knee until I heard fingers cracking. Prowler screamed; I found a pair of Jockey shorts on the counter, shoved them in his mouth, and kept applying pressure with my knee. More bone crack; amputation coming up. I eased off and let the man collapse on his knees.

The shitbird was stone-cold out. I kicked him in the face to keep him that way, turned on the wall light, and prowled myself.

It was just a crummy bedroom, but the interior decorating was *très* outré: Jap nationalist posters on the walls – racy shit that showed Jap Zeros buzz-bombing a girl's dormitory, buxom white gash in peignoirs running in terror. The one table held a stack of Maggie Cordova phonograph records – Maggie scantily attired on the jackets, stretch marks, flab, and chipped nail polish on display. I examined them up close – no record company was listed. They were obvious vanity jobs – fat Maggie preserving her own sad warbles.

Shitbird was stirring; I kicked him in the noggin again and trashed the place upside down. I got:

A stash of women's undies, no doubt Bad Bob's B&E booty; a stash of *his* clothes, assorted switchblades, dildos, French ticklers, tracts explaining that a Jew–Communist conspiracy was out to destroy the world of true peace the German and Japanese brotherhood had sought to establish through peaceful means, and – under the mattress – seventeen bankbooks: various banks, the accounts fat with cash, lots of juicy recent deposits.

It was time to make Shitbird sing. I gave him a waistband frisk, pulling out a .45 auto, handcuffs, and – mother dog! – an L.A. sheriff's badge and ID holder. Shitbird's real monicker was Deputy Walter T. Koenig, currently on loan to the County Alien Squad.

That got me thinking. I found the kitchen, grabbed a quart of beer from the icebox, came back and gave Deputy Bird an eyeopener – Lucky Lager on the *cabeza*. Koenig sputtered and spat out his gag; I squatted beside him and leveled my gun at his nose. 'No dealsky, no tickee, no washee. Tell me about Murikami and the bankbooks or I'll kill you.'

Koenig spat blood; his foggy eyes honed in on my Roscoe. He licked beer off his lips; I could tell his foggy brain was trying to unfog an angle. I cocked my .38 for emphasis. 'Talk, shitbird.'

'Zeck – zeck – order.'

I spun the .38's cylinder – more emphasis. 'You mean the executive order on the Japs?'

Koenig spat a few loose canines and some gum flaps. 'Zat's right.'

'Keep going. A snitch jacket looks good on you.'

Shitbird held a stare on me; I threw him back some of his manhood to facilitate a speedy confession. 'Look, you spill and I won't rat you. This is just a money gig for me.'

His eyes told me he bought it. Koenig got out his first unslurred words. 'I been doin' a grift with the Japs. The Government's holdin' their bank dough till the internment ends. I was gonna cash out for Murikami and some others, for a cut. You know, bring 'em to the bank in bracelets, carry some official-lookin' papers. Japs are smart, I'll give 'em that. They know they're goin' bye-bye, and they want more than bank interest.'

I didn't *quite* buy it; on reflex I gave Koenig's jacket pockets a toss. All I got was some women's pancake makeup – pad and bottle. The anomaly tweaked me; I pulled Koenig to his feet and cuffed him behind his back with his own bracelets. 'Where's Murikami hiding out?'

'1411 Wabash, East L.A., apartment 311. Bunch of Japs holing up there. What are you gonna—'

'I'm going to toss your car and cut you loose. It's *my* grift now, Walter.'

Koenig nodded, trying not to look grateful; I unloaded his piece and stuck it in his holster, gave him back his badge kit, rounded up the

157

bankbooks, and shoved him toward the front door, thinking of Lorna accompanied by Artie Shaw and Glenn Miller, the two of us enjoying Acapulco vacations financed by Axis cash. I pushed Koenig down the steps ahead of me; he nodded toward a Ford roadster parked across the street. 'There, that's mine. But you ain't—'

Shots cut the air; Koenig pitched forward, backward, forward. I hit the pavement, not knowing which direction to fire. Koenig slumped into the gutter; a car sped by sans headlights. I squeezed off five shots and heard them ding metal; lights went on in windows – they gave me a perfect shot of a once-rogue cop with his face blasted away. I stumbled over to the Ford, used my pistol butt to smash in a window, popped the glove compartment, and tore through it. Odd papers, no bankbooks, my hands brushing a long piece of slimy rubber. I held it up and flicked on the dash light and saw a paste-on scar – outré – just like the one eyewitnesses at the bank job said one of the heisters had.

I heard sirens descending, blasting like portents of doomsday. I ran to my car and highballed it the fuck away.

My apartment was in the wrong direction – away from leads on Maggie into Lorna. I drove to 1411 Wabash, found it postmidnight still, blackout black – a six-story walk-up with every single window covered. The joint was stone quiet. I ditched my car in the alley, stood on the hood, jumped up, and caught the bottom rung of the fire escape.

The climb was tough going; mist made the handrails wet and slippery, and my shoes kept slipping. I made it to the third-floor landing, pushed the connecting door open, padded down the empty hallway to 311, put my ear to the door and listened.

Voices in Jap, voices in Jap-accented English, then pure Americanese, loud and clear. 'You're paying me for a hideout, not chow at two-fucking-A.M.. But I'll do it – *this time*.'

More voices; footsteps leading toward the hall. I pulled my gun, pinned myself to the wall, and let the door open in my face. I hid behind it for a split second; it was shut, and Caucasian-san hotfooted it over to the elevator. On tippytoes, I was right behind him.

I cold-cocked him clean – wham! – grabbed his pocket piece while he hit the carpet and dreamsville, stuffed my display handkerchief in his mouth and dragged him over to a broom closet and locked him in. Two-gun armed, I walked back to the door of 311 and rapped gently.

'Yes?' – a Jap voice – from the other side. I said, 'It's me,' deliberately muffled. Mutters, the door opening, a jumbo Buddhahead filling the doorway. I kicked him in the balls, caught his belt mid-jacknife, pulled forward and smashed his head into the doorjamb. He sunk down gonesville; I waved the automatic I'd taken off the white punk at the rest of the room.

What a room.

A dozen slants staring at me with tiny black eyes like Jap Zero insignias, Bob Murikami smack in the middle. Arkansas toad-stabbers drawn and pointed square at my middle. A Mexican standoff or the sequel to Pearl Harbor. Kamikaze was the only way to play it.

I smiled, ejected the chambered round from my pilfered piece, popped the clip, and tossed both at the far wall. Jumbo was stirring at my feet; I helped him up, one hand on his carotid artery in case he got uppity. With my free hand, I broke the cylinder on *my* gun, showing him the one bullet left from my shootout with Walter Koenig's killers. Jumbo nodded his head, getting the picture; I spun the chamber, put the muzzle to his forehead, and addressed the assembled Axis powers. 'This is about bankbooks, Maggie Cordova, Alien Squad grifts, and that big heist at the Japtown B of A. Bob Murikami's the only guy I want to talk to. Yes or no.'

Nobody moved a muscle or said a word. I pulled the trigger, clicked an empty chamber, and watched Jumbo shake head to toe – bad heebie-jeebies. I said, 'Sayonara, shitbird,' and pulled the trigger again; another hollow click, Jumbo twitching like a hophead going into cold-turkey overdrive.

Five-to-one down to three-to-one; I could see Lorna, nude, waving bye-bye Hearns, heading toward Stormin' Norman Killebrew, jazz trombone, rumored to have close to a hard half-yard and the only man Lorna implied gave it to her better than me. I pulled the trigger twice – twin empties – shit stink taking over the room as Jumbo evacuated his bowels.

One-to-one, seven come eleven, the Japs looking uncharacteristic-ally piqued. Now I saw my own funeral cortege, 'Prison of Love' blasting as they lowered me into the grave.

'No! I'll talk!'

I had the trigger at half pull when Bob Murikami's voice registered. I let go of Jumbo and drew a bead on Bad Bob; he walked over and bowed, supplicant-samurai style, at my gun muzzle. Jumbo collapsed;

I waved the rest of the group into a tight little circle and said, 'Kick the clip and the Roscoe over.'

A weasel-faced guy complied; I popped one into the chamber and tucked my Russki roulette piece in my belt. Murikami pointed to a side door; I followed him over, a straight-arm bead on the others.

The door opened into a small bedroom lined with cots – the Underground Railway, 1942 version. I sat down on the cleanest one available and pointed Murikami to a cot a few yards over, well within splatter range. I said, 'Spill. Put it together, slow and from the beginning, and don't leave anything out.'

Bad Bob Murikami was silent, like he was mustering his thoughts and wondering how much horseshit he could feed me. His face was hard-set; he looked tough beyond his years. I smelled musk in the room – a rare combo of blood and Lorna's Cougar Woman perfume. 'You can't lie, Bob. And I won't hand you up to the Alien Squad.'

Murikami snickered. 'You won't?'

I snickered back. 'You people mow a mean lawn and trim a mean shrub. When my ship comes in, I'll be needing a good gardener.'

Murikami double snickered – and a smile started to catch at the corners of his mouth. 'What's your name?'

'Spade Hearns.'

'What do you do for a living?'

'I'm a private investigator.'

'I thought private eyes were sensitive guys with a code of honor.'

'Only in the pulps.'

'That's rich. If you don't have a code of honor, how do I know you won't cross me?'

'I'm in too deep now, Tojo. Crossing you's against my own best interest.'

'Why?'

I pulled out a handful of bankbooks; Murikami's slant eyes bugged out until he almost looked like a fright-wig nigger. 'I killed Walt Koenig for these, and you need a white man to tap the cash. I don't like witnesses and there's too many of you guys to kill, even though I'm hopped up on blood bad. Spiel me, Papa-san. Make it an epic.'

Murikami spieled for a straight hour. His story was the night train to Far Gonesville.

It started when three Japs, bank-building maintenance workers pissed over their imminent internment, cooked up a plot with rogue cop Walt Koenig and a cop buddy of his – Murikami didn't know the guy's name. The plot was a straight bank robbery with a no-violence proviso – Koenig and pal taking down the B of A based on inside info, the Japs getting a percentage cut of the getaway loot for the young firebrands stupid enough to think they could hotfoot it to Mexico and stay free, plus Koenig's safeguarding of confiscated Jap property until the internment ended. But the caper went blood simple: guards snuffed, stray bullets flying. Mrs. Lena Sakimoto, the old dame shot on the street the next day, was the finger woman – she was in the bank pretending to be waiting in line, but her real errand was to pass the word to Koenig and buddy the split second the vault cash was distributed to the tellers. *She* was rubbed out because the heisters figured her for a potential snitch.

Double cross.

Bad Bob and *his* pals had been given the bank money to hold. Enraged over the deaths, they shoved it into Jap bank accounts, figured the two whiteys couldn't glom it, that the swag would accumulate interest until the internment was adios. Bob stashed the bankbooks at his crib and was soon to send the white boy fronting the getaway pad over to get them – but he got word a friend of his got greedy.

The friend's name was George Hayakawa, a vice warlord in the Rising Sons. He went to Walt Koenig with a deal: he'd get the cash for a fifty-fifty cut. Koenig said no dealsky, tortured the location of the bankbooks and the address of the hideout out of Hayakawa, snuffed him, chopped off his dick, and sent it over in a pizza delivery box. A warning – don't fuck with the White Peril.

I pressed Murikami on Maggie Cordova – how did she fit in? The epic took on perv-o overtones.

Maggie was Bad Bob's sister's squeeze – the femme half of a dyke duo. She was the co-finger woman inside the bank; when Mrs. Lena Sakimoto got shot to sukiyaki, Maggie fled to Tijuana, fearing similar reprisals. Bob didn't know exactly where she was. I pressed, threatened, and damn near shot Murikami to get the answer I wanted most: where Maggie Cordova got 'Prison of Love'.

Bad Bob didn't know; I *had* to know. I made him a deal I knew I'd double-cross the second Lorna slinked into view. You come with me, we'll withdraw all the gelt, you take me to T.J. to find Maggie and the money's all yours. Murikami agreed; we sealed the bargain by toking a big bottle of laudanum laced with sake. I passed out on my cot with my gun in my hand and segued straight into the arms of Lorna.

It was a great hop dream.

Lorna was performing nude at the Hollywood Palladium, backed by an all-jigaboo orchestra – gigantic darkies in rhinestone-braided Uncle Sam outfits. She humped the air; she sprayed sweat; she sucked the microphone head. Roosevelt, Hitler, Stalin, and Hirohito were carried in on litters; they swooned at her feet as Lor belted 'Someone to Watch Over Me'. A war broke out on the bandstand: crazed jigs beating each other with trombone slides and clarinet shafts. It was obviously a diversion – Hitler jumped onstage and tried to carry Lorna over to a Nazi U-boat parked in the first row. I foiled Der Führer, picking him up by the mustache and hurling him out to Sunset Boulevard. Lorna was swooning into my arms when I felt a tugging and opened my eyes to see Bob Murikami standing over me, saying, 'Rise and shine, shamus. We got banking to do.'

We carried it out straight-faced, with appropriate props – handcuffs on Bad Bob, phony paperwork, a cereal-box badge pinned to my lapel. Murikami impersonated over a dozen fellow Japs; we liquidated fourteen bank accounts to the tune of $81,000. I explained that I was Alien Squad brass, overseeing the confiscation of treasonous lucre; patriotic bank managers bought the story whole. At four we were heading south to T.J. and what might be my long-overdue reunion with the woman who'd scorched my soul long, long ago. Murikami and I talked easily, a temporary accord in Japanese-American relations – thanks to a healthy injection of long green.

'Why are you so interested in Maggie, Hearns?'

I took my eyes off the road – high cliffs dropping down to snow-white beaches packed with sunbathers on my right, tourist courts and greasy spoons on the left. Baby Tojo was smiling. I hoped I didn't have to kill him. 'She's a conduit, kid. A pipeline to *the* woman.'

'*The* woman?'

'Right. The one I wasn't ready for a while back. The one I would have flushed it all down the toilet for.'

'You think it will be different now?'

Eighty-one-grand seed money; a wiser, more contemplative Hearns. Maybe I'd even dye a little gray in my hair. 'Right. Once I clear up a little legal trouble I'm in, I'm going to suggest a long vacation in Acapulco, maybe a trip to Rio. She'll see the difference in me. She'll know.'

I looked back at the highway, downshifted for a turn, and felt a tap on my shoulder. I turned to face Bad Bob and caught a big right hand studded with signet rings square in the face.

Blood blinded me; my foot hit the brake; the car jerked into a hillside and stalled out. I swung a haphazard left; another sucker shot caught me; through the sheet of crimson I saw Murikami grab the money and hotfoot it.

I wiped red out of my eyes and pursued. Murikami was heading for the bluffs and a path down to the beach; a car swerved in front of me and a large man jumped out, aimed, and fired at the running figure – once, twice, three times. A fourth shot sent Bob Murikami spiraling over the cliff, the moneybag sailing, spilling greenbacks. I pulled my Roscoe, shot the shooter in the back, and watched him go down in a clump of crab grass.

Gun first, I walked over; I gave the shooter two good-measure shots, point-blank to the back of the head. I kicked him over to his front side and from what little remained of his face identified him. Sergeant Jenks, Bill Malloy's buddy on the Alien Squad.

Deep shit without a depth gauge.

I hauled Jenks to his Plymouth, stuffed him in the front seat, stood back and shot the gas tank. The car exploded; the ex-cop sizzled like French-fried guacamole. I walked over the cliff and looked down. Bob Murikami was spread-eagled on the rocks and shitloads of sunbathers were scooping up cash, fighting each other for it, dancing jigs of greed and howling like hyenas.

I tailspinned down to Tijuana, found a flop and a bottle of drugstore hop, and went prowling for Maggie Cordova. A fat white lezbo songbird would stick out, even in a pus pocket like T.J. – and I knew the heart of T.J. lowlife was the place to start.

The hop edged down my nerves and gave me a favoir-faire my three-day beard and raggedy-assed state needed. I hit the mule-act strip and asked questions; I hit the whorehouse strip and the strip that featured live fuck shows twenty-four hours a day. Child beggars swarmed me; my feet got sore from kicking them away. I asked, asked, asked about Maggie Cordova, passing out bribe pesos up the wazoo.

Then – right on the street – there she was, turning up a set of stairs adjoining a bottle-liquor joint.

I watched her go up, a sudden jolt of nerves obliterating my dope edge. I watched a light go on above the bottle shop – and Lorna Kafesjian doing 'Goody, Goody' wafted down at me.

Pursuing the dream, I walked up the stairs and knocked on the door.

Footsteps tapped toward me – and suddenly I felt naked, like a litany of everything I didn't have was underlining the sound of heels over wood.

No eighty-one-grand reunion stash.

No Sy Devore suits to make a suitably grand Hollywood entrance.

No curfew papers for late-night Hollywood spins.

No PI buzzer for *the* dramatic image of the twentieth century.

No world-weary, tough-on-the-outside, tender-on-the-inside sensitive code-of-honor shtick to score backup pussy with in case Lorna shot me down.

The door opened; fat Maggie Cordova was standing there. She said, 'Spade Hearns. Right?'

I stood there – dumbstruck beyond dumbstruck. 'How did you know that?'

Maggie sighed – like I was old news barely warmed over. 'Years ago I bought some tunes from Lorna Kafesjian. She needed a stake to buy her way out of a shack job with a corny guy who had a wicked bad case on her. She told me the guy was a sewer crawler, and since I was a sewer crawler performing her songs, I might run into him. Here's your ray of hope, Hearns. Lorna said she always wanted to see you one more time. Lor and I have kept in touch, so I've got a line on her. She said I should make you pay for the info. You want it? Then *give*.'

Maggie ended her pitch by drawing a dollar sign in the air. I said, 'You fingered the B of A heist. You're dead meat.'

'Nix, gumshoe. You're all over the L.A. papers for the raps you brought down looking for me, and the Mexes won't extradite. *Givesky*.'

I forked over all the cash in my wallet, holding back a five-spot for mad money. Maggie said, '881 Calle Verdugo. Play it pianissimo, doll. Nice and slow.'

I blew my last finnsky at a used-clothing store, picking up a chalk-stripe suit like the one Bogart wore in *The Maltese Falcon*. The trousers

164

were too short and the jacket was too tight, but overall the thing worked. I dry-shaved in a gas station men's room, spritzed some soap at my armpits, and robbed a kiddie flower vendor of the rest of his daffodils. Thus armed, I went to meet my lost love.

Knock, knock, knock on the door of a tidy little adobe hut; boom, boom, boom, as my overwrought heart drummed a big-band beat. The door opened – and I almost screamed.

The four years since I'd seen Lorna had put forty thousand hard miles on her face. It was sun-soured – seams, pits, and scales; her laugh lines had changed to frown lines as deep as the San Andreas Fault. The body that was once voluptuous in white satin was now bloated in a Mex charwoman's serape. From the deep recesses of what we once had, I dredged a greeting.

'What's shakin', baby?'

Lorna smiled, exposing enough dental gold to front a revolution. 'Aren't you going to ask me what happened, Spade?'

I stayed game. 'What happened, baby?'

Lorna sighed. 'Your interpretation first, Spade. I'm curious.'

I smoothed my lapels. 'You couldn't take a good thing. You couldn't take the dangerous life I led. You couldn't take the danger, romance, the heartache and vulnerability inherent in a mean-street-treading knight like me. Face it, baby: I was too much man for you.'

Lorna smiled – more cracks appeared in the relief map of her face. She said, 'Your theatrics exhausted me more than my own. I joined a Mexican nunnery, got a tan that went bad, started writing music again, and found myself a man of the earth – Pedro, my husband. I make tortillas, wash my clothes in a stream, and dry them on a rock. Sometimes, if Pedro and I need extra jack, I mix margaritas and work the bar at the Blue Fox. It's a good, simple life.'

I played my ace. 'But Maggie said you wanted to see me – "one more time," like—'

'Yeah, like in the movies. Well, Hearns, it's like this. I sold "Prison of Love" to about three dozen bistro belters who passed it off as their own. It's ASCAP'd under at least thirty-five titles, and I've made a cool five grand on it. And, well, I wrote the song for you back in our salad days, and in the interest of what we had together for about two seconds, I'm offering you 10 percent – you inspired the damn thing, after all.'

I slumped into the doorway – exhausted by four years of torching, three days of mayhem and killing. 'Hit me, baby.'

165

Lorna walked to a cabinet and returned with a roll of Yankee greenbacks. I winked, pocketed the wad, and walked down the street to a cantina. The interior was dark and cool; Mex cuties danced nude on the bar top. I bought a bottle of tequila and slugged it straight, fed the jukebox nickels and pushed every button listing a female vocalist. When the booze kicked in and the music started, I sat down, watched the nudie gash gyrate, and tried to get obsessed.

Also in Arrow . . .

A STAINED WHITE RADIANCE

James Lee Burke

A bullet shot through the window of Weldon Sonnier's house propels Dave Robicheaux back into the lives of a family that he's not sure whether he wants to be reacquainted with.

As a man whose CIA-influenced past has led to dangerous commitments, including debts to local mob boss Joey 'Meatballs' Gouza, Weldon may have put himself in the line of fire. And it is left to Lyle Sonnier, television evangelist and faith healer, to fill Dave in on a violent family history – a history that intersects menacingly with Dave's own. But overshadowing the manoeuvres of Gouza's lethal gang of thugs is the spectre of racial politics in the modern South, and it is former Klansman Bobby Earl who proves to be Dave Robicheaux's most elusive enemy.

This is the fifth highly-acclaimed novel in the series featuring the Cajun detective, Dave Robicheaux.

'American crime fiction has no finer prose stylist than James Lee Burke, and he has never been better than in *A Stained White Radiance* . . . An intricate plotter with all the narrative gifts of a born storyteller'
– Los Angeles Times Book Review

'A complex brew, dark and strong . . . if you haven't read James Lee Burke, he's worth discovering . . .'
– USA Today

FOREIGN EXCHANGE

Larry Beinhart

Europe in the 1990s – a nervous place where power shifts as swiftly as an Alpine avalanche.

Brooklyn PI Tony Casella, on the run and lying low in the Austrian Alps, just wants to avoid trouble. But when a good-time American blonde and a rich Japanese mogul are crushed in an avalanche, events snowball. Casella wants nothing to do with it. But with the CIA on his tail he may not have a choice.

On a wild trek from Vienna to Prague and Budapest, across a new Europe where economic forces are murderously taking shape, Casella is forced on a desperate hunt for information some would kill for. Are killing for . . .

'This witty, near perfect caper makes merry with European cuisine, customs, currencies and politics'
– **Publishers Weekly**

'Knock-out fun, top-drawer plotting. This'll burn away the night' – **Kirkus Reviews**

THE BLACK DAHLIA

A chilling novel based on Hollywood's most notorious murder case.

Los Angeles, 10th January 1947: a beautiful young woman walked into the night and met her horrific destiny.

Five days later, her tortured body was found drained of blood and cut in half. The newspapers called her 'The Black Dahlia'. Two cops are caught up in the investigation and embark on a hellish journey that takes them to the core of the dead girl's twisted life . . .

'One of those rare, brilliantly written books you want to press on other people' – **Time Out**

'A wonderful tale of ambition, insanity, passion and deceit' – **Publishers Weekly**

BESTSELLING FICTION FROM ARROW